HIDDEN DREAMS

What Reviewers Say About
Shelley Thrasher's Work

Autumn Spring

"Thrasher's unique and exquisite take on romance in a small town offers a new and welcome perspective on mature relationships. ...The focus on the empowerment of older women serves to underscore both the charm of life at a slower pace and the sweetness of new relationships. Readers will find it deeply refreshing to see female characters who are defined as much by their kindness and grace as by their chosen roles in life."—*Publishers Weekly*

First Tango in Paris

"So initially I read this book to indulge in my love for Paris; that was the defining factor in my choice of novel. I didn't know what the subgenres of the book were (incidentally they are LGBT, family drama, history, romance etc) but what I got was a captivating story of love, not only of another person but also love of oneself. The historical elements of the story are fascinating. ...This subject makes for interesting reading and made me want to read further into some of the key figures in French history. I really enjoyed *First Tango in Paris*. The storyline flowed with effortless ease and the characters had me rooting for them. I can't ask for much more in a novel."
—*Lisa Talks About...Blog*

"Great debut novel. Easy read, likeable characters and good thoughtful plot."—*Rainbow Book Awards*, Honorable Mention

The Storm

"*The Storm* is very well researched and Shelley Thrasher does an excellent job weaving together fact and fiction. The references to historical events such as the Galveston hurricane, the Spanish Flu epidemic and the suffrage movement add depth and interest to the overall storyline. Overall an entertaining and enlightening read that fans of historical romances will enjoy."—*Library Thing*

"The Orient Express" Short Story in *Women of the Dark Streets*

"Fantasy and dreamlike story aboard the Orient Express, is imaginative and super sexy. Bon voyage!"—Rainbow Book Reviews

Visit us at www.boldstrokesbooks.com

By the Author

The Storm

First Tango in Paris

Autumn Spring

Hidden Dreams

HIDDEN DREAMS

by

Shelley Thrasher

2021

HIDDEN DREAMS

ISBN 13: 978-1-63555-856-2

This Trade Paperback Original Is Published By
Bold Strokes Books, Inc.
P.O. Box 249
Valley Falls, NY 12185

First Edition: May 2021

Credits
Editor: Cindy Cresap
Production Design: Susan Ramundo
Cover Design By Tammy Seidick

Acknowledgments

It has certainly taken a village to create and deliver this novel.

I wouldn't have gone to Cambodia if my friend Caroline Sanchez hadn't agreed to travel with me on an adventure tour. And I wouldn't have gained so many insights into the culture, history, and beautiful people of this small country in Southeast Asia without the companionship of a young Swiss woman, seven intrepid Aussies, Caroline, and our native guide, Kom.

Before I flew to Cambodia in early February 2020, I'd had a vague idea for the plot and characters of the novel I wanted to write based on my upcoming experience. And after my return two weeks later, everything slowly began to fall into place. Covid-19 had just begun to be taken seriously worldwide, and it wasn't too much of a stretch to begin fleshing out my two major characters, Barbara and Dara.

After writing several chapters, I formally proposed the novel to Sandy Lowe, who replied that if I'd send her a title, she'd send me a contract. Radclyffe's choice of Sandy as our senior editor was an inspired one.

As usual, I discussed my blossoming ideas with Connie Ward and sent bits and pieces to author Justine Saracen for her always helpful input. Luckily, I also enticed author Karen Williams to be a beta reader as well, and she shared her vast knowledge of many subjects and her considerable writing skills so extensively that at times I considered her my co-author. Justine faithfully chimed in throughout the process, with her usual keen insights, as did Connie, whom, at that point, I especially leaned on for medical insights. I also had considerable long-distance help from Chantha Nguon, a native Cambodian activist since the Pol Pot era, and now, among other meaningful projects, the author of her upcoming memoir, *Slow Noodles*.

As the novel evolved, the title kept changing from its original one: *Corona*. Also, I added another major contributor: fellow author Andrews, of Andrews and Austin fame. She painstakingly reviewed what I considered my near-final draft and contributed her keen insights and expertise with her trademark wit and grit. Near the end of the writing phase, Connie listened to me read the manuscript aloud, informing me when I was too wordy, or obvious, or scholarly, or descriptive, or whatever. And she came up with the final title, *Hidden Dreams*.

Cindy Cresap, my editor, zeroed in on several major points of plot and character, as well as numerous small items so easy for an author to miss, and I gratefully took her advice during the revision process. The typesetter did her usual meticulous job, as did the faithful proofreaders that BSB is so fortunate to have. Ruth Sternglantz and Carsen Taite added their talents to help with the company's outreach to readers, and of course, you faithful readers are the main point of all the efforts we make at BSB to provide you with quality books.

To everyone I've mentioned and those I've forgotten—so many friends, reviewers, and fellow authors who provide support, comfort, and inspiration—thank you.

Dedication

I'm brave in many ways, but without Connie Ward, I'd probably never have had the courage to email Radclyffe back in 2005 and ask if she would hire me to be a BSB editor. I'd also probably still be tinkering with my first novel, *The Storm*, if Connie hadn't insisted that I soldier on and submit a manuscript, no matter how rough it was.

Connie, you've read all my manuscripts and offered such helpful advice, endured me spending many hours alone in my office editing books for BSB, and participated enthusiastically at practically every GCLS conference, Women's Week in P-town, BSB event in Palm Springs and elsewhere, and all the other book-related gatherings we've attended during these past sixteen years.

You've also helped me get ready for trips to Egypt, France, and Cambodia, phoned and Skyped and FaceTimed with me daily while I was abroad, and welcomed me back home enthusiastically, sometimes even bringing the dogs with you to the airport.

Because of all this support, and much more, I dedicate this book to you.

THE BALLAD OF BARBARA ALLEN

T'was in the merry month of May
when flowers were a-bloomin'.
Sweet William on his deathbed lay
for the love of Barbara Allen.

Slowly, slowly she got up,
and slowly she went nigh him.
And all she said when she got there,
"Young man, I think you're dying."

"Oh yes, I'm sick and very low,
and death is on me dwellin'.
No better shall I ever be
if I don't get Barbara Allen."

"Don't you remember the other day
when we were in the tavern.
You toasted all the ladies there
and slighted Barbara Allen?"

"Oh yes, I remember the other day,
when we were in the tavern.
I toasted all the ladies there,
gave my love to Barbara Allen."

The more she gazed, the more she mourned,
until she burst out crying.
"I beg you come and take him away,
for my heart now too is dyin'."

He turned his pale face to the wall,
and death was on him dwellin'.
"Adieu, adieu, my kind friends all,
be kind to Barbara Allen."

As she was walkin' through the fields,
she heard the death bells knelling,
and every toll they seemed to say,
"Hard-hearted Barbara Allen."

She looked east, she looked west,
she saw his corpse a-comin'.
"Lay down, lay down the corpse," she said,
"and let me gaze upon him."

"Oh Mother, Mother, make my bed,
Oh make it long and narrow.
Sweet William died for me today;
I'll die for him tomorrow."

Sweet William died on a Saturday night,
and Barbara died on Sunday.
Her mother died for the love of both
t'was buried the next Monday.

They buried Willie in the old churchyard,
and Barbara there anigh him.
And out of his grave grew a red, red rose,
and out of hers, a briar.

They grew and grew in the old churchyard,
tll they couldn't grow no higher.
They lapped and tied in a true love's knot.
The rose ran 'round the briar.

PART I

BARBARA

CHAPTER ONE

Barbara Allan lounged in her thick-cushioned beach chair, water as blue as a Siamese cat's eyes stretching east toward mainland Cambodia. She scooped up a handful of sugary sand and let it filter through her fingers, transferring it from one hand to the other as if playing with an hourglass. Its warmth, combined with the sun's, mesmerized her. How long had these waves rolled onto these shores?

In the distance, a figure appeared, strolling along the beach. A young woman, all curves and black hair. Who was this stranger? Not a tourist. Apparently, a Cambodian. Something about the way she moved, the tilt of her head, reminded Barbara of one of the few photographs she'd found of her mother—whom she'd always called *Meatea*—after her funeral four months ago. She rubbed the sand between her thumb and forefinger, watching the woman pass.

Her mother could have walked along this shore some seventy years ago, before meeting the handsome American soldier who whisked her away from this kingdom of wonder—only to let her wither for decades in the harsh climate of Texas high society.

She brushed her palms together, the sand dropping back onto the beach. Her heart clenched. If only she could have made this trip sooner—while Meatea was still alive.

She grasped the objects hanging around her neck. One, a shell, was a precious memento her mother had always kept, obviously a reminder of her girlhood in Cambodia. The other, heart-shaped, was new.

Thinking of her mother's life and death made her feel as empty as the shell she wore. She sat up and burrowed her feet in the sand, then wiped them off and turned around to watch the spreading purple, pink, and yellow in the west. The glassy infinity pool to her right reflected towering palm trees as the sun plummeted toward the rain forest of Koh Rong. The pool created the illusion that the forest never ended, that this gorgeous locale would last forever. But it wouldn't. Nothing ever did.

She touched her salty face. It was hot. She rolled her sore shoulders and back muscles, which protested. She needed a massage first thing in the morning. Why had she insisted on carrying her own scuba tank to the beach today? She was getting too old to dive, but it had been so quiet and peaceful under the water. And the purple coral and crowds of yellow and blue fish as she swam near them had soothed her.

A familiar voice drifted over from near the restaurant attached to the resort. "Hey, Barb." It was Roland Greer, the gay guy from San Francisco she'd met during her brief flight here this past Sunday. She enjoyed bantering with him. "Want to meet me at the bar for a drink in a bit?"

"Sure," she said, brushing the sand from her bare feet. "But I need to shower first."

After draping a silk sarong around herself, she eased into black flip-flops and headed over to her thatch-roofed cabana with its own pool. Foregoing its lure, she peeled out of her damp, black one-piece and stepped into her shower. Water from its twelve-inch-square, silver-plated showerhead pounded her sunburned back and briny hair, which she washed with a special shampoo to lengthen the effectiveness of her hair dye. As she sudsed her head, she studied the bamboo and rock walls surrounding her.

She was accustomed to this type of luxury, not the flimsy showerheads of the second-class hotel rooms she'd stayed in during the two-week adventure tour she'd booked on a whim and was currently resting from. Yet how she wished she could rewind the clock, relive that experience.

❖

"Hi there," Roland said as Barbara strolled into the cozy open-air bar attached to the hotel restaurant. Only about fifteen bottles were displayed on the few wooden shelves lining the room's newly constructed cement walls, but the bartender was apparently a magician.

Short, dark, and quick, he pulled out a chair for her at the small round table where Roland sat, then mixed her a mango daquiri and presented it to her on a tray. French and German phrases floated around, though she had also encountered tourists from Sweden, Belgium, and Israel here at the resort. So far, she and Roland were the only Americans on the premises, and she enjoyed being in the minority for a change. It made her feel anonymous and somehow special in a perverse sort of way.

Australians had dominated the gritty adventure tour she'd finished this past Sunday, and being with such avid travelers had made her experience even more pleasurable. Unlike these Australians, most Americans abroad, at least in her circles, valued high-priced hotels and ridiculously expensive food. Like her new acquaintances from Down Under, she wanted to get to know the real Cambodia, not its Hollywood version.

Roland sipped his drink, his gaze patrolling the room before settling on her. "Girl, I bet every lesbian in Dallas drools when you wear that white, tailored boyfriend shirt. It makes your brown eyes even darker and dreamier, especially with that gold monogram." He fanned his face. "And those tight pants cup your ass just right." He shook his hand like his fingers were on fire.

"Oh, I wish." She laughed at him. "I'm well past my prime, you know."

"Don't fool yourself. My ancestors came from Britain, so I know who Barbara Allen really is." He fingered his neat chin stubble.

"What do you mean?"

"She's just the most famous heartbreaker in the history of folk music. The beautiful woman in the ballad who hardened her heart against her suitor."

"That's actually correct, except our last names are spelled differently. My father was Scottish, and he sang that old song to me practically every night before I fell asleep." A gust of cool air blew in from the rain forest, and she shivered.

Roland just kept talking, like he was telling her something she didn't know. "The man in the ballad told Barbara Allen he was dying of a broken heart because she'd rejected him. He begged her to forgive him for accidentally slighting her, and she essentially told him to piss off." Roland sighed loudly. "So he did just that. He died, and everyone blamed her. So she joined him."

She shook her head, tempted to laugh at the tragic expression Roland twisted his features into. "It's only an old song, and it's just what my name turned out to be. No connection. End of story."

"Okay. You win." He grinned and looked out the window toward the beach. "Say. I've been wondering about that shell you always wear around your neck, along with that heart. Was it a gift from a forsaken lover?"

She fingered its smooth surface. "It's a cowrie shell I found among my mother's things after she passed last year. Pretty, don't you think?"

"Oh. Sorry to hear about your mom. That shell is stunning. I understand why she kept it. The deep brown with all those sparkling gold flecks in it sets off you and your outfit perfectly. Which reminds me. How was your scuba trip today?"

"Amazing. I'm so glad I certified to dive all those years ago in Texas. I was afraid I'd forgotten the routine, but my guide stayed beside me, and I relaxed quicker than I expected to."

He nodded approval, and she finally sipped her daquiri, savoring its sweet tang. Then she rubbed her left shoulder. "Though I wish I'd let him carry my gear to and from the boat, like he offered."

"The independent American, eh?" Roland quirked an eyebrow.

She rubbed her sunburned cheek, which was beginning to sting despite the lotion she'd slathered on herself earlier. "The independent *older woman*."

"The *sunburned*, independent older woman. You better be careful, or your skin will be redder than your hair."

"Don't worry about it. I always carry a little magic bottle to remedy that situation myself."

He put his hand over his mouth to stifle a mock gasp. "Do tell. So you're not a natural redhead? Could have fooled me."

"Don't tell anyone." She leaned across the table, whispering. "I'm a natural brunette. Always have been."

"Why the change? Want to stand out even more from the crowd?"

"We'll have to know one another way better before I confide in you about that." She turned her drink glass in her hand. "Why don't we change the subject?"

Roland glanced over at the waitstaff, which didn't seem to be paying any attention to them now. "What would you rather talk about?"

"The Cambodians. They seem to be a tolerant lot." She ran her fingers along the curve of her cold glass, tempted to lift it to her heated forehead, but its stem made that maneuver difficult.

"Hmm. Maybe they're tolerant because you're a wealthy foreigner who's helping improve their economy." He tapped her hand with a tanned finger and motioned with his head toward the staff. "The natives themselves seem to still be stuck in the get-married-and-procreate rut."

She studied the wrinkles on Roland's forehead, his receding hairline. "What about the ones who've passed that stage of life?" Possibly he was old enough to know what she was referring to.

"You mean the gay men past their prime? The ones who can't still attract someone older to pay their bills and are forced to either settle down with a suitable partner or support someone younger?" He frowned, most likely dreading both alternatives to being young and handsome.

She gazed past him into the sudden darkness that had dropped like a curtain outside, the surf a rough growl. "You men may think like that, but we women are different." The breeze cooled her cheeks. "As we age, we become increasingly invisible. So we're free to do exactly what we want, instead of what society expects of us."

Roland shrugged, his white, pleated guayabera pristine. "And what do *you* want to do?"

She recalled dark eyes and gleaming straight hair. Dara Dith stood in front of their tour group at Ta Prohm, part of the world-famous Angkor Wat temple complex, pointing out the amazing strangler fig trees that threatened to destroy the ancient structure. Her voice was soft yet clear, so near Barbara had detected Dara Dith's freshness, the silver hairs lightening the dark ones. If Dara were here, would she flinch away from Barbara's touch or turn those walnut-brown eyes on her, draw her into a foreign, mysterious world?

The breeze rattled the palm fronds that comprised the roof of the bar, where she sat staring through the gaps at the inky sky. She shook her head, her face even hotter. *I'm flying back to Texas soon, far away from Dara.*

"What I want to do, dear one," she told Roland, responding to his intrusive question, "is yet to be revealed."

He steepled his fingers under his prickly chin, his gaze steady.

She motioned the bartender over. "Another round, please."

❖

Barbara lay in the shade of several sugar-palm trees, stretched out on a lounge chair. The ocean air and steady cadence of the waves had almost lulled her to sleep. It fascinated her how waves could change so fluidly from being separate entities to reuniting with the ocean and losing their individuality. What a Zen thought, she mused.

"Hey, Barb. Thought you were taking a jungle tour today. Missed you at breakfast."

She raised her sunglasses and looked up at Roland, whose yellow drawstring swim trunks hit about two inches above his knees. "I canceled the tour and slept in."

"Feeling lazy, eh? Want some company?" He dropped into a nearby lounger, adjusting his trunks.

"Yes. I was a little tired this morning so decided to rest all day. After all, that *is* what vacations are for." She fingered her black-and-gold, square-frame Versaces.

"Good idea. Aren't you flying back to Dallas before long?"

"That's the plan, though I'm not too gung ho."

"Really? You're not tired of all this?" He motioned at the resort. "To be honest, I'm getting a little bored. Not enough action, if you know what I mean."

She nodded. "I know, but that's not why I came to Cambodia." She replaced her glasses.

Roland took a swig from the can of Angkor beer he'd brought with him. "Why did you?

She rolled over on her side to face him, adjusting her black swim bottom. "Are you gathering information for a book?"

He flushed and laughed. "No. I'm just a nosy queen."

She couldn't resist his honesty. "It's complicated, but I'll give you the CliffsNotes version."

"I'm all ears," Roland said, rubbing his hands together as if expecting a juicy story.

"I hate to be a downer, but didn't I tell you my mother died four months ago?"

He took a drink of beer and lost his grin. "Yes. And you wanted to come here why? Did she have some sort of connection to Cambodia?"

She leaned forward and brushed a bit of sand from her foot. "I'd say so. She was born here and didn't leave until she was in her late teens."

Roland spewed beer from his lips. "I don't believe it. You're half Cambodian? You don't look like it."

"I don't feel like it either. My father saw to that." She didn't want to sound too bitter, so she lightened her tone. "I'm tall like him and have the same-shaped long nose and light skin." She rubbed her nose. "But my eyes are dark like my mother's, and my hair used to be, before I started dying it."

Roland stared, as if seeing her for the first time. "You seem so all-American."

She shrugged, fingering her tiger-striped tankini top. "I have my father to thank for that too."

"I sense a story there. Do tell."

She drew a deep breath of fresh sea air and exhaled forcefully. "I'd rather not." She didn't want to even think about those early years, much less talk about them. She had only shadowy memories anyway.

A slim, attractive waiter walked over to them. "Another beer, sir? Water, madam?"

Roland shook the can he'd just sipped from. "Sounds good to me. Give me about ten minutes, and I'll be ready."

The waiter nodded, and she asked for bottled water.

Roland kept his eyes on the young waiter as he walked gracefully away, and she enjoyed the silence.

Even Roland didn't start talking again, just settled back in his lounger.

She let her mind wander, still musing about the waves, then finally turned toward him. "Are you awake?"

He nodded, lowering his blue-lensed Maui Jims. She had his attention.

"We were talking about my mother earlier. Still interested?"

"Mmm-hmm," he murmured, as if waiting for her to continue.

"I called her Meatea. That's Cambodian for 'mother.'"

"Got it," he said, his tone encouraging her to continue.

"I've been thinking a lot about her since I've been here, and I've learned how very friendly and kind the Cambodians are."

Roland nodded. "I haven't interacted much with them on a social level, but from what I've observed, you're right. Everyone I've seen has the most beautiful smile."

"Yes. But Meatea didn't have much occasion to smile."

Roland shifted in his chair. This conversation was nothing like their usual banter, but she felt more somber than usual.

"Why was that?"

She hadn't seen this serious side of Roland before yet didn't want to bore him. "That's a long story. But I'm not too eager to leave because of the usual reason."

His eyes lit up. "A woman?"

"You got it."

"A beautiful one?"

"Of course."

He clapped, his gold rings glinting in the sunlight. "How old?"

"What a gauche question. But I'll answer it anyway." She rubbed her neck, where some type of stinging insect had just bit her.

"She's sixty-two."

"Cambodian?"

She nodded.

"I bet she doesn't look her age."

She studied him, a virtual stranger. Why not answer all his nosy questions? "You're right. I don't know how she does it. I'd have pegged her for fifty."

He took a long, last drink and slowly crushed the can. "Is she older than you?"

Go ahead, she thought. Tell him the truth. He's a stranger, and we're in a strange land. He'll forget all about you as soon as he returns to the States.

"She's younger."

He gave a mock gasp. Evidently, her dyed hair and face work hadn't fooled him for a second. "No! All of two months younger, I bet."

She enjoyed his obvious attempt to flatter her. "Try eight years."

He jumped up and started pacing. "You have got to be kidding me. No way you're seventy."

"Way," she said. "Sit down. You're making me tired."

"So, this Cambodian woman. She's beautiful and what? Where did you meet her? At least you were able to talk to her in her own language and impress her."

She grimaced. "I can't speak a word of Cambodian, and she was my tour guide."

"Ah. Well educated."

"Why do you say that?"

"Didn't you know tour guides over here are required to have a university degree? And a large majority of them are men, so she must be something special. Is she married?"

"I don't know. Anyway, she was my guide, which made her unavailable, to me at least."

"That's the best kind. The challenge makes it more fun." He paused, playing with his glasses. "Your mother didn't teach you to speak her own language? Why not?"

He stopped interrogating her for a second, but then his mind must have leapt back to his major interest. "Did you sleep with her? Your guide, I mean."

She shook her head. "Is that all you guys think about? She has no idea how much I like her, even though we roomed together for two weeks. She might have gotten together with one of the younger Australian women though. One of them couldn't stay away from her. Sat in the front of the tour bus right across from her every day and hung on every word she said."

"What? You didn't put the make on her? She must be special. What's her name? I'm going to phone her this instant and tell her to get down here and put you out of your misery."

"Don't you dare." She pretended to be indignant just to make him laugh.

"What's her name?" he asked, evidently playing along with her.

"Dara Dith. Or Dith Dara, if you're using the Cambodian custom of putting a person's last name first."

"And her phone number?" Roland took his cell from his pocket and pressed it on.

She rattled off the number just to keep their little scenario going. She'd memorized it in case she got lost on the tour. Right. She'd memorized everything she could about Dara. Her dark eyes shining when she told them the stories behind the intricate friezes at the Angkor Wat temple carved eight hundred years ago. Her laughter the time they got lost and ended up at the wrong hotel. How cute she looked in knee-length shorts. Barbara had stored a collage of memories away, both in her mind and on her phone camera, and had already replayed them endless times.

"Got it," Roland said, pressing his phone case shut. "Don't be surprised if she shows up tonight, ready to relieve your boredom." He rubbed his palms together in apparent excitement.

She wished she could tell him how she really felt about her situation with Dara. She would say, "I'm so tired of being in relationships that don't work out." But she would also tell him, "I'm too old to attract anyone nearly as attractive as Dara Dith."

Roland would sober and simply ask, "What do you mean?"

Then she would be completely honest. "I've always been on the outside of love, peering through a window, watching other happy couples yet never quite understanding what it's like to be emotionally involved with someone. It's frustrating, like hearing a foreign language but not comprehending a single word."

The conversation she would like to have with Roland unrolled in her head like a screenplay.

Barbara: "I want to change, be able to feel love, joy, hope—all those things most people seem to enjoy with someone special."

Roland (taking her hand): "I understand. But what's keeping you from smashing that window and doing something instead of always just watching?"

Barbara: (shaking her head): "I've been with so many women. In fact, when I was about forty, I made a listed of what I wanted in the perfect woman. But no one ever had every single quality I wanted, so I always compromised."

Roland: "And every time, things started out fine but finally crashed and burned. I know about that."

Barbara: (squeezing Roland's hand): "So what do we do?"

Roland: "Don't quit looking, and next time, don't compromise. She has to be perfect for you, and you have to be perfect for her. Maybe then, together, you can find what you're looking for."

"Are you asleep?" Someone shook her arm. "The waiter's back. Here's your water," Roland said.

She took a swig, the bottle cool in her hand. She pressed this one against her neck, her cheeks, her forehead, then took another drink. God, the water tasted so good.

"Thanks for listening, Roland," she whispered. She barely dared peek at him now. Had she told him too much? "If it's okay with you, I need to sleep now. The sun and the water are working their magic. I'm glad we've met. You're special."

She couldn't keep her eyes open any longer and felt only a soft kiss on her forehead before she drifted off there in the shade, the cool breeze whispering around her, the waves lapping the shore.

Barbara's cheeks were burning when she woke up the next morning, as was her forehead. In fact, she had thrown off her top sheet during the night and was as soaked as if she'd been swimming in her private pool. Her face was blazing, on fire, even though she'd used sunscreen yesterday and worn a floppy hat what little time she'd spent on the open beach and in the water. Water. She needed something to cool her parched throat.

She turned over and grabbed the stainless tumbler she carried everywhere with her, which stood next to the pitcher of pure water the staff provided daily. She'd been so thirsty last night, she'd brought it into the bedroom with her. Her hand shook as she filled the container and emptied it, but her throat still scratched like she'd swallowed sand. She licked her dry lips, downed another full bottle, and fell back against her pillow, exhausted.

After she worked up enough energy to turn onto her side, the same muscles seemed even sorer than they had yesterday and the day before, after she went scuba diving. In fact, every other one in her body seemed to have joined them. She throbbed all over, as if she'd played tennis all day in a grueling July tournament with no warm-up. But this was even worse. She felt as if she'd been the tennis ball that Amazons had swatted back and forth over the net.

Her legs and arms were cramping, her back and neck muscles knotted, and her hands reminded her of claws. The light filtering through the shutters attacked her eyes, and the sudden shriek of the young boy vacationing at the neighboring cabana with his parents assaulted her ears. Her head ached, as did her throat, which now had to be raw, almost bleeding. And then she coughed from deep inside her lungs, a forest fire suddenly raging in them.

She obviously was ill, and all alone in Cambodia. Well, at least she'd picked a beautiful place to die, she thought as she sank into oblivion.

Barbara woke up and reached for her thermometer. She wasn't sure how many hours or days had passed, when a persistent knocking finally got her attention. "Barb? Where are you? I missed you at the bar last night and at breakfast and lunch today. Are you okay?"

It's Roland. So I haven't died after all.

"I'm here," she called, too weak to crawl out of bed at first. But then she staggered to her front door and opened it. She immediately backed away and called, "You better not come in."

"Don't be ridiculous. I've had so many tropical diseases I can't count them. Malaria, Japanese encephalitis, dengue fever…On second thought." He paused and took a step backward, peering through the outer doorway to her suite. He seemed so far away, the noonday sun almost blinded her as she glimpsed him.

"I just took my temperature, which was 103.7 Fahrenheit, and I'm aching all over. I didn't get much sleep. Excuse me a second." She coughed until her lungs ached and then lurched back into her bedroom. There, she emptied her pitcher of water into a glass, spilling some of it on the floor before she reentered her living area. "Would you tell the management to bring me more water and leave it outside my door? And some soup as well. I might feel like choking some down later."

"What's wrong? Hung over?" Roland called. "Naughty girl. Did you find someone else to party with?"

"Of course." Teasing him took her mind off her battle with whatever was trying to pummel and roast her into submission. She dropped onto her sofa. "She was gorgeous, by the way. And incredibly sexy."

He rested a hand on the frame of her front door but didn't attempt to come any closer. "You don't say. I haven't met anyone by that description staying in this vicinity. Are you sure you weren't dreaming?" He was on to her ruse immediately.

She tried to smile but managed only a retort. "She slid down a moonbeam into my room last night, and we had quite a time of it. A dream come true, you might say."

Suddenly, she was too exhausted to joke with him any longer. "Seriously, Roland, I think I'm ill. Maybe with that new virus, the one that's killed so many people in China lately."

He jerked his hand away from the door sill and jumped back, her revelation dissolving whatever comeback he'd been formulating. "You mean the Corona virus?" His banter had changed into apparent disbelief. "How ghastly." He half turned, as if to leave. "I've heard that in China they're quarantining everyone who has it and isolating everyone who doesn't. It's wildly contagious." He took a half step backward.

She let her shoulders slump as she confronted the reality of her situation. "And often fatal, especially for those of advanced age."

"Which we are." Roland obviously knew she could bear the truth. Apparently, he could too.

"Yes." She drew a long breath to slow the cough lurking in her chest. "It appears I'll have to extend my stay here in paradise until I either die or beat this virus. It's been a pleasure to meet you, but I'm afraid this is it." She managed to stand but wished he would leave so she could go stretch out in bed again. The waves slapped the beach in the distance, until Roland finally spoke so softly she could barely hear him.

"I wish I had a magic cure for you, Barbara Allen. But I better cut my trip short and return to the City immediately." He sounded stone sober. "If I've picked up the same bug you have, at least I'll be able to try to survive it in a more medically advanced environment." He put his hand on the doorknob. "Can I do anything to help you before I leave?"

She couldn't keep from coughing again, and when she finally finished, she said, "Aside from the water and soup, just tell the management what's happened and that I'll need to lengthen my stay. I hope you make it home to San Francisco safely and don't catch this virus. It's been fun knowing you." By then, she was barely holding herself upright.

"Likewise." He gave her a little salute. "Best of luck. Be careful. Let's try to keep in touch. You have my cell number."

And with those empty words, he closed the door and was gone. Another friendly face in the crowd of acquaintances with whom she'd always filled her life had vanished.

Coughing, she stumbled back to her bed with its wrinkled, sweat-stained sheets and prepared to fight for her life, alone.

Chapter Two

Barbara startled awake. Lying on her side, she reached up to the head of her bed and grabbed a vertical, round rod. Where was she? She opened her eyes. The room was dark, the only light outlining a rectangle. Daylight. She let go of the rod and moved her hand to the right. Another one, identical to the first. She gripped the frigid, knobbed metal. If only she could put it against her burning forehead and cheeks. She jerked up the sheet covering her and stretched one foot as far as she could. More cold bars at the end of the bed.

Her heart raced. *Where am I?*

"Barbara. Are you all right?"

She pried her eyes open. She knew that voice. Could it be? "Dara?"

A shadowy figure approached and placed a chilly hand on her forehead. "How are you?"

"Where are we?"

"On the island of Koh Rong. You flew down here from Phnom Penh after our tour ended."

Bus rides. Climbing ruins in the heat. Eating with several women. Rooming with this woman—Dara—every night. "The tour. Are we still on it?"

A soft laugh, the cool hand on her forehead. "No. Our tour ended. You and I are the only two left in Cambodia."

"Are we roommates? Where are we?"

The hand moved slowly to her cheeks, her nose, her chin, then down to her shoulder. So calming, so firm.

"I just told you. You are vacationing on a beautiful tropical island." Dara's voice had sharpened and sounded alarmed.

"The metal rods above my head and at my feet. At least I'm lying on something comfortable."

"Oh," Dara said. "You are in a quite fancy bed. In a cabana, in a very nice resort. Should I investigate?"

She nodded. Her brain seemed to roll around in her skull like a ball.

"Keep your eyes closed. I will switch on your reading lamp."

She yawned.

Click.

Light filtered through her eyelids, looked dusty rose. The cool hand left her shoulder, the slap of feet sounding like waves on the beach. Her bed moved, tilted. Dara must have sat down.

"What's the metal I felt?"

"You must have been touching your bedframe. It is decorated with stainless-steel cylinders on each end."

She inhaled, then her throat constricted. "Why can't I move?"

"You probably have a high fever. I need to take your temperature."

"Anything to help."

Dara sat beside her again. "Open your mouth. Good."

A beep, then silence. "How much is it?"

"When did you last take it? How high was it then?"

"I don't know. It could have been yesterday, and it was over 103 degrees. That's Fahrenheit, you know."

Dara got up, her steps still like waves lapping the floor, eddying onto the sandy beach, then back out to the all-engulfing sea. After forever, Dara said, "Here. Please swallow these."

Dara took her hand and put something in it. Pills of some sort.

She clutched them, her chest tight, explosive.

She finally quit hacking.

Dara said, "These should bring down your fever. Maybe rest will help that cough."

She squinted and glimpsed Dara's hand. The pills she offered were red, like candy. She'd taken them other times when she was sick, and they'd been sugary. But these had no taste.

"Here. Drink this."

Dara rested her hand behind her head and helped her sip from a cold-rimmed glass. The water didn't have any flavor either. Several days ago, it had been sweet, like Dara's lips would surely be.

She finished drinking, and Dara washed her steaming face with a damp cloth. Then Dara pulled the sheet up over her, and she slept and saw her dream lover, who'd slid down a moonbeam and come to life.

She had dark hair and eyes, a soft voice, and firm lips. Dara and she ran into the surf and played in the turquoise waves together. Then they lay side by side on the sand, arms wrapped around one another, and melted into each other.

Barbara stayed in her lovely dream for an eternity. The beach disappeared. Tall buildings shot up all around—horns honking, people talking, laughing in restaurants, department stores. Dallas.

Her father walked toward her—red hair flaming, stern voice insisting.
"Barbara. Come be with me."
"Father."
"Come be with me."

Weak, alone, afraid. Where was she? They'd buried him six months before Meatea died. He couldn't be here.

Red—everyone called him that—had always been strong, sociable, fearless. He must have arisen. No. Impossible. He was dead. He wanted her to be too.

"I've missed talking to you."

His voice was the same, yet wheedling now. He always got his way.

"Please keep me company."

He was begging her. She'd always found it impossible not to give him what he wanted.

But then another voice floated toward her. Meatea. Mother.

"Such a lovely part of Cambodia. Get well, precious daughter. You stay in my country. Learn its wonders. Listen to people's stories. Share their lives. Share their happiness. See me. Find you."

Something bubbled up inside her. Meatea had visited her bedside one night when she was a child, and Meatea's blanket of love had warmed her all over. She was burning now, the flame from her mother she'd rejected all those years ago searing her inside. Was it destroying or cleansing her? She let it blaze, lay wrapped in it, sighing.

"I love this country, Meatea. But don't you want me with you? Father does."

"Of course. I long for you."

"Why should I stay here?"

"Half of you belongs in Cambodia. You and your father will never admit it. He says you are all American. He is too strong for me to fight. I will stay with you as long as I can. You can choose now. Get to know Cambodia. Accept it, what my people can teach you."

She lay still, her face cooler now. Gentle lips touched her forehead.

"Come be with us later." Meatea's voice trailed away, the tail of a cirrus cloud.

"Can you hear me?"

Another Khmer accent. Dara?

"Can you open your eyes? You need to drink. Maybe eat something. Just a bit."

Barbara struggled, her eyelids heavy—fluttering like the bats that swooped over the jungle near twilight. She tried to open her eyes, but light stabbed her. She clamped them shut.

"Come on. You can do it," Dara said.

Raising her lids seemed easier this time. The fog-like figure hovering over her was smiling—so pure, fresh. "You're actually here, not a dream?"

Dara slowly nodded. "I am not a dream."

"How did you get here?"

"Your friend Roland. He called me. Said you gave him my number. He seemed—what is the word?—panicked. He told me you were sick, alone. He had to go back to America. He thought you had the new virus, needed help. So here I am."

"Oh. Thank you. I do feel terrible."

"You almost died last night. But then you came back. I called a doctor in Sihanoukville. He brought medicine and showed me how to take care of you."

"You're glad I didn't die?"

"Of course. You are a very nice person."

Her head ached, and the light still hurt her eyes, but she did feel better. "I dreamed about my mother and father."

"What did you say?"

"My parents visited me, seemed as real as you do right now. It must have been a vision."

Dara sat on the bed beside her and took her hand. "Describe what you saw."

She recalled her conversations as clearly as she could, and Dara listened as if she might believe her.

After she finished her tale, she relaxed into her pillow. Then her shoulders tensed. She looked up at Dara, still sitting there calmly, holding her hand.

"They're both dead, so they couldn't have been here, could they?" she asked. "You must think I've lost my mind."

"No. I do not. But you are very ill and need to rest. We can talk about your vision later. Is that all right?"

Dara's hand felt so good. She relaxed again. Dara didn't think she was crazy. She could sleep now and not be afraid.

Several days later, Barbara asked Dara, "Do you think my vision of my parents was real? Or did my fever cause it?"

Dara shook her head. "Many Cambodians believe in the spirit world, along with their faith in the Buddhist way. Maybe you could stay here in my country, meet some of the believers. You could ask them to teach you the things your mother talked about."

She lay still, trying to absorb the experience she'd had. Dara's understanding and acceptance soothed her.

"You know, Dara. When my parents were alive, my mother acted more like my father's servant than his wife. But now, in the spirit world, as you call it, the situation seems reversed. She appears more powerful than him, as if she's gained strength. And he's more servile, like his energy has somehow dried up. Isn't that strange?"

"Maybe. But it might not be that uncommon," Dara said. "In Buddhism we say that if you mix three tablespoons of salt into a glass of water, it becomes undrinkable. But if you throw the same amount into a river, it makes no difference."

What was Dara talking about?

"Perhaps your father's heart was the size of a glass and your mother's as big as a river."

Dara's words rang true, though she suddenly said, "We can discuss this again, after you are better. Things will be clearer then. Would you like to clean up? You have been in that bed for a while."

She got up, her legs weak, and sat on the edge of the bed, its tangled sheets wrinkled.

Dara said, "Maybe you can do what your mother suggests. Explore Cambodia. But you need to get well first. All right?"

Dara left the bedroom. But she returned soon, carrying a basin of water she set on a nearby table, and moved a warm, soapy washcloth over Barbara's face. Then she lay on the bed again while Dara rinsed the cloth and slid it down her right arm, her hand, and her other arm.

How divine. This is like having a massage. The surf was washing the distant beach. Maybe Dara would never stop washing her chest, breasts, stomach, hips, legs, and feet either.

She must have fallen asleep, because now metal clinked on glass, and a tray appeared on her side table. Dara lifted a tumbler, gave her water to drink, then offered something warm from a bowl, spoonful by spoonful. Pure liquid. Perhaps broth? It had no smell, no taste. Her raw throat eased, as did her stomach.

"Can you sit over here in this chair," Dara asked, "while I change your sheets? Would you not rather I do it than let a stranger?"

She nodded. She would never be able to repay this debt. "Yes. Thank you."

After a while, Dara helped her slide back into her clean bed and into a deep sleep. Then Dara was talking to someone, probably on her cell phone. "Have you heard anything?" Dara was asking. "I will be in touch when I get back."

Time passed. Dara had to leave too soon.

Barbara could get out of bed and stand under her huge silver showerhead without help. She walked through her cabana for the first time in what seemed like months. How spotless everything was. Dara must have cleaned the entire place before she left her alone. How kind, thoughtful.

Barbara probably would have died without Dara—so gentle and patient. When she returned to Phnom Penh, before she flew back to Dallas, maybe she could contact Dara, find some way to thank her. But how could she ever repay such generosity of spirit?

Barbara folded the last one of her freshly laundered shirts and slid it into her four-roller suitcase. Soon she would travel from Sihanoukville to Phnom Penh. A cab to the ferry, an hour and a half to cross to mainland Cambodia, another taxi to the local airport, and then a mandatory wait for her flight. In five hours, she should be back where this adventure began, several pounds lighter and perhaps now immune to this novel Corona virus, which she'd learned to respect.

Where she'd contracted it didn't matter. But whom she might have infected did. She hadn't posted a warning message to their tour group on WhatsApp. But Dara assured her that she had already warned everyone.

A voice sounded outside her cabana. "Taxi, ma'am?"

"Yes. I'm coming." She visually swept the bedroom, then rushed into the bathroom to check it. She'd become acquainted with this seaside cabana much better than she'd wanted to. Yet leaving its safety gave her a jolt. Its French owners had kept their distance but provided for her needs. Only Dara had been near her. But she seemed to have been a dream. No real person could possibly be that kind, that thoughtful.

"Ma'am. We need hurry or miss ferry." The taxi driver's voice shook her from her foggy memories. She grasped the very real handle of her roller bag, hooking her fringed backpack over one shoulder. She glanced at her suite, where she'd been confined too long, and opened the door. The sky and sea seemed so blue, almost blinding.

She drew a deep breath of salty air, let the driver manage her bag, and walked to the office. There she settled her accounts, including a large gratuity in small denominations. "Please share this with everyone who treated me so well. I hope this virus doesn't hurt your business. I've already recommended your resort to my virtual friends and will tell my actual ones about it after I return to Dallas. You've been so hospitable and understanding."

The Frenchwoman smiled. "Thank you, madam. I am sorry you grew so ill during your stay. We will wash your bedding separately. Air out your room. After you grew ill, you encountered no one who works here, oui? Only the doctor from Sihanoukville and the Cambodian woman? If they were the only ones, God willing, perhaps we will all be safe from this scourge."

She nodded. "I'm so sorry this had to happen."

"Do not blame yourself," the woman said. "Your struggle has inspired us. If the virus attacks, we will fight valiantly also. But be careful not to fall ill again."

With a wave, Barbara walked to the white Lexus that served as a taxi. She hated to leave this tropical paradise, but something was urging her toward the capital of Cambodia—Phnom Penh.

Barbara glanced around the empty pontoon boat she had just boarded. It had been full of tourists chatting in a babel of languages on her ride over to the island of Koh Rong. Most of them had flown in the same little plane with her from Phnom Penh. By luck, she and Roland had been seated side by side in it and had immediately sensed an affinity.

How quiet the ferry was now. She'd become friends with silence during her long illness, yet this nearly empty boat depressed her. Would the airport and Phnom Penh itself be this transformed?

At the other end of the ferry sat a petite woman, her shining black hair streaked with silver. Dara? She almost got up and walked down the center aisle. But then the woman turned her head, her nose and chin nothing like Dara's.

Now that she was well, the thought of Dara bending over her made Barbara tingle. What would have happened between them if she hadn't been ill?

The boat reached Sihanoukville quickly, the tourist mecca bristling with skyscrapers. How different from the rain forest on Koh Rong.

An SUV rapidly drove her to the airport. On her trip to the island, huge trucks hauling construction materials and concrete had dominated the SUVs, tuk-tuks, and motor scooters darting around them. Now, traffic was a trickle. Half-completed gas stations, hotels, office buildings, and factories along the main highway appeared to be deserted.

The SUV driver's eyes shone as she handed him twenty dollars for her fare. And after she added a large tip, his smile was much bigger than the one she'd received on the trip down. "Thank you, madam. Not many people come here from China now. No much tips like before." He pulled her roller bag from the back of the vehicle and set it carefully in front of the terminal.

The airport was much less lively now. According to Roland, before the virus in Wuhan made headlines, flights from all major cities in China had landed here, as had ones from nearby Vietnam, Thailand, and Malaysia. But now it seemed desolate.

She pulled her bag into a near-empty waiting area, where she lingered to check in for her flight to Phnom Penh. Eventually, she strolled down the broad, deserted corridor. But, exhausted, she soon returned to wait to board the plane. A few other travelers lounged nearby, almost all wearing face masks. Most were tall, light-skinned under their obvious tans. One short woman with dark hair sat with her back to her, and she tensed. *Dara.*

She almost pulled herself to her feet. But the woman turned her head, and she again realized her mistake. Everyone around her kept their distance, glancing repeatedly at the reception counters and the clock.

She slowed her breathing and recalled soft, capable hands and a soothing voice.

CHAPTER THREE

The brief flight to Phnom Penh was uneventful, the plane almost empty. Barbara dozed but awoke when the prepare-for-landing announcement sounded.

After she descended the metal staircase, she grabbed her roller bag, already waiting on the tarmac, and headed for the terminal. Several irate Americans stood around inside it, surrounded by luggage and almost screaming.

A bald man with a scruffy beard yelled to no one in particular, "My flight was canceled with no notice yesterday. So here I am again. I called the 800 number until I was blue in the face. No damn answer." He scratched his nose. "I thought if I came out here, I could track down somebody to tell me when I can get the heck out of Dodge. But so far, no luck." The man looked like he'd slept in his T-shirt and shorts, his sandals scuffed, his oversized plastic luggage dented.

Should she join this crowd of frantic tourists? She could explain that she'd been ill, buy another ticket, and probably be on her way to Texas before the sun set. Or, if the situation was as desperate as the bald man said it was, she could stay in a nearby airport hotel. Surely the airlines were still operating. A first-class ticket would probably be easier to come by than one in economy, where most of this crowd would likely be sitting.

An older Khmer woman walked by, staring at the noisy, unruly group. What must she think of them?

Meatea! Why had her mother told her to stay here, to visit Cambodia? Even if her suggestion had been only a dream, it must somehow be important. Besides, she couldn't bear to sit in a plane to Taiwan, then in the terminal there, and after that, spend hours crossing the Pacific. Even the final hop from Houston to Dallas would be too much.

Other knots of people, seeming either furious or despondent, crowded the terminal lobby. She sent them good vibes as she walked out to where tuk-tuk and taxi drivers clustered. "Please to help you, madam?" an older-looking Cambodian man asked.

"I'd like to go to the White Iris Hotel downtown." It was the first name that came to mind.

She might enjoy the Raffles, the historic luxury hotel where writers, royalty, and entrepreneurs had stayed since the 1920s. But something pulled her toward the clean, convenient White Iris. She had such fond memories of staying there with the tour group, especially Dara. She'd go there and rest. Then she'd worry about arranging a flight back to Texas.

"I think White Iris still open for business," the man said. "It was last time I drive by, but you never know." He took her bag and rolled it toward a bright-yellow tuk-tuk, which resembled a Smartcar, though it had only one front wheel, which belonged to a motorcycle.

She stopped. This was his vehicle. She looked around for a cab. The poor driver gave her a wary smile, and she followed him. He obviously needed her fare as much as she needed a reliable ride. He tucked her bag securely in the rear of the tuk-tuk, and she held her backpack in her lap. This little contraption wasn't very different from the large, heavy American or European cars used as taxis that she usually rode in. In fact, she seemed to arrive at the hotel more quickly than in a cab.

"We in luck, madam," her driver said, pulling up in front of the tall staircase fronting the White Iris. "Hotel seem open. You have no problem getting room."

She doubled his modest fare, and he grabbed her bag and lugged it up the steep flight of steps. Every time he glanced back at her, a grin stretched his lips.

Inside, the lobby was just as she recalled. The huge glass chandelier loomed high overhead, the framed portraits of Prince Sihanouk and his wife hung above the reception desk, the statue of the happy Buddha crouched to one side. She sighed. How wonderful to be in familiar, friendly surroundings.

She booked a king room from an obliging desk clerk and then glanced at the cozy sitting area to her right. She almost expected to see Dara and her six companions from her recent tour lounging there. They'd held their first meeting and introduced themselves in that spot. She'd said, "I'm Barbara Allan, from Dallas, Texas. My dad used to own a major sports team there, and I'm a big fan of competitive events. I also enjoy traveling to intriguing parts of the world, so I suppose I'm in the right place."

The others in the group had chuckled, Dara appearing rather startled. Had the word competitive bothered her? She hadn't seemed very competitive. In fact, "meditative" might best describe her. Dara—short and plump, her straight black hair streaked with silver—had guided the group discussion with skill, providing just enough information to keep it moving and let all of them immediately become acquainted.

Reserved yet friendly, Dara had large brown eyes that drew Barbara in yet kept her at bay. Would Dara fall for her charm and money? But why had she even asked herself such a question?

To be honest, from the instant she saw Dara, she could barely breathe. Her presence had invaded her more quickly and fully than the virus had. She'd felt feverish, at a loss for breath, and hadn't cared if Dara was gay or straight and obviously younger than she was. She was certain of only one thing. She wanted to be near Dara for as long as she could manage.

In their small group, two single women who were traveling together, as well as a married couple, each shared a room. And two other women, unacquainted, had been assigned as roommates.

Barbara had paid extra for the hotel's best accommodations, so she and Dara had been scheduled to stay in the same suite. She rarely shared a room with anyone and had planned to protest that arrangement. But after she saw Dara, she'd changed her mind. In fact, she'd rejoiced. She'd thought this trip might be more interesting than she'd even dreamed but kept her feelings to herself.

During the two weeks on tour, nothing had happened between her and Dara except polite conversation about varied subjects. Dara had immediately established firm boundaries, which she had been forced to respect. Dara was her guide, and she had followed where Dara led.

Had things changed between them after she fell ill on Koh Rong and Dara had showed up unexpectedly? *She saved my life.*

She couldn't grasp the immensity of that thought, was still grappling with Dara's generosity. She had felt so protected and trusted Dara with everything. She couldn't leave Cambodia without seeing her again. She needed to be sure Dara had returned here safely and would be all right in the middle of this worldwide crisis.

Now, as she settled into her room with its view of the hotel's huge infinity pool and Phnom Penh's distant skyscrapers, the memory of Dara's dark eyes engulfed her. She looked at the other king bed in the room and immediately pictured Dara lying there—so near yet so far away.

She located Dara's name and number in her contacts and phoned her, her breath coming faster but almost catching in her throat.

❖

"Hello."

Dara's voice lacked its usual upbeat energy.

"This is Barbara. Are you all right?"

"Barbara. Thank goodness. I have been uneasy but did not want to bother you. Are you finally back from Koh Rong?"

"I'm fine. At least I will be. I'd like to thank you more fully for what you did for me there."

Dara's voice gained strength. "Oh. That was no problem. I was glad to help. Are you feeling well now? Where are you?"

"At the White Iris. In the first room we shared on the trip. And yes. I'm much better."

"Are you staying overnight? Would you like to meet somewhere later today? Have a meal together?"

She inhaled as deeply as she could, though her lungs still felt a bit ragged. "That would be wonderful. Where's good for you?"

"I need to discuss something with the manager of the White Iris late this afternoon. How about you and I meet at the café just down the street from the hotel? The one where the group ate our first dinner together?"

"Perfect." She recalled how Dara had sat on her right, showed her the various denominations of Cambodian rials, explained that dollars were just as welcome in the country as rials were, though most people preferred ones and fives to anything larger. Of course, she had already known about the currency from her pre-trip research, but she enjoyed hearing Dara's soft accent as well as sitting so near her.

Dara interrupted her reminiscence of their first of many meals together. "Want to meet there at five thirty?"

"Looking forward to it. I'll be the worn-out woman sitting in the corner."

Dara chuckled. "I will be the worried one searching for the brave woman who conquered the virus. Or, should I say Covid-19?"

Warmth flooded her as if she'd stepped into the sunshine. She'd just thought Koh Rong's beaches and rain forest had been relaxing. Being connected to Dara again surpassed being on that magical island south of Cambodia.

She didn't care that the streets of Phnom Penh were still as littered as she recalled and that the city pulsed at a much higher speed than Koh Rong's languid pace. Dara was here. That was all that mattered.

Maybe she should pay more attention to her mother's advice about staying longer in Cambodia.

Chapter Four

The café wasn't fancy. It contained only five tables, the decor not at all memorable. But it donated some of its profits to local charities and trained former street kids to serve regional Cambodian food to tourists with a conscience who wanted to experience what the natives ate.

Barbara had arrived early, pushed her sunglasses up into her hair, and sat in the back at one of the two tables she and her fellow adventurers had shoved together a month ago.

Dara strolled in at exactly five thirty, wearing a red silk blouse and black pants that showcased her generous hips. Barbara's deep breath traveled in and out of her stressed lungs a bit easier this time. But she wouldn't feel like climbing any steep temple steps for several more days. Simply gazing at Dara was strenuous enough.

She started to get up, but she felt feverish again, and her legs were shaking—but not from the virus. She didn't trust them, so she sat there and let Dara come to her.

Dara moved slowly, as if in a dream. Barbara gripped the edge of the table, as if she were in a dive boat on a rocking sea.

"Hello," she managed to say. "So good to be with you again."

She'd wanted to say, I haven't thought about anything but you since you left Koh Rong.

But when Dara bent beside her and hugged her with one arm, she went rigid. During their entire two weeks traveling together, sharing a room each night, they had never intentionally touched, as if following a strict protocol.

Dara hadn't seemed to mind making physical contact with the other group members: a quick pat, a hand guiding someone toward the correct location, the usual meaningless gestures that communicated basic responses, such as, you did well, you need to head this way, and so forth.

But Dara had never touched her like that during the tour. Had she sent out an invisible "hands off" message, or had the occasion simply never arisen?

Everything had changed in Koh Rong. Dara had made contact with her in ways she'd never expected. Washed the stench from every inch of her feverish skin. Cleaned her face with a wet cloth. Brushed her hair. Helped her eat, get out of bed, walk to the toilet and the shower.

Now the soft press of Dara's fleshy hand against her own lean shoulder warmed her again, this time with embarrassment. What must Dara think of her? She'd seen her at her very worst. The length of Dara's arm against her back and across her spine now, as swift as a hummingbird's kiss, made her throat tighten.

The hug vanished as quickly as it had come. She could think of nothing but having it return. Yet she needed to respond in a civilized manner.

"Hello," she said. English seemed like a foreign language.

Dara pulled a chair close. "Hello to you." Her eyes grew large, then narrowed. She resembled a doctor probing a patient. "Are you feeling all right? Have you seen a specialist? Our medical facilities do not compare to what you are used to. But I can recommend someone you can trust, who studied in the US."

She relaxed back into her chair, still warm both inside and out. "I'm okay. Not quite back up to speed yet. But I'm a tough old bird. Plus, I've always taken good care of myself. That gives me an advantage."

Dara searched her gaze, as if taking her fever and feeling her pulse rate. Finally, she nodded, appearing satisfied. "I did not want to tell you, but I believe I had the virus also."

She went rigid again, sitting forward in her chair. "I must have given it to you while we roomed together. During my long layover in

Taiwan on the way here, I was exposed to tourists from all over the world, some apparently from China."

"Or it could have been the opposite. A lot of foreigners *have* landed here ill or contagious, and our government has fussed that they are spreading the virus. Yet we native Cambodians can contract and share it too. I had a very light case."

What was Dara saying?

"That is why I did not hesitate to come to you when your friend Roland phoned. I was almost certain I had immunity. He said you were very ill and all alone. He had to leave right then."

So Roland *had* cared enough to call for help. Had Dara already told her that, on the island? She couldn't remember. But she was certain Dara had traveled all that way just to help her.

Her mind spun with the too-fresh memories. Dara cleaning her room, caring for her—someone she'd known only two weeks. What kind of person would do that?

No wonder her mother had advised her to get to know these people. They had to be saints.

When she could finally speak, she said, "I'll never be able to thank you enough."

Dara smiled and reached across the table and clasped her arm. "You are more than welcome. You needed someone, and I could help. That is enough thanks for me." She sounded sincere.

"Why did you do it?"

"Like I just said. You were sick and alone, and you needed me."

"You weren't working?"

"The tourist industry in Cambodia is very weak right now. All the foreigners are trying to catch a plane away from here. Were you not at the airport earlier?"

She recalled the knots of people, the angry bald man. "Yes, but I didn't realize it was that bad."

"You have not already secured a flight back to Dallas?"

"No."

"But surely you plan to."

"Perhaps. Perhaps not."

Dara stared at her.

Suddenly, a young waitress, wearing tight jeans and a black T-shirt, stood at their table. "Good evening, ladies. Welcome. What can I get you?"

"A large bottle of water, to begin with," Barbara said. "And what would you recommend?"

She liked this teenager. She seemed just nervous enough to arouse compassion yet confident enough for Barbara to tease.

The girl didn't hesitate. "You cannot go wrong with our national dish—fish amok in a banana leaf, with rice."

"And what makes you think it would be right for me, a picky American?"

"You appear to be adventurous."

"How can you tell?" She was truly curious.

"Oh, from your quirky eyebrows and the way you wear your red hair sort of parted in the middle. It looks like it might fall in your eyes any time, except your sunglasses are holding it back."

She smiled at Dara. "I like this kid. Let's adopt her. Her English is great."

Dara's head jerked back for a second, but then she replied. "I already have two children. You keep her."

Oh. I didn't know that. Is Dara married? How could I have missed that detail?

She glanced at the waitress again. "Would you like to go to America with me?"

The girl narrowed her eyes. "Would you buy me a big Mercedes and let me eat hamburgers every day?"

She and Dara laughed. "That's what you think all Americans do? Ride around in fancy cars and eat junk food?" Barbara asked.

"Yes, ma'am." The teenager stared at her as if convinced she was right. She even put her left hand on her hip.

"You're not far from the truth, though not everyone has a Mercedes." She closed her menu. "I'm not going back to America for a while. But if you keep working hard, maybe you'll be able to visit me there one day. I'll have the fish amok you recommended. And don't forget my water, the biggest bottle you have. Plus a glass of mango juice, on ice."

The girl took Dara's order as well and hurried off to the kitchen, no doubt thinking she'd earned a big tip by putting up with the crazy American lady. And she would be right.

After they were served, Dara turned to her, her somber brown eyes still seeming to search for something. "So you feel well now?"

"Fit as a fiddle, as my dad would say." She stretched both arms out to her sides. "See? Same long arms and legs. Though I'm sure I'd have to stop a few times to catch my breath if I tried to do anything strenuous."

"And I would be right beside you. I plan to relax for a while."

Soft hands washing my clammy face, strong hands holding my tumbler so I can drink from it, spooning soup into me, urging me to rest, to sleep.

She laid down her fork. The tender white fish steamed in creamy coconut milk and loaded with spices and herbs was the first food she'd enjoyed since she became sick, though it was still rather tasteless. "You truly don't have any groups to lead?"

Dara stared at her. "Are you serious? Where have you been? On a deserted island without internet?"

She stared back. Now she was the one being joked with. "That's not far from the truth. I rarely looked at my phone while I was sick. In fact, I didn't do anything but focus on getting well and ingesting as much liquid as I could get."

"This virus has shut down tourism in Cambodia—and the rest of the world."

"You're serious? I did notice the traffic has dropped off, and the airplane from Koh Rong was practically empty. It's actually that bad?"

"Worse. When you were first here, many of our Chinese tourists had stopped visiting. You do not remember? Now our government is trying to send everyone back home, so I am definitely out of work."

She crossed her arms and peered at Dara. "What will you do?"

Dara shrugged. "Whatever I can. I have some savings. When that runs out…who knows? I am exploring my options, as you would say."

"Would you like to work for me?"

"For you?" Dara put down her own glass of iced mango juice and stared at her. "What do you mean? I assumed you would be leaving soon."

She sat up straighter in her chair. "Why would you assume that? Do you think a virus can scare me away? Besides, my mother wants me to discover more of Cambodia before I leave. Now that I'm better acquainted with your country, I'd love to set my own itinerary and spend more time with some of the people here."

"Why would your mother want you to stay here? She should tell you to hurry back to Texas. You will be safer there. What kind of mother would want that for her daughter?"

"One who's from Cambodia."

"What?" Dara stared at her, fish-mouthed. "How did that happen?"

"Even I don't know much about it."

"Why not?"

"No one ever discussed my nationality. Everyone tried to forget it. My mother associated only with the hired help, and for as long as I can remember, my father acted as if he didn't have a wife. I suppose, in the 1950s, the stigma against marrying an Asian woman was so strong he chose to ignore her. He might have been afraid of being disinherited if he openly treated her like his wife."

"So you never really had a mother." Her eyes clouded, as if she were feeling the pain that she imagined a girl in her position might experience.

She nodded. "Apparently, I had a nursemaid who took care of me when I was a baby and a toddler. I assume now that Meatea, which is what I called my mother, wasn't allowed to have anything to do with me." She couldn't remember her mother ever doing anything for her or with her except sit at the same dinner table and eat with her and her father when she was young.

"Father tucked me into bed every night and read me stories. He even sang to me. Evidently, he tried to take her place, but that plan didn't work out very well. I lack some basic attributes." Her chest felt as heavy as it had during her illness.

"Your mother never showed or told you she loved you?"

She stared at Dara. "No. She seemed sad, apologetic, but mainly scared. Far from affectionate, especially when my father was around us, which was most of the time."

"And what did you think?"

"What does any child in such a situation think? That something was wrong with me. Otherwise, Meatea would treat me better."

"And it never got any better between the two of you?"

"Not for a long time. I was six when they put me in an expensive boarding school. There, I realized my mother wasn't like the other girls', the *white* girls' mothers. She looked different, talked different, even dressed different." She shrugged. "When I was older, she moved into a small apartment on the grounds of the main house, so she could come and go as she wanted. I rarely saw her unless I spotted her working in the flowerbeds or shared an occasional evening meal."

"How did being so separated from her affect you?"

"When I was growing up, I was ashamed of her for being so different, and of that part of myself. I did everything possible to look like the other girls, and luckily, I didn't have to do much because I resembled my father much more than her. Tall, with a straight nose. I couldn't do much about my brown eyes, but I cut my long, dark hair and started dying it red as soon as I could manage to buy the dye and apply it myself. Father loved it and took me to a top stylist in Dallas, so I've never quit."

"How sad. And how sad your mother must have been all those years."

"Yes. Our lives could have been so much happier if it hadn't been for those prejudiced snobs who disapproved of her."

Dara put her warm hand over hers as it lay on the table. "Think of the bright side. You say your mother managed to tell you that she wants you to search for what both of you lost here, in the country she left, among the people she probably longed for and loved while she was in exile."

She pushed aside one of her bangs, which had escaped the confines of her sunglasses. "I still wonder why she never left Texas. Why she didn't come back here."

"I wonder that too. If I decide to take this trip with you, maybe we can understand better."

"Maybe. Only she would know for certain, but it won't hurt to try. I really do want to follow her advice, do what she wants for me just this once in my life. I'll pay all our expenses and give you three times as much as you earn for leading a tour. Plus, you already know what a great tipper I am." A burst of energy shot through her.

Dara flinched, but then her clouded eyes cleared. She took a deep breath, and finally, she smiled. "How can I resist such an offer? I was beginning to wonder if I would be able to pay my rent this month."

"Do you live near here?"

"Yes. On the outskirts of Phnom Penh. My place is small but all I need, since I travel so much."

"Can you leave soon?" She had almost concluded that Dara must live alone. Whether she was in a relationship with someone was still unclear.

"How about in the morning? But would you not rather wait until we are sure you have recovered fully?"

She grabbed the ticket the young waitress had just slipped onto the table, held out her glass, and Dara raised hers. "I want to go now, as soon as possible. I'm sick of just lying around. I have so much left to see. We can rest on the way, somewhere quiet, away from this noisy city." They clinked glasses. "To a wonderful trip. I can't wait."

"Me either," Dara said. "But how do you want to travel? Rent a car and driver? Take public transportation? Ride my cycle?"

She twisted her mouth to one side. "I don't want to bother with having a driver, and public transport's too inconvenient and crowded. Hmm. I enjoyed my tuk-tuk experience this morning, so your bike option sounds like fun. After surviving that horrible virus, I feel like living dangerously. You never know which day might be your last. I've seen four or five people riding on one motorbike. Of course, several of them are usually children. Just the two of us, with a backpack each, should fit fine."

Dara stared at her. "Are you sure? I was not serious when I mentioned that as an option. But it *is* the main way I, and most people, get around, so I feel very comfortable driving a motorcycle."

"That's good enough for me. I'll pack a few clothes that'll dry overnight and be good to go. If we forget something, we can always buy it somewhere. Besides, if I get tired of what I'm wearing, I'll leave it for the help and buy some of those loose-fitting Cambodian outfits I've been admiring in the markets."

She jumped up from the table, her energy stronger every minute. As she handed a few large bills to the cashier, she felt even more excited than she'd been when she left Texas to fly over here.

She and Dara were going to have a wonderful time!

Chapter Five

Barbara studied the stack of clothes heaped on the bed and frowned. *What was I thinking?* How could she carry everything she needed for her adventure in this tiny suede backpack? *Stop. What do you absolutely have to have?*

She ran her tongue across her teeth. She hadn't brushed after dinner. *Toothbrush and toothpaste. Makeup bag.* She began to pile items on her extra bed and shoved her fingers through her bangs, which were falling in her face. She really needed a haircut. *Comb. Scissors.* They went on top of the tooth-brushing equipment. *Sunscreen.* At least she wasn't susceptible to sunburn and freckles, not being a true redhead. But this Cambodian sun could be brutal, especially with summer on its way.

Two pairs of underwear. No bra. Three shirts and two pants, preferably dark so they wouldn't show dirt. Bottle of all-purpose liquid soap, for herself and her clothes. Body lotion. Bathing suit. Her brownish, floppy Panama hat. What else? Passport, credit card, and a huge amount of dollars in her money belt, plus the wallet she wore around her neck. A tiny flashlight and her phone with its charger. And, of course, her water bottle, with its mesh carrier so she could snug it around her waist. She carefully placed everything in her backpack, amazed when it all fit. She retrieved the few items she needed for tonight and left the rest intact.

As she dumped everything else into her large suitcase, she remembered her sleep shirt. Of course if she could sleep nude on this trip, she could lessen the weight of her pack. Wouldn't that be fun?

She grinned. But sleeping in the nude while rooming with Dara? Her own heart couldn't take the strain. *We're still just roommates and likely to stay that way.*

She fanned her face with a pamphlet from the hotel lobby. Two mature, middle-aged women touring Cambodia on a motorcycle because one of them wanted to honor her dead mother's suggestion? Right.

Forget the "mature" part. Whatever. They were doing what they wanted.

Suddenly tired, she closed her suitcase and locked it. Maybe that would keep her from being tempted to sneak anything else into her backpack.

After a long shower, she slathered lotion on herself, brushed her teeth, and slid into bed. Tomorrow night she'd have Dara to talk to, review their day's activities with, but for tonight, all she wanted was sleep.

❖

"Do not worry about your bag, Miss Allan," the hotel manager said the next morning as Barbara stood at the marble reception desk in the lobby. "We will store it for you as long as you need."

"Thank you for everything." She glanced around at whomever the manager had shifted his gaze to.

There stood Dara, like a vision in her capris and orange T-shirt that said ANGKOR WHAT?! in big white letters. *I get to sit behind that and put my arms around that waist!*

She slung her own fringed backpack over her shoulder and pulled on her sunglasses, her lightweight denim jacket draped over her arm. "Well, if it isn't my tour guide/driver/traveling companion all wrapped up in one neat package."

She hoped she didn't sound like the lascivious old lady she felt like, but she couldn't help herself. The open road beckoned, a gorgeous siren luring her toward the sea cliffs if she weren't careful. But she wasn't Odysseus. And Dara was no Circe. Or was Dara tempting her to forget about flying home to Dallas, where she belonged?

Dara handed her one of the two gleaming helmets she'd been holding. "Ready to do this?"

She didn't hesitate. She intended to visit the real Cambodia, as her mother had recommended. Mothers always knew best, didn't they?

❖

"Do you still want to take my cycle?" Dara asked as they walked down the steep flight of stairs toward the busy side street.

"I'm not completely sure, but I want to try."

"Me too. We can always turn around. There is my bike, over there." Dara pointed at a gleaming red machine with a black leather seat, its chrome almost blinding in the morning sun.

"Wow." Was this really going to be as much fun as she'd imagined last night?

She stared at the bike. It wasn't nearly as big as the ones she'd seen parked at rest areas and truck stops back home. She'd barely noticed how tiny the two-wheeled contraptions most people over here drove were.

She took a big breath and shrugged into her jacket. It wasn't leather, like she imagined real bikers wore. But it suited this warm climate better. "What are we waiting for? What should I do first? Where are we going today?"

Dara settled her backpack in place and helped her do the same. Before they pulled on their matching red-and-black helmets, Dara handed her a black face mask. "Here. Put this on. Required. It'll filter out practically everything. I brought extras too."

"Only if you wear one."

"I thought you might say that." Dara tugged hers from where it had been hiding under her T-shirt and settled it over her nose and mouth. "We are twins."

"Great," she said, though she wasn't sure Dara could hear her.

Dara looked her up and down. "Good thing you have long legs. I will get on first, to steady the machine. Then you sling your right leg over the saddle and ease on behind me. It will be a tight fit. But we should be able to make it to Kampong Cham today."

"How far is that?"

"About one hundred and thirty kilometers. Eighty miles."

"That's not bad."

"In Texas, on an interstate, it is probably nothing," Dara said. "Two hours at most. But here, if you remember from our other tour, it will not be so easy."

She winced. How could she have forgotten that first day on the road with the adventure tour? "Oh, yes. I'll always remember that." She lowered her mask so she could talk more easily. "Dust, construction, traffic, bumps, holes, more dust, ruts. It was like riding over a dirt road in Texas in the back of a pickup."

Dara laughed. "Did you ever do that?"

"Yeah. When I was a kid."

"You are an adult now. But let us do this." Dara settled into the space in front of her, adjusted her backpack, and then kick-started her cycle. It roared to life immediately. "Ready?" she shouted.

"You bet. Let's go." She put her mask back in place and secured her sunglasses.

The Honda lurched over the curb, and she grabbed Dara around the waist. What have I gotten myself into, she wondered for the umpteenth time as they darted down the crowded side street, heading for the broad avenue ahead.

CHAPTER SIX

B arbara kept her eyes closed during the first thirty minutes. Hearing the squeal of brakes, the roar of engines, and the whoosh of air as they darted through the busy traffic was enough. This wasn't anything like taking a slow ride in the back of an old pickup as a child.

She leaned first one way and then the other, wrapping her arms around Dara's tiny waist and burrowing her face into Dara's knapsack. At least the stench of oil, gas fumes, and garbage wasn't as bad as it could have been, but her sense of smell was returning, and she almost had second thoughts. Almost. The thrill that tingled through her at what she was doing overwhelmed the discomforts of riding this bike.

When she finally opened her eyes, she was glad she was wearing her sunglasses. With them on, plus the clear plastic shield on the helmet Dara had given her, she could look around without getting dust in her eyes.

Not that the landscape was exactly stunning here north of Phnom Penh. Instead of the vivid-green rice fields and lush banana plantations she'd expected in this country, the landscape looked barren, dry, dusty. Dust was the key word. Duh. Dry season—dust. Wet season—mud. The reality of the tropics. The sooner she wiped her tourist vision from her mind, the sooner she'd be able to uncover the real Cambodia where her mother grew up.

Yet surely her mother hadn't ridden over roads like these—broad strips of asphalt, or whatever surface they were made of. Houses as colorful as the ones she'd seen in Mexico; billboards mainly advertising beer; and gas stations—some already established and others under construction—lined the roadway. She rested her head against Dara's backpack again, wishing she'd slept better last night. But she'd been too excited.

After a while, the lull of the road turned to the spit of gravel as they crunched to a stop. "Ready for a break?" Dara asked after she turned off the engine.

She rolled her shoulders as best she could. "I'll say. My face is sweating under all this gear, and I'm numb you know where."

Dara laughed. "I understand. You will gradually get used to the hard seat." She dismounted and booted the kickstand into place. "Here. Let me help you off."

"All right. But I need to learn to do that by myself."

"Of course. You are independent, but you need to relax, learn how to be on the road like this."

Her legs almost gave way, and she grabbed Dara's arm. "Whoa. I understand what you mean. Is it like getting your sea legs?"

"Exactly." Dara gestured toward the tents and booths nearby. "This is the same roadside market where we stopped with the group. I like it and have good connections with some of the women who have food stands here."

She scowled as she glanced around. "Is this where you showed us all those spiders and snakes and other insects, even bats, that people around here eat?"

"Yes. You did not like it? Usually tourists enjoy seeing all this."

"Not this one. It just made me sad."

They'd been walking across the gravel parking area toward the large tented area where women stood behind covered tables lined up in a huge rectangle. Boiling pots steamed, skillets hissed, and women of all ages called, offering samples.

"Why sad? Everyone else I stop here with is either disgusted or fascinated. But sad? No."

"Maybe it was because we'd been to the killing fields the day before, and to the museum that showed what all those poor people who were thrown into prison and tortured had to endure."

"I do not understand. What is the connection?"

"Millions of people starved to death during the Khmer Rouge period, right?"

"Yes."

"If I were starving, I'd finally decide that roasted snakes and fried spiders tasted pretty good too."

"I appreciate your point. It bothers you for tourists and natives to laugh about things so many people once had to eat just to survive."

She nodded. "That's right."

Dara looked around the large market. "Would you like to leave? Or does anything here appeal to you?"

"Let's stay a short time. I recall exactly what I bought here, and I'd like to have some more." She glanced at the other side of the market area, where open-air tables sprawled under large shade trees. "Over there. And that's the same woman who waited on me. She was very nice and let me take her picture." She led Dara to the booth she'd been talking about.

"Honey mangos?" Dara asked.

"Yes. I love them. And to be able to buy them from someone who probably picked them off her own tree this morning is a real treat." She held up three fingers to the broad-faced woman who stood behind her table smiling. "I doubt if she remembers me, but I definitely remember her."

The woman wore her black hair in a bun on the crown of her head and had her large purse draped across her chest and zipped securely. Her gaze level, she spoke a few incomprehensible words.

"She wants you to choose the three best ones," Dara said.

Barbara pointed them out.

The woman pushed them to one side and spoke again.

"Now she is asking if you want her to peel and slice them for you, like she did the last time," Dara said.

"What a memory. It's been almost a month since we were here."

"This is how she makes her living. If she wants to survive, she has to notice everything."

"Well, please tell her I'd love for her to peel two of them. I'll save the third one for later."

Dara engaged the woman in a brief conversation, which ended with both of them laughing.

As the woman held the mango in her left hand, which she'd covered with a plastic bag, she flicked her shiny knife over the fruit in short strokes, bits of the orange-yellow peeling dropping into a large dish on the wooden table in front of her. Then she sliced the mango into bite-sized pieces and enclosed them in the same bag she'd held it in. In another minute, she'd finished a second piece of fruit.

After Barbara took the baggies, she held out two one-dollar bills. The woman shook her head.

"That is too much," Dara said, interpreting. "She charged you only one dollar last time."

"Tell her that's her reward for having such a good memory."

But again, the woman shook her head, her gaze direct and clear, her chin held high. And once more she spoke to Dara.

"She said her mangos are not worth two dollars. She likes you and wants you to come back. So she does not want you to pay too much."

Barbara slowly slid one of the bills into her pants pocket and held out the other one. "*Orkun*," she told the woman, a familiar sensation filling her.

Meatea was sitting beside her childhood bed, with its pink satiny bedspread, saying this word. "Orkun." She struggled to pry up the memory. Why had Meatea even been there with her? Had Red been out of town and the hired help not doing their job? And what had she been thanking her for?

The word orkun reverberated in her head. Then it came to her. Meatea had slipped into her room, probably thinking she was asleep, and simply sat beside her bed. She had heard her mother come in and pretended to be asleep, and when she thought Meatea wouldn't be looking, she'd eased her eyes open and peeked.

Tears were oozing down Meatea's cheeks, leaving tracks on her rich, tan skin. Barbara had wanted to wipe them away but didn't want to draw attention to them. Instead, she slipped her own hand out from under the sheet and bedspread and placed it on Meatea's. With a quick breath, Meatea covered her hand with her other fleshy one, and that was when she heard her mother say orkun.

Such a simple memory, but it left her so weak-kneed, she had to grasp the edge of the table where the mango seller stood, appearing as patient as a bird on her nest.

"Orkun." She could almost taste the sound of the once-forbidden word, hear Red tell Meatea over and over, "Don't teach her to speak Cambodian. It's a waste of time and will just confuse her. She's an American. Not a damn foreigner." Barbara wasn't sure how much of his tirade her mother had understood, but his words and their message had stayed hidden within her.

Suddenly, someone was clutching her arm, steadying her. "I think the woman heard you the first time, and the second, and even the fourth." The voice sounded half a world away from the way Red's had all those years ago—not angry at all but pleased, though concerned. "Practicing your Khmer?"

She glanced to one side, still half lost in her memory. "Dara? What did you say?"

"Are you well? Have you had too much sun?"

The fruit-seller gazed at them and beamed. "Soum unjaown." She was responding to the word orkun, which she had evidently just stood there and repeated like an idiot.

Soum unjaown, the woman had said. Now she chewed on that sound, its bizarre collection of letters, the way the woman pursed her lips at the beginning of it and then crooned the final syllable, like she was hushing a baby or a toddler.

"Your thanks evidently meant more to this woman than an extra dollar would have," Dara said. "You showed that you respect her for her honesty. And it pleased her that you tried to speak her language."

"It pleased me too. It made me remember something that must have been buried so deep, it has taken this many years to unearth it." Her throat clenched, but she pushed past the tightness. "I know it sounds ridiculous, but it has to do with speaking Khmer. That's what you call it, isn't it? It's the main language in Cambodia, but not the only one."

Dara focused on her, her gaze intense. "Correct. But what problems do you have with speaking it?"

"During our first tour, I was always afraid. I wanted to learn a few words or phrases, but even before I tried, I stopped myself." She paused. Then, feeling a little more confident because Dara appeared interested, she tried to clarify what she'd just said. "I felt like I'd be punished if I spoke it."

"How strange. After we reach the hotel and rest, maybe you can explain what you just said."

Dara spoke several more words to the woman, who stood there watching them.

As they turned to leave, she waved good-bye, and the woman smiled. How amazing that exchanging only those few words with this stranger had created an unforgettable bond. Red couldn't have chosen a better way to keep Meatea and her apart.

Obviously, he'd taught her to use money instead of words. "Give someone a tip, and they'll do whatever you want," he'd told her over and over." But his advice didn't work with everyone.

As they walked back to the motorbike, she handed Dara one of the baggies and pulled a slice of mango from the one she kept. Dara grinned as they stopped under a nearby tree and bit into the tangy, sweet fruit. After they finished, Dara pulled a paper wipe from her pocket and dabbed the juice of the ripe fruit from her chin and cheeks before she offered it to her for her messy hands.

She did the same for Dara, tracing the tissue over each of her sticky dimples and her full, moist lips. The sun suddenly seemed brighter, even in the shade of the tree and wearing sunglasses, and when she glanced back at the mango seller, she couldn't decide if she was smiling or frowning.

But Dara was definitely smiling, and the words orkun and soum unjaown circled through Barbara's brain as they remounted the bike and headed north again. She had to try to help Dara understand why this simple exchange with a stranger had affected her so strongly.

Yet how could she explain why she felt so afraid and panicky every time she tried to speak her own mother's language? Her reaction would probably seem silly to Dara, but she had to try. Dara might understand, or at least try to.

"How long before we reach Kampong Cham?" Barbara asked. They stood in the parking lot of a gas station drinking a canned soda.

"About an hour. How are you holding up?"

"I can maybe last that long. But after that, I'm not guaranteeing I'll make it. I'm hot and covered with dust, and my rear end feels like I've been riding a bucking bronco for two days."

She took a long swallow, still vibrating from the cycle's constant motion. "Aren't you tired?" Dara had been driving all day, and though the traffic wasn't too congested along this strip of highway, she'd had to navigate a few stretches of gravel that made Barbara nervous. What if they skidded? She didn't even want to think about how painful that would be.

"A bit." Dara finished her drink and tossed the can into a nearby bin. "But I am too used to my bike to think about it."

"What *do* you think about?"

Dara looked around and pointed at a golden spire gleaming in the distance. "That temple, for example. I wonder who built it, and when, and how, and who goes there, and why. I let my mind wander, and that way I am never bored. I suppose that is part of being a guide too. Always something to learn."

Dara looked so cute in her capris and orange T-shirt, her face smudged with dirt and her hair mussed from her helmet. She wanted to touch Dara's face, her shiny hair.

Did Dara ever want the same? Did she wonder about her, crave to learn more about her like she did about Dara?

Chapter Seven

"This hotel is not the best in Kampong Cham, but if you recall, it was one of the better ones on our tour," Dara said. She had just checked them in and stood chatting for several minutes with the desk clerk. She always seemed so at ease with every stranger or short-term acquaintance she met, a trait Barbara admired. "Remember, on the tour, we were originally supposed to stay in a dormitory. This last-minute substitution was quite a step up."

"Yes. All this shiny woodwork here in the lobby and the hardwood panels, carvings, and statues throughout the country take my breath away."

Dara smiled, her expression making the room seem even more breathtaking. "Items like this are beautiful but becoming rarer every day. When we toured, did we not discuss Cambodia's crisis with its forests?"

"That's right. It makes me sick." Barbara suddenly felt tired. "Could we go up to our room now? I need to at least wash my face and lie down for a while."

Dara pressed the button for the elevator. "We are staying on the third floor. Are you sure you want to share a room? I can pay for my own."

"Don't be silly." She shifted her backpack from one side to the other as the door slid open and they entered the elevator. During their slow ride up, she almost panicked at the thought of not sharing a room. "I stayed by myself all that time on Koh Rong, except for the days you were there while I was so sick. Now that I'm well, I'd enjoy your company." The elevator stopped.

She stepped into the hall and stood searching for their room. She wanted to share this experience with Dara in every way—laugh together and enjoy trying to discover the Cambodia her mother grew up in. "Back to deforestation. Can you imagine what this country looked like during the 1930s and 40s, when Meatea lived here?"

Dara gazed at her with her usual thoughtful expression, as if ready to help in any way possible. "It depends on where she lived. By the way, do you know her Khmer name? That might give us a clue." She pointed to the sign in the hall. "We are in 308. This way."

"Unfortunately, I never learned her real name." The admission saddened her. What else about her mother was she ignorant of? "Red called her Maria. I have no idea why."

"That is not a Khmer name."

"I realize that." She tried to consider the bright side. At least she was finally trying to find her mother's roots. "But let's talk about where she might have lived. If it were near the southern coast, the beaches wouldn't have been so littered. A lot more shells and no empty plastic bottles."

Dara stopped in front of their room and swiped her keycard. "And they would have used metal keys at the hotels." Dara always managed to present a side of a situation that would never have occurred to her.

"Tourists were rare, I imagine." She was already feeling better since she and Dara had begun this guessing game. She tossed her helmet onto the bed but had second thoughts after she watched Dara put hers in the closet. After all, it was covered with dust and a few winged creatures she didn't want to sleep with. She retrieved her own, planning to clean it later. Then she laid her fringed backpack on a rattan table next to Dara's and picked up the thread of their conversation. "And a visitor like me would have carried a suitcase instead of rolling it or wearing it on her back."

Dara nodded, seeming absorbed in their game too. "Very few cruise ships would visit here because of the Great Depression and World War II. The majority of tourists would be rich or part of some fighting force."

She immediately walked into the bathroom, relieved to have access to an American-style toilet instead of an Asian-style one like she'd squatted over at the last gas station where they'd stopped. After she finished, she washed her grimy face and hands, nudging open the door with her elbow. She called out to Dara. "Oh. This water feels so good. Sorry. But I couldn't wait. I've been thinking about what you said though."

She dried herself on a fresh towel and then returned to their bedroom. Dara was already unpacking, placing her few possessions in an open drawer. "You're exactly right about the tourists in this area. My father was taking the long way home from Japan when he came here and met Meatea. I do know that for a fact."

Dara closed the drawer, then walked to the window and drew back the heavy drapes. "I am sorry to change the subject, but what about that view?"

"I remember." She walked over and stood beside Dara. "That's the Mekong River. And that bridge that spans it is more than a mile long."

"Excellent. You recall one of my small stories."

"Of course. I recall practically everything you said." She gazed at Dara but then caught herself.

Dara had no idea how attracted to her she had been during those two weeks on tour, and she resisted the urge to put her arm around Dara and hug her now, though they'd practically been one person on the motorcycle most of the day. Dara was simply being kind, doing a job, and she had no right to throw her sloppy personal feelings into the mix. Instead, she simply stood beside her and enjoyed the view.

"While we are here, do you want to ride a bicycle again, like we did with the group?" Dara was grinning, clearly oblivious to what she was thinking.

She laughed. "No, thanks. The traffic on the main street down there was bad enough during our last visit here." She pointed at the busy street below. "The bicycle I got stuck with on the tour was probably new when my father was here. And having to push it through all that sand and over that endless bamboo bridge almost did me in."

Dara joined her laughter. "That part of the trip was geared toward the younger group members."

She glared at Dara playfully, who held up her hands in mock self-defense. "You and I did a good job of keeping up. But I could tell you did not enjoy bicycling as much as they seemed to."

She nodded. "You're right. I felt wobbly at first, and the pedal kept hitting my shin when I had to walk and push the bike. I'll pass on a replay of that activity."

"Do you want to do anything this afternoon? Or would you rather rest?" Dara turned toward their beds.

She scrubbed her face with both hands and headed toward the bed nearer the bathroom. "A long nap's at the top of my list. Then maybe we can revisit that remote area where we bicycled?" She shook her head. "But on the motorbike this time. I'd like to spend some more time with that little old lady who was cutting banana leaves into squares."

Dara nodded. "Ah, yes. I remember her. And some rest sounds good. My first day on a trip like this is usually tiring. Plus, the heat and the dust were intense today." She stretched her arms over her head and yawned, her lips full and inviting. "I will clean up and join you."

Barbara lay down, her bed seemingly miles away from Dara's. What would it be like to share one with her? As she fell asleep, she hugged the possibility to herself.

The sun wasn't as hot now as it had been when they arrived in Kampong Cham. As they approached the motorbike, they pulled on their freshly cleaned head gear and their sunglasses. "Thank you for washing this," Dara said, tapping her own helmet. "I do not like to let the bugs and dust build up too much."

"Both of them were filthy, and since you're doing all the driving, it was the least I could do." She elbowed Dara playfully. "I'm not just along for the ride."

"You are paying me to drive you around my country." Dara stopped and turned toward her, unsmiling, her posture rigid.

"Of course. But I'd prefer to think of us as two friends enjoying a vacation together instead of employer and employee."

Dara still didn't smile. Instead, she simply stared at her.

"Please don't think I'm being too presumptuous. You literally saved my life." *Or would she have done the same for anyone, even a stranger?*

A line creased Dara's forehead. "Are you certain you want to act like we are friends?"

"Of course. I'm very fond of you." Just the idea of being this near Dara, alone, for an extended number of days was making her jumpy. Was her pretense of wanting only friendship too transparent?

"I am poor, and you are rich," Dara said. "When this trip ends, we will say our good-byes. Then you will fly away, just like you flew here. We might even text each other for a while, or be Facebook friends. But you will return to your routine and I to mine. We are literally from two different worlds."

She removed her helmet as Dara's words grabbed her attention. Good to know that Dara didn't want to become too involved.

She wasn't sure what she wanted, so she just stood there, gazing across the street at the Mekong River. She'd heard its name so often during the Vietnam War, when she'd rebelled against Red and protested that controversial conflict. Who knew she'd ever be standing here, talking to this attractive Cambodian woman?

"Everything you say is true except the last part, about us being from two different worlds."

"What do you mean?" Dara asked.

"Look at that bridge across the Mekong." She pointed at it, silver and shining in the sun.

"Did you ever expect something like that here—so long and well-built and, uh, beautiful?"

Dara shrugged, her lovely shoulders expressive. "I never thought about it, but no. It is quite a piece of engineering, especially in a poor, war-torn country like ours."

Dara looked grim now, as if recalling the atrocities that had weakened her country during the past two centuries. She frowned.

"Maybe this is a good time for you to explain what you meant back at the market about being afraid to speak Khmer," Dara said, pulling off her own helmet.

She took a deep breath. "Okay. I'll try. Though you'll probably think I'm simply imagining things. Sometimes I'm afraid I am. But it'll be good to get some of these memories out of my head and into the light." The sun's heat was making her sweat almost as much as this conversation with Dara was.

Dara pointed to a nearby shady bench across the street, on the riverbank, and they walked over and sat down. "You talk, and I will listen. Okay?"

"I've always considered myself an American." She stated the obvious.

Dara grinned. "And sometimes you act like the stereotype of one. Rich, bossy, and—how do you say it?—a know-it-all."

She bumped Dara gently. "I'm trying to be serious."

"Okay. Sorry. Just trying to make the mood lighter."

She stared across the river at the bridge. "The longer I stay here, in Cambodia, the more I realize how divided I've always felt inside."

"Because of your American father and your Cambodian mother?"

"Yes. It wasn't easy to be of mixed race, even during the 1960s in the US, and even though my father did everything possible to make sure few people thought of me that way."

"I understand. And Texas was probably not the most liberal place to live back then."

"Still isn't. But the family I was born into was on the far right. You know. Extremely conservative." She grimaced at the memory of some of her grandparents' rabid political friends. "Maybe Red tried to escape his upbringing by being overseas during the war and seeing different parts of the world after it ended. But after he returned to Texas, he evidently fit right back in with the family who raised him."

"So that made your mother a big problem for everyone."

"Absolutely. I could tell you all kinds of stories about that situation, but for now, I just want to explain why I've been so bottled up about learning Khmer."

"He would not let you speak it with your mother when he was nearby?"

"He refused to even let me learn the language. And he never encouraged Meatea to learn English, though she eventually managed to pick up a good conversational vocabulary."

"Why? And how?"

"I had nursemaids, and sitters, and nannies, and whatever else you want to call them. They were always around me, supposedly to spare Meatea the trouble of taking care of me, but actually to make sure she didn't teach me Khmer."

"That does not make sense."

"But it does, in a perverse way, though I'm probably being charitable. Maybe he didn't want me to think of myself as mixed. He certainly didn't want others to. Perhaps that's why he kept Meatea and me apart in the most obvious way. If we couldn't communicate, we'd grow apart. And it worked."

"But at the market you told me it scared you to try to speak Khmer."

"Yes. From the first time I can remember, he'd burst into the room whenever my mother managed to find some time alone with me. And if she was trying to talk to me, he'd scream at her to stop." She grimaced. "He must have had plenty of free time, because it happened a lot. I would just begin to relax and listen to the strange words she was saying, and there he'd be again, his face as red as his hair, almost foaming at the mouth."

"Did you not hate him, think he was crazy?" Dara looked at her intently.

"Yes. In a way. Especially at first. But it didn't take me long to quit trying to learn the words she was evidently trying to teach me. Every time she said a Khmer word, I visualized his red face and put my hands over my ears. Meatea finally stopped trying." She took a deep breath. "Maybe I hoped that would make him quit yelling at her, and I suppose it did."

A longboat speeding down the river churned up waves, and one of them seemed to wash through her.

"How old were you?"

"I can't remember. I haven't dwelt on all this in so long. Not until that breakthrough with the mango lady. Maybe more memories will surface." The river calmed as the boat disappeared under the bridge.

"If they do, be sure to tell me."

"I will. And if you get tired of listening, just let me know." She wanted to put her hand on Dara's thigh, to reassure herself that Dara meant what she said, but that move felt too intimate.

"Okay." Dara shifted from one hip to the other, seeming restless on the concrete bench.

Barbara rotated her neck from one side to the other, listening to its familiar popping.

"Talking helps me start to bridge the huge gulf between these two parts of myself. I truly appreciate your interest."

"Soum unjaown," Dara said.

"Oh. I should have said *orkun*. I'll try to do better. But one more thing while we're on this subject." She took another deep breath. "I've always felt like I was too divided inside between my parents for one side to even know the other existed. And it seemed impossible they could ever be joined. But now I can at least see across the divide."

"That is a start," Dara said. "And I am glad to help."

She stood and stretched, then gazed across the river. "If a group of people can build a bridge like this, then surely I can build something similar inside myself." She sighed and forced herself to continue. "Maybe then you and I can get to know and understand each other better. At least we could overcome our employer/employee status. Me being half Cambodian should help too, though I agree the entitled-American part of me can be a real pain."

Dara finally smiled, then laughed. "You are right about that." She covered her mouth with her hand. "Oops. I did not mean it. I meant—"

She gently moved Dara's hand and squeezed it. "It's okay. You're right. I can be a royal pain in the—"

"Do not get carried away. It is hard not to think of you as my rich boss from America. But I will try. Are you ready to go visit a little old lady?"

"You bet."

They walked back across the street, put on their helmets once again, mounted the bike, and headed east, along the side of the river. Relieved, she sighed. Dara had listened closely to her story about her mother and still seemed to accept her.

Chapter Eight

R iding a motorcycle was much more pleasant than being on a bicycle. Barbara didn't have to struggle to keep up or watch for the cars and motorcycles whizzing along the busy street.

Yet when she had pedaled a bicycle a month ago, foreign-sounding music had filled the air. It had first blared from a wedding reception taking place in a white tent that, at one point, covered half the street and all the sidewalk. And after that, the minor-key sound of a Muslim call to worship had bewitched her.

Now, though, only the sound of Dara's motor, muffled by her helmet, engulfed her. Nearby, people strolled down the busy street and along the bank of the river—arms linked, talking and laughing.

On the outskirts of town, Dara turned left onto a secondary road and headed toward a wooded area. There, the road narrowed into a rutted lane overhung with trees, and Barbara recognized a Buddhist temple where they'd stopped last month to talk to some orange-robed monks and watch a young one perch high on scaffolding near the top of an ornate red-and-gold column, touching up its red spire with a paintbrush.

Wooden houses built on stilts lined that road. With their tin roofs and variety of bright colors, they invariably had cloth hammocks hanging in either the large, open space under the house itself or between two nearby palm trees. A few people lay stretched out in them, apparently sleeping, but most were empty, the occupants burning brush, tending gardens, etc. Before her trip she'd imagined the rural women still wearing native dress, such as sarongs. But almost all the older people here wore Western-style clothes, and all the kids did.

Barefooted youngsters were everywhere. When she'd ridden a bicycle down this narrow road, the children had all waved and smiled, some running along beside her and holding up a hand for a high five. But on the motorbike, she and Dara blended in with the other traffic, the kids rarely noticing them.

Dara made another turn and slowed, pulling to a stop in front of the house Barbara had thought and wondered about many times since she'd first been here. It hadn't changed. Back in Texas, she would have called it a shack, because it was so weathered, with several barefooted children running around its littered yard. But the family who lived here, whom Dara had asked for directions when they got lost, had for some reason haunted her ever since she'd seen them.

When she'd earlier asked Dara if they could visit this particular family, Dara had appeared puzzled. But then she'd said, "Why not? If that's what you want to do." And now she still wasn't sure what she was looking for.

But they were here, so after they stopped and parked in front of the house shaded by mango, banana, and sugar-palm trees, she felt strangely calm.

"Is it okay if we just ask the women here a few questions? Maybe I'll understand then why I have such an urge to communicate with them."

Dara acted as if such requests weren't unusual. "Sure. As we go along, just tell me what you want to know, and I will be your interpreter."

The old woman who lived here didn't seem to have moved since the last time Barbara saw her. She wore the same loose-fitting, dark-blue pants and black blouse, trimmed with a black-and-white checked strip of material and a worn turquoise grappa, which practically every Cambodian woman and man wore. Attractive, it seemed to serve as a scarf, a mask, a purse, a handkerchief, or whatever other function the wearer wanted or needed.

The old woman squatted on her large bare feet, her knees in the air and her buttocks almost touching a faded wooden floor built up several feet from the ground. Her leg muscles had to be like steel. As they walked toward the house, she looked up with no apparent surprise.

Dara spoke to the women, apparently making introductions.

A middle-aged woman, who sat on the floor at the back of the open-air ground floor where they were working, gazed at them with seeming indifference.

Dara spoke again, and this time she seemed to ask a question.

The younger woman of the two inclined her head as if she were a celebrity agreeing to an interview.

Dara nodded at Barbara and sat on the wooden floor near them, gesturing for her to do the same.

Their process would be cumbersome, with Dara having to interpret everything they said. If only Red had let Meatea teach her Khmer when she wanted to. But that was the past, and now maybe Dara could help her make up for that lost opportunity.

Dara told the women her own name and said the name Barbara, then turned to her. "Say hello."

"*Chum reab sour.*" Barbara spoke slowly, putting her palms straight up and together, positioning the tip of her middle fingers at the same height as her lips and looking down.

The middle-aged woman dropped a gummy-looking substance back into a red plastic bowl full of what looked like dough and returned Barbara's traditional greeting. The old woman, who hadn't quit cutting large green leaves into squares the size of a sheet of typing paper since they got here, suddenly stopped and greeted her and Dara in the same fashion.

What a difference three words and a gesture could make.

Dara questioned the younger one about what she was making.

The women never stopped working.

"They're preparing sticky rice, a popular dessert here in Cambodia. They wrap it in the pieces of banana leaves the older woman is cutting."

Dara handed her a freshly made piece of the confection from a stack near the younger woman. "Here. They want you to try it and tell them how you like it."

She carefully untied the piece of twine that kept the little green packet closed and pulled it open. The square of congealed white rice inside stuck to her fingers as she pinched off a bite and tasted it. "Umm. This is really good. It's sweet, but not too much, and it's soft and moist. I like it."

The women had evidently been watching her reaction, but when Barbara glanced at them, they quickly returned to their chores. "What's the word for 'delicious,' Dara?" she asked.

As best she could, she repeated the Khmer word that Dara provided, and both women gave a faint smile.

"Please tell them I'd like to buy some," she said, and after Dara did, the women both smiled again, as if this was business as usual.

After that transaction, one of the barefooted children, probably two or three years old, his rounded stomach hanging over his jeans shorts making him resemble an infant, wandered into the front yard. His black hair pulled into a topknot and little tufts, holding a half-eaten ear of corn on the cob, the child cut his eyes at her, lips pursed in a tight smile.

"That little one looks well fed and happy," she murmured to Dara, who smiled and seemed to be talking to the women about the child and an older little girl who had showed up, wearing a blue dress with a cat applique and holding a plastic bag full of something to drink. She didn't gaze at Barbara directly, but to the side, appearing wary rather than frightened.

The children's brown skin and almond-shaped eyes reminded her of her mother. Had she lived in a place like this? And had she been as contented and well-nourished as these children seemed to be?

"The youngsters belong to the daughter of the woman I have been talking to," Dara said. "She works in Kampong Cham as a seamstress and brings home money regularly."

"So the old woman is their grandmother?"

"Their great-grandmother."

"Oh. Did you ask how old she is?" With her drooping, leathery skin and graying short hair, she appeared to be at least eighty-five.

"I did. I thought you would be interested." Dara glanced at the old woman and whispered, almost as if she could understand what Dara said, "She's sixty-three."

Barbara's knees almost buckled, and her lower jaw actually dropped. "Are you sure you heard right?"

"I asked twice."

"She's only a year older than you are, Dara."

"Right. I was shocked too."

"So she was, what, eighteen in 1975, when the Khmer Rouge took over the country?"

"Yes. Older people like us are rare," Dara said. "Pol Pot and his followers murdered almost a fourth of the population, between one-and-a-half and two million people."

"But why does she appear so ancient and you so young?" The contrast still shocked her.

Dara shrugged. "It could be many things. For one, I was lucky."

"Because you left Cambodia before things got so bad? I remember you telling us about how you and your parents flew to the States just before everyone was forced to leave Phnom Penh."

"Yes. That decision probably saved our lives. Plus, I was lucky to be able to go to college in California and stay in the States as long as it was so dangerous to live in Cambodia."

Barbara glanced back at the women, who were steadily working. "I'd like to know more about these women now, if you don't mind. But later, I'd love to hear more about the time you spent in the US."

"That is fine. What do you want to ask them?"

"What it was like to live here during the Khmer Rouge regime, how the older woman likes living here with her daughter and her offspring, what they think of America, and what their favorite food is."

"You put some thought into this visit."

"I don't encounter people like this every day, so I have a million questions. But these are the ones that most interest me. I'm sure these women don't want us to bother them all evening."

"Okay. Let me try to get some answers." Dara sat near the old woman and spoke to her in a soft, gentle tone.

At first the old woman's expression hardened, and she looked almost scared. But when she finally started talking to Dara, she seemed unable to stop. Tears began to trickle down her withered, sagging cheeks, and Barbara suppressed an unfamiliar urge to take her in her arms and try to comfort her. *That could have been Meatea.* At least Red had done her a favor by keeping her with him in Dallas all those years, especially during that terrible time. Meatea would have been in her thirties then, and who knew if she would have survived.

Dara turned to her, one hand on the old woman's arm. She'd finally stopped working and sat there unmoving, her dusty, weathered cheeks streaked with tears.

She told Dara, "I'm not sure the woman wants to talk any more. That subject seemed to have taken a lot out of her. Why don't you just ask her about her favorite food?"

The old woman's face brightened, and she didn't hesitate to answer Dara's query.

"Ice cream," Dara translated. "She has had it only twice. But why that question, of all the ones you mentioned earlier?"

She had an idea. "Do you know of any place close enough for us to bring some back here before it melts?"

Dara paused. "Maybe. Is that what you want to do?"

"Absolutely. Can you explain, and then we better go before it gets much later."

Dara sped back into the outskirts of Kampong Cham, where they located a large container of ice cream, had it wrapped in some insulating foil and put in three paper bags, and flew back over the last bumpy stretch, Barbara clutching the precious package and hoping the ice cream wouldn't be a gooey mess when they got there.

But it was still firm enough to eat, and she'd never seen anyone enjoy anything as much as the women and children clearly did, their faces shining and sticky.

Their good-byes were as friendly as their hellos had been indifferent, and Barbara couldn't recall many visits she'd enjoyed as much as this one. She would never forget the dignity, the sorrow, the strength, and the joy she'd detected in this Cambodian family. And the handful of dollar bills she handed the old woman made her smile almost as much as the ice cream had.

After they returned to their room, Dara asked, "Are you hungry?"

"Eating that huge breakfast at the hotel in Phnom Penh, then the mango at the market where we stopped on the ride seems to have happened in another century. I'm starving. Any ideas about where to go?"

"Do you want something fast or more leisurely?"

"As fast as we can make it happen."

Dara ran a comb through her mussed hair. It fell past her shoulders, straight and shining, though it had been crammed under her helmet much of the day. Barbara took the comb from her and repaired the part in her hair. "There," she said.

She'd never touched Dara's hair before, with its mixture of black and silver. White hair usually signaled that a woman was ageing. But it simply enhanced Dara's level of maturity. She'd seen a Disney movie ages ago, with Glenn Close—*101 Dalmatians*. The actress had played the villain, as she did so well, her hair entirely black on one side and silver on the other. The combination had made the character seem sophisticated and exciting instead of old and dowdy.

The texture of Dara's hair stayed with Barbara as she quickly combed her own. Dara's wasn't as coarse as she'd imagined, though it certainly wasn't fine. Thick, with no indication it would ever thin, it shone in the light, appearing alive, vital.

She put down her comb. "So. Suggestions?"

Dara gave a slight jerk, her thoughts apparently far away. "Suggestions? Oh, yes. Food. Let me see. Did you ever eat at any of the local food stands during the tour?"

"No. The group always wanted to try some special café, so we never got around to it. I was curious but a little afraid something would upset my stomach. Is the food at the stands safe for spoiled Americans?"

Dara nodded. "If those Americans are with a local. At least have a look. If nothing appeals to you, we can always find a tourist restaurant nearby. Foreigners taking a cruise down the Mekong often stop here."

"Okay. I'm more than ready. Let's go." She patted the center of her chest. She carried smallish amounts of money in a wallet hanging there, for unexpected purchases such as souvenirs. She hadn't noticed many pickpockets, but it didn't hurt to be careful.

When their tour began, Dara had warned them about occasional thieves in Cambodia who rode motorcycles and snatched purses and cameras and backpacks from careless tourists as they drove by them. Barbara tried to be alert on the street.

Dara grasped her arm after they left the hotel, and they walked in the direction they'd ridden earlier. "We could go down toward the market." Dara let go of her arm long enough to gesture in the other direction. "But the street vendors are probably moving from there to the area where we saw that large group exercising together earlier." Dara took her arm again.

Barbara's arm throbbed where Dara held it, but she tried to ignore the sensation. "The people walking along the riverbank, under all those trees? Who were they? Do they do that every day?"

Dara slowed them to a stroll, her hand warm on her arm. "Those were the locals, mostly townspeople. A lot of them have repetitive jobs, like the old woman and her daughter making sticky rice, though truly poor people like them are rare in such a group. The people who work in town—"

Barbara glanced over at the river, its smooth surface reflecting the setting sun. "Sorry to interrupt. But why does the river have so little boat traffic?"

"Ah. Because of the bridge. It replaced the ferries that took an hour to make the trip from one side to the other and—"

"Look. The exercise group up ahead of us. It must be just breaking up. What were you saying about it?" Barbara couldn't decide whether the feel of Dara's gentle hand on her arm or all the commotion around them interested her more.

"Many Asians enjoy group activities. They're not like you independent Americans, who prefer to have private guides they can interrupt as many times as they want."

Dara grinned, and Barbara elbowed her gently. "You better believe it. I love having you all to myself."

Dara's head jerked a bit, and she stiffened.

God. Did I actually say that?

But Dara kept on walking, not breaking contact. Then she stopped and pointed. "Look. Here we are at the promenade, and the food sellers are setting up. We should have some good choices soon."

"Not everybody is as lucky as I am to have her own personal guide." *Especially one as beautiful and appealing as Dara.*

"Of course not. Only a rich woman from Texas can afford my services." Dara tossed her head in a mock-flirtatious way, her sheaf of luxurious hair reminding Barbara of the all-purpose grappas the natives used.

Dara took her arm and quickened their pace.

"Do you prefer leading a group or an individual?" Barbara wanted to know how Dara felt about her on a personal level but couldn't think of any other way to ask.

"Hmm. It depends."

"On what?"

"How attractive and demanding the individual is."

She stopped. "How demanding am I?"

Dara briefly touched her cheek. "Not very."

Then Dara took her arm again, guiding her toward a knot of people where a variety of pleasant smells was coming from. Barbara wished she could enjoy them full strength. "I would rather show my country to an individual, especially if her mother is Cambodian." She smiled. "And if she dreams of discovering more about her mother's background, that is even better." Dara stopped and gazed at her. "Such a person is my preferred client."

Satisfied, she smiled back. "Good. And now, since we've solved that mystery, how about something to eat?"

"That sounds good to me. Let me show you the best choices available."

PART II

DARA

Chapter Nine

I cannot stay quiet any longer. Yet I need to share some background about this situation. Then perhaps you would like to ride along with me and watch it unfold.

In early February, I spent two weeks rooming with an American woman named Barbara Allan. I was leading a group for an adventure-tour company that is eco-friendly and does not have a big profit margin. We had seven participants—four Australian women, a married couple also from Down Under, plus this older woman, Barbara, from Dallas, Texas. At least she was older than the rest of the group.

She is seventy, although she is in good shape. She is also obviously rich but seemed eager to travel in a more basic way than she was accustomed to. She refused to explore Cambodia only from a cushioned seat in a tour bus. She also did not want to stay in the most expensive hotel in town. And she preferred to eat some of the things native Cambodians enjoy.

But back to why I was rooming with her. Basically, the company wanted to save money. And I was shocked when she agreed to their suggestion. On tour, I usually have a room to myself. But lately, Chinese travelers, who make up most of our business, have not been visiting Cambodia like they used to. In response, my supervisor proposed this scheme.

"You are only eight years younger than this Barbara Allan. That should help," he told me. "You two should get along well. Also, it will be good for you to observe a tour from the viewpoint of one of our clients—blah, blah, blah."

I still hesitated. I like my privacy.

"If you cooperate, we will give you a nice bonus," he finally said.

So I agreed, against my better judgment. My savings are not what they should be, however. Also, after my divorce, I no longer have a husband to support me. I could ask my two grown sons for help. But they are married and live abroad. They have their own families to provide for, so I try to take care of myself.

Besides, I wanted to determine if I could endure sharing a room with this foreign woman. I also wondered how much extra she would tip me if we got along well.

The members of the group had an interesting age range. The younger two single women were in their thirties, the other two in their forties. And the couple was mid-to-late fiftyish. That left Barbara and me, both in our sixties. But she had just turned seventy and seemed conscious of that fact.

The arrangement turned out better than I expected. She was never late for any of our activities, which is always important to a guide. She consistently reached the top of any steep incline we faced last, but always smiled about it. The sun was often broiling, but she never complained. These traits are also important to a guide. She was friendly with the other group members but often reserved. That quality did not bother me at all.

On our hikes through several villages, and once when we visited a cave and a pepper plantation, I noticed her lagging behind the rest of the group. Often she would converse with only one other woman. At those times, she seemed to talk as well as listen. I sometimes wondered what the two of them were so focused on.

She missed a few activities—an evening river cruise in Kampot, a brief ride on a unique "bamboo train" near Battambang, an impromptu card game at our homestay. She said she was tired, needed to rest, or was simply not interested. But usually she participated in whatever was planned.

She had problems only during our bicycle trip here in Kampong Cham. She explained later that she was last in line to choose her bicycle and ended up with the oldest, most outdated of the rentals. "I once rode a hundred miles in one day," she also confided to me that night after our ride, "but that was a long time ago."

Was she sad because she realized she was ageing? She had trailed behind the younger group members as we rode down the busy streets of the town and said she had to concentrate so much on riding, she barely saw anything except the traffic.

In the countryside, she stayed in the rear, clearly enjoying the slower pace and frequent stops. She marveled over the local homes built on stilts, the busy natives, and the friendly children. And an old woman and her daughter and great-grandchildren we met briefly seemed to intrigue her.

But during our return trip, we ended up on a sandy road. She clearly did not enjoy trying to ride her bicycle through its deep ruts. And then we all had to push our bikes across a long bridge made of bamboo. The locals rebuild it each year and let it wash away when the nearby Mekong River overflows during the rainy season. Pushing anything over large canes of bamboo lashed together above a muddy landscape is not easy. She did it.

Several days later, in Battambang, we took a second bicycle tour. But she chose to ride in a tuk-tuk, behind the rest of the group. She enjoyed that experience much more than pedaling a bike. When we asked her why, she said she could experience all the sights and sounds and smells of the city much better that way.

She did not talk much at meals. Do not get me wrong—she was full of questions about the people and their history. But she did not often share her personal reflections. Sometimes she seemed far away, so I left her to herself.

Breakfast is usually included at tour hotels, and every day I had to go down early to talk to the hotel management. Then I ate with our driver, to discuss our route and any detours or special stops not printed in the itinerary. She would usually show up later and consume a leisurely breakfast, seeming occupied by her own thoughts.

During our first tour together, when we had free time in the larger cities—Phnom Penh, Siem Reap, Battambang, and Kampot— she told me she walked all over each one. She liked to experience everything, even the garbage that littered the sides of the streets and the thick bundles of electric power lines. She wanted to hear the other pedestrians talking, get lost in the crowds. She never seemed frightened or reported any problems. At times she would mention a visit to a museum or a library or a market, though she rarely bought anything. I wondered if she had anyone at home to purchase souvenirs for or if she was as solitary in Dallas as she was here.

She and I did not spend much time together during the tour. When we traveled, she sat in the back of the bus, usually by herself. She would stare out the window of our van and rarely complained about how all the road construction made our ride so rough. I was usually either telling the group my small stories about whatever attraction we were passing or scheduled to visit or providing other types of information common on tours. The rest of the time I chatted with the bus driver or answered questions from nearby group members. When I did notice her, if she was not looking out the window, she was jotting something in a little notebook she always carried. Or she would consult her guidebook. As the tour progressed, she sometimes chatted with one of the other women sitting nearby, but that was rare.

She and I did talk some when we were in our room, getting ready for bed at night or for the day ahead. She confided about her bicycle experience then, but this was the level of our typical conversations. We discussed Cambodia—its history, its people, its beauty—which was why she chose this tour, she said. She wanted to experience this country as fully as possible.

I found myself admiring the simple outfits she wore—lightweight, loose-fitting clothes made of cotton. And she rinsed some of them in the bathroom sink every few days. "I don't want a lot of luggage to haul around," she said. I appreciated her attitude. But I was surprised she would wash her own clothes. She could have sent them to the laundry for almost nothing, or bought new ones. But she insisted it was not a problem. At home, she had watched her maids sometimes rinse out things by hand and said she thought it would be fun to try. Like Marie Antoinette playing milkmaid, I suppose. I wrote off her odd behavior as an eccentricity.

Neither of us spent much time trying to make ourselves beautiful. Though one evening I did unexpectedly come in early from a meeting with the hotel manager and caught her touching up the roots of her red hair. When I walked in, she seemed startled, almost guilty. But I understood. Asians supposedly respect their elders more than Westerners do, yet people emphasize youth and beauty worldwide.

If she wanted to try to make herself seem younger than she was, I supported her attempt.

The strangest thing about her, however, was her reluctance to try to learn Khmer. Every morning when we first got on our little bus, I would introduce the group members to several common words they might want to use that day. *Please, thank you, hello, good-bye*—that sort of thing. We would practice pronouncing them for a few minutes. Then, during the day, when they had an opportunity, they were supposed to try them. She never did, that I could see.

Yet she seemed genuinely interested in the locals we encountered, even the insistent ones selling T-shirts and silk scarves at the popular tourist venues. She was good with the nonverbal greeting I showed them the first day, bowing her head and putting her hands together like she was praying. She even remembered to hold her clasped hands higher at times, depending on the status of whomever she interacted with. The higher the status, the higher the hands. But she rarely tried to communicate with the native Cambodians in any way except with that hands-together gesture. And she paid whatever they asked for an inexpensive, compact souvenir she occasionally showed an interest in, though the vendors in the bazaars and on the streets usually expected tourists to bargain at least a bit. If she photographed anyone, she did so at a distance, as if the locals made her nervous or even frightened her.

She did confide in me one afternoon during a break that her mother had died several months earlier. So I suspected she was grieving and preferred to be alone. At times, I caught her looking at me with a strange expression, but I did not think much of it. She never tried to challenge my authority as the leader of the group—which older people, especially men, in other groups sometimes do—or my knowledge of whatever site we might be visiting. She seemed fairly knowledgeable of my culture, and I suspected she had thoroughly read the guidebook she always carried with her.

I have met a lot of women during my twenty years as a tour guide. They come from all over the world to visit our kingdom of wonder. The majority are young, athletic, eager for adventure of any sort—from Europe, Australia, primarily Asia, and occasionally America. I admit I have flirted with several of them, even been attracted. But

I always keep my distance. After all, it is not easy to find such an enjoyable job. And though a few intrigued women have intrigued me in return, at the end of the tour, they always board their plane and fly away.

Yet I kept noticing little things about Barbara. The joy that sparked in her dark eyes when she gazed out the bus window, even if she was looking at only beer signs and service stations. The way she would flip through her guidebook after I shared a small story about some site we were passing. Her obvious unrest when she watched two teenage girls making rice cakes. "Can you imagine spending all day, every day, doing the same thing over and over like this," she had whispered to the woman standing next to her.

"Do these girls ever switch jobs?" she then asked me. After I shook my head, her angry expression made me wonder why she was so interested in them, and in women in general. She seemed to focus on all the females we came across during our travels.

One afternoon, when I noticed her drop behind us with one of the other women in our group, chatting with so much animation, something tingled inside me. What *were* they discussing so intently? At such times, I barely recognized her as the aloof, solitary figure I originally considered her to be. She truly seemed to love her own gender. Hmm.

By the end of the tour, I had grown fond of her and was surprised and grateful when her tip was double the one suggested for my services as a guide.

The day after Barbara and the others left Phnom Penh, twelve members of an Italian family from a town near Milan canceled their tour. A relative had been hospitalized for a flu-like condition and died, and it scared them. Some of them had been exposed, so they all decided to stay home with him. I was disappointed to miss two weeks of income. Yet when I read the newspaper reports about how rapidly the strange new virus from China was spreading throughout Italy, I was glad the group had decided not to travel with our company.

About that time, I had come down with a fever and body aches. I recovered after several days but wondered if I had succumbed to a mild version of the virus. If so, I should be immune now. This all happened just before I received a call one evening from someone named Roland.

"Is this Dara Dith?" a man with an American accent asked.

"Yes."

"Thank goodness." The stranger sighed heavily. "My name is Roland Greer. I'm contacting you about Barbara Allan, who was part of your last tour group. She's currently at a resort on Koh Rong and is very sick."

"What is wrong?"

"That's why I'm calling." His voice rose with what sounded like alarm. "Do you have any contacts listed for her? I'm afraid she might have this Corona virus that's going around. I've decided to return to the States immediately, so I'll be near my own doctor if I catch whatever she has."

"A wise decision," I said. *Are any of the Aussies sick too?* "To answer your question, I do not have access to her insurance and other travel records right now, but I will retrieve them."

On tour, we rarely have serious medical problems, and I was frank with this Roland fellow. "I do not know any doctors in Sihanoukville who could treat her effectively, but I will try to locate one." The ones I usually use deal with tourists who drink too much or almost drown. We also deal with occasional food poisoning or severe sunburns, but with a highly contagious virus like this—

"It's almost two hours by ferry and taxi from here to the nearest hospital." He raised his voice. "I don't know what to do. Any suggestions? I'm really worried."

"I do know where she is staying, and I have just recovered from what might be the virus."

"You've had it and are all right now? Would it be possible for you to check on her? I mean, could you come down here for several days and help her through the worst of it? I'm sure she'd reimburse all your expenses. And if she needs to be hospitalized, perhaps you could arrange the details."

I scratched my head, frantic and terribly guilty. I might have been contagious during the tour and infected others, I did not have any other plans, and Barbara had been nothing but pleasant and generous.

"I will check her contacts in Texas for someone to consult in case she is severely ill." I looked around for my backpack and began to plan what to take on this unexpected trip. "I should be there some time tomorrow. And thank you for letting me know."

"God bless you, or the blessing of Buddha be with you, or whatever's appropriate," he said, obviously trying to be sensitive to our cultural differences.

"Have a safe flight to America, Mr. Greer," I said.

"And you have a safe trip down here. Thanks again for taking care of her. That's a load off my mind."

With that, he ended the call, and I threw a few clothes and other necessities into my backpack, including a bag of simple medical supplies I rely on when someone on tour has a mishap. Finally, I made certain my little Honda motorcycle was equipped to carry me more than 225 kilometers south to Sihanoukville and then on the ferry to the island of Koh Rong.

Early the next morning, I pulled on a pair of new jeans and one of my favorite T-shirts. It is black—displaying a huge red, white, and blue tree and its vast root system—also red, white, and blue. In white lettering, it states, AMERICAN RAISED WITH CAMBODIAN ROOTS.

That is my story in five words, for I spent almost twenty-five years in the US and nearly came to think of myself as an American. But I do not often discuss my past. The notorious reign of the Khmer Rouge has affected my life unbearably. I prefer not to recall that terrible time.

I am not an American, though. I am Cambodian, through and through. My country is poor, yet after I returned I knew this is where I belong. My roots in this country are everything to me now.

I fastened my backpack to the rear of my motorcycle, pulled on my helmet, and headed south from Phnom Penh. Semis, tuk-tuks, and other cycles surrounded me as I traveled through the vast construction sites south of the city. The Chinese have invested so heavily here in Cambodia, that in twenty years, my country will probably be considered a suburb of theirs. I sped past concrete pilings and the shells of huge factories. Every time I ride along this stretch of highway, the future becomes more real.

The traffic was light as I finally drove through Sihanoukville and reached the dock in time to catch the Koh Rong ferry. The largest island off the southern coast of Cambodia, it no longer has the thatched huts I remember from childhood trips here. Fashionable resorts, filled with tourists from around the world, have taken their place. And plastic bottles keep defacing the beach.

But the turquoise water still rolls onto the blinding white strip of sand the resorts cling to. And the jungle that lurks behind the new resorts has not changed much. It keeps trying to dominate the shoreline again.

After the ferry bumped against the dock, I rolled my cycle down the vibrating metal gangplank. Then I took off for the resort where Barbara was staying. Her friend Roland had provided good directions, and I did not have to drive far. Soon I entered the bar that doubled as an office.

"How may I help you?" a middle-aged man with a French accent asked.

"You have a guest named Barbara Allan?"

"But of course." He glanced at my jeans and T-shirt, apparently unable to make a connection.

"I was her tour guide."

"Ah, yes. Mr. Greer told me you might arrive. And I am delighted you are here. Madame Allan seems rather indisposed and is, unfortunately, alone. We have supplied her with an abundance of water and some soup. But that is all she has requested at present."

"Have you seen her today?"

"Alas. No. My wife is out of the country, and I am quite occupied without her assistance. I was not sure when you would arrive. And, to be honest, it slipped my mind."

Slipped his mind? Barbara could be dead by now. I bet that would not slip his mind. I refrained from saying what was on my own mind. "Would you please show me where to find her?"

Once outside again, I grabbed my backpack and arranged for a safe place to park my cycle. I had no idea how long I would be here and wanted to protect it from the sand and salt spray.

"This way," the owner said, directing me to one of the two largest cabanas in the row of twelve that dotted the curved beach.

Once there, he tapped on the bright-yellow door. "Madame Allan," he called softly.

I knocked then, more loudly. "Barbara. It is Dara. Are you all right?"

Nothing. I pounded on the door and called again, practically screaming. I tried to open it, but it was locked.

This time I heard a noise, enough to think she might be still alive and conscious. "Would you unlock the door, please," I asked, and the manager quickly did so. "She probably would rather not see any strangers right now."

He nodded, apparently relieved to leave the matter of Madame Barbara Allan to me.

❖

I spoke to the manager quietly as I eased the door open. "I will phone you soon and tell you what I will need to take care of Madame Allan. Please have whoever brings it knock and leave it here." I gestured toward a bench to my right.

Already I dreaded what I might find inside. Was Barbara sprawled on the floor—helpless, injured, perhaps almost dead?

She had been alone overnight and much of today. But perhaps she had simply slept. I was glad her friend had called. Of course, this could be a false alarm. If she was seriously ill, would she not have phoned me? As her guide, even after the tour, I was still her major contact in Cambodia. Why had I not heard from her? Had she already forgotten me? The possibility made her dimly lit room seem even darker.

I stood in the doorway and peered into the stale-smelling room, outraged at these unpleasant conditions. But then I heard a moan.

"Barbara. Are you all right?" I kept my tone pleasant. That one sound had made my anger vanish.

"Dara?" she asked, her soft voice childlike. She sounded so alone that I teared up, imagining a lost puppy or kitten. I inched into a living area with a large couch, my eyes gradually adjusting. After creeping into the bedroom of this spacious suite, I made out a shadowy figure hunched in a huge bed. The air conditioner was working well, but the space smelled of sweat and stale air. I quickly turned all the overhead fans to full speed.

"Barbara. It is Dara. I have come to visit you." I tried to be positive, but she said something strange.

"I'm sorry, Father. I won't let her say anything to me again."

What was she talking about? She sounded like a frightened little girl that someone had just scolded.

I switched on a table lamp, and she stared at me.

"What the hell are you doing here," she cried. "How did you find me? The tour's over. You're done babysitting me."

Not exactly the greeting I had expected after driving all that way. I gritted my teeth. Her brown eyes looked larger than normal, wild. Did she recognize me? Her normally straight bangs looked like horns, the rest of her hair both flattened and sticking up. And her lips were white, scaly, peeling. This was not the rational woman I had been with almost constantly for two weeks. But her fire drew me. What was she seeing?

"Barbara. I am Dara."

I stepped toward her, but she pulled her legs close to her chest, her crumpled sheet covering them. "Go away. I don't want you here. I can take care of myself."

Where was the aloof, private person I had first noticed on our trip? I had never suspected either the softness or the fury I had just witnessed. Of course, I had known her only a brief time.

Yet she needed help, so I assumed a caring approach. I found her thermometer and took her temperature. Dangerously high. I gave her some pills from my medical kit and asked, "Are you thirsty? When did you last drink anything?"

I had glimpsed a refrigerator behind the bar in the living room and returned to it. Several bottles of sparkling water sat on the bar, clean glasses nearby. In the freezer compartment I found several old-fashioned trays of ice. After filling two glasses, I walked into her bedroom again.

She still hunched in the far corner of her king bed, though appearing less wary now. "How about a nice cool drink?" I held out a glass. "It is very hot out there, and I am thirsty. What about you?"

She shook her head. But then she licked her parched lips. "I guess I am...Who are you?" The child was back. She reached out and took the glass.

After she emptied it in one long pull, she thrust it toward me. "More?" Her eyes no longer flared, so I gave her the other one. She drank the entire contents again.

"More." Seeming insatiable, she consumed almost two large, full bottles. Then she straightened her legs, lay down, drew a deep breath, and fell asleep.

To be safe, I called a doctor in Sihanoukville whom I had discovered, and he eventually arrived and checked her over. She was quite groggy, and he left some medicine and instructions for her care.

Then, relieved I had helped her this much, I sat beside her, holding her hot hand and stroking her forehead with a damp cloth. She twitched and turned in her sleep, and I studied her long, straight nose, her tousled red hair, her chapped lips. She didn't wake the remainder of the night, and I slept on the couch—listening, feeling more responsible for her than I had for my own twin sons when they were ill.

During the next few days, her fever began to drop, and she coughed less.

At first, she said, "I'm so grateful you're here." She even briefly touched my arm. "It really *is* you, isn't it? I was afraid I was dreaming. I've had some strange experiences lately."

She stared around the room, as if making sure of where she was, her face almost glowing. Whether she still had some fever or something else was happening to her, I could not tell. When she spoke again, her voice was strong, clear. "I had a vision. I think it was the day you came here," she said. "My parents appeared to me, and my mother, Meatea, suggested that I remain in Cambodia."

"Maybe you should consider her suggestion." What else could I say? That she was imagining things? She seemed so convinced that I did not want to upset her. I simply cleaned her as best I could with a washcloth, and she fell asleep.

She was groggy when she woke up this time. "Did you eat anything the day before I got here?" I looked around for dirty plates or other signs that she had eaten and saw only one crusted bowl that probably had contained the soup the manager had mentioned.

She shook her head.

"Are you hungry?"

She nodded.

She was obviously dehydrated, so I ordered some broth, and she drank most of it.

After that, she seemed more like herself, though her cheeks were still flushed. Because she began to finger her hair, I said, "Want me to brush that for you? It got a little untidy while you were asleep."

She stiffened but then said, "That would be nice. Thank you."

After I finished, I replaced her soiled sheets with clean ones, and she fell asleep again. She had changed from wild to tame in such a short time, I hoped she would be well soon. Who knew she would be so sturdy?

When I was not tending to her, I tried to read one of the magazines I found in her cabana. But I could not concentrate. So I walked the beach, not straying far in case she needed me. I thought of my own mother, so far away. She had been living in California when she died. I longed for her to appear and give me some advice.

The days flowed by. After Barbara felt stronger, I helped her to her bathroom with ease. When I first saw it, with its huge showerhead and, just outside, a private pool large enough for a dozen people, it amazed me. Was this how she lived back in Texas?

As she showered, I rummaged through the items scattered on the granite countertop. Finally, I located her hairbrush, the one I had used earlier. *Nieman Marcus* was stamped on the back of it, the name of an ultra-expensive department store. No one with her wealth would want to associate with a hard-working guide in a poor country for very long.

After her bath, wearing a fresh, blue sleep shirt that said DALLAS COWBOYS, she let me brush her tangles, reminding me of a purring cat. I did not want to leave. I enjoyed taking care of her. And being with her gave me a sense of belonging I had never felt with anyone before. Yet she would be flying away from my country soon. I needed to tend to myself instead of wish for something I could never have.

Back in her bedroom, she lay relaxed against her pillows, half asleep. "I have to go back to Phnom Penh, Barbara. You are well enough to manage on your own." I placed a wet cloth on her forehead.

She whispered, "Thank you," and I pressed a quick kiss on her cheek, murmuring good-bye. Would I ever spend time with her again? I hoped so but did not expect to. We lived in two different worlds.

Back in the city, everything had changed—fewer tourists, a sprinkling of face masks, more tours canceled, less traffic. A new term dominated the news and everyone's conversation: Covid-19. Barbara had conquered it, but could the world? The death count from China and Italy made headlines. I assumed I had gained immunity. But no one was certain of anything about the virus. If she had exposed me a second time, was it only a matter of days before I became one of the small but growing number of Cambodians who had the disease, again?

Yet at this point, I was more uneasy about not being able to pay my bills than growing ill. That was when she checked back in at the White Iris and phoned me and, at dinner that evening, offered me this job.

Now, once again, I am doing what I love best, content to spend time with this intriguing woman.

CHAPTER TEN

"Dara?"

Barbara's voice, and the noise of people talking and laughing, wakes me from my dreaming memories of how she and I began this journey together.

"Huh?" I smile at her, aware again of hundreds of aromas. The food vendors have set up their woks and grills on the streets of Kampong Cham.

"I'm hungry. What do you think I'd like? I bet everything smells great."

"So can you detect many odors yet?"

"Yes. How could I not?"

I head toward a row of tiny portable metal buildings, each of them attached to a motorcycle that pulls them from one location to the next. "What are you in the mood for tonight?" I ask her. "Seafood, chicken, vegetables, noodles, beef?"

"Not beef," she says. "Texas has the market cornered, and I doubt I'll ever find anything that compares to a big, juicy steak like Dallas is famous for." She glances at each steaming container as we walk past. "What's that? It looks good."

We stop at a stand where the vegetables appear fresh from the garden and the meat looks high quality. "Lok lak. You might have had it in Thailand, but we do not like it as hot as the Thai people do. Since you have been bragging about Texas beef, would you like to compare ours to yours? We usually cut our steak into bites, stir-fry it, and put tomatoes, lettuce, cucumbers, and onions on it. Then we season it with lime juice and our world-famous black pepper."

She stops and watches a smiling woman whisk cubes of meat around in a large wok. "Hmm. That looks and smells great. I agree to a comparison test. Do you want some too?"

I shake my head, wanting to browse longer, so she holds up one finger to the vendor. "What do you say when you want one of something?" I ask her, like a teacher reminding a student to do her homework. She has begun to try to speak Khmer, and I want her to progress, not regress. She screws up her mouth, then finally says, "*Muy.*"

The woman cooking the beef for her lok lak smiles and stirs faster, then replies. Barbara stares at me, the rush of words obviously overwhelming her.

"It is okay. She just assumed you speak her language more fluently than you do. That is a compliment. She asked if you want your lok lak Cambodian style."

"What's that?"

"Wrapped in a big lettuce leaf. Kind of like a taco."

"Hmm. Sounds delicious. Tell her yes."

I stand my ground. "Tell her yourself."

She flinches, then squints, her tongue peeking from her mouth, and retrieves the correct word. "*Baht.*" She grins at me. "I sound like a sheep."

The cook covers a huge plate with three lettuce leaves, piles them high with vegetables, scoops the steaming contents of her wok on top of them, and hands the dish to Barbara.

"Wow," she says, as I order the same thing. "This is like a hamburger, but totally different. Hey. I thought you planned to shop around some more."

"I did," I admit, as I place a large bill on the narrow counter in front of the grill. Barbara has asked me to take care of all our business transactions except for the most trivial. "But I am hungry, and this looks even better than I expected."

The woman hands me my own plate and tries to give me our change, but Barbara nods for me to include a large tip, as always. So I comply, especially since the shortage of tourists is probably hurting even local businesses like these.

Barbara and I find a concrete bench near the river, sit down, and pick up one of the filled lettuce leaves. "God, this meat is so juicy and tender," she says. "And the spices are perfect. I'm glad I bought some of that Kampot pepper at the plantation the group toured."

"It is a major export item," I remind her. "No self-respecting chef, here or abroad, prepares a meal without it." I cannot stop praising the strengths of my country. It may be small, but we do have a few things to brag about, and our pepper is probably the best in the world.

After she devours her lok lak, and I leisurely finish mine, we sit and watch a green dragon boat speed up the river. "It is practicing for a big race coming up soon," I say.

"Oh, yes," she remarks. "You weren't with us, but a local village guide showed us a boat like that in a shed on their local temple grounds. It must have been a hundred feet long. I found it strange for a religious organization to own a boat."

"It is common, a major way for villagers to raise money to maintain their temple and its grounds. A team races for prize money in large regional cities like the one we are visiting. The winner gets money, usually several thousand dollars, and gains prestige too."

She studies the next boat that flies past us. "Red—my father— would have loved to watch a race like that," she murmurs, almost to herself.

I do not respond but let her linger with her memories. She finally says, "He loved any kind of competition. His mother once said, when she couldn't get him to budge from the television set, where he was always watching some sporting event, 'You'd rather watch two flies screw than do something worthwhile.'" She claps her hand over her mouth. "Oops. Sorry to be so crude, Dara."

I laugh. "No need to apologize. I have heard the same thing before, in several different languages."

"Really? And how many languages do you speak?"

"Hmm. Let me see. Khmer. That is my native tongue, as you say. I learned French while growing up here in Cambodia, because we were a colony of France for so long."

"That's right. I'd forgotten. So, when you were young, everyone spoke French?"

"Not everyone. We gained our independence five years before I was born, so all the educated adults spoke the language. I learned it from my parents and other family members."

"I'm impressed. I studied it in school but didn't retain much. Not too many people in the US learn anything but English. It's all we need."

I nod. "Except in the immigrant communities in large cities."

"In Dallas I didn't have much opportunity to visit any communities like that. Come to think of it, Meatea did befriend most of our yard workers, who usually spoke a foreign language. If I'd paid more attention to what she was interested in, I might have picked up some Spanish, at least."

The wind blowing off the Mekong has turned a bit cool, so I gather the plastic plates the vendor served our lok lak on. "We need to take these back. I like to eat on reusable ones like these for the sake of the environment.."

Barbara jumps up. "Sure. Let's go."

After we have disposed of our dishes, I take a good look at her. "What do you think?" I point at the crowds milling along the riverfront, enjoying the cool of the evening. "Want to walk a bit? Or are you ready to call it a day?"

"*A day*," she says, smiling. "Sorry. I couldn't resist. Didn't you ever hear that old joke? It was mainly among the kids, I guess, when I was growing up."

"I guess it had died out before I moved to the US. Or maybe it was popular in Texas and did not make it to California."

"Most likely the opposite," she says. "California's been the trendsetter as long as I can remember." She shrugs. "Doesn't matter. I should have just told you I'm tired. This has been a really long day. Is it okay if we just go back to the hotel?"

"I was about to suggest that. I was not nearly as sick with the virus as you were, yet I am very tired."

As we walk the few blocks to our hotel, Barbara stumbles on a crack in the sidewalk, so I take her arm, and we stroll along like one of the other couples. She is a head taller than I am, but that does not matter. She shortens her stride, I lengthen mine, and we move as one, tired and full. The way she bumps against me and almost stumbles again tells me she is as ready to reach the hotel as I am.

❖

I have just finished my shower, put on my clean sleep shirt, and walked into our bedroom toweling my hair dry. Barbara is already clean and stretched out on her bed, scrolling through her messages. She looks up. "How many languages did you say you speak?"

"Where did that come from?" I plug in the hotel hair dryer and dry my hair as quickly as possible.

She watches me until I finish. "I'm impressed. I don't know many people who speak three languages fluently. Should I be even more impressed?"

I chuckle. "It is nothing. My mother loved them and encouraged me to learn as many as I could."

Something clouds her expression, but it quickly passes. "Back to my question. How many?"

I rub some cream on my face and arms. "Let me see. I have mentioned Khmer, French, and, of course, English."

"You lived in the US how long?"

"Uh, from 1974 till 1998, so twenty-four years."

She nods. "So that's why you speak English as well as I do."

"I would not say that, but I already knew quite a bit when I got there. That made it easier to try to pick up the slang. You know how teenagers are. They want to fit in."

"Yeah. I know." She seems to retreat into her own thoughts but then refocuses on me.

"I knew quite a bit of Russian and German when I got there too," I say, hoping I do not sound like I am bragging. "So I improved my skills and ended up with a triple major in Russian, German, and Chinese in college."

She shakes her head. "Now I really am impressed. That's how many—six? I do well to speak one. You must think I'm a real dunce, as much trouble as I have learning Khmer."

And there it is. Did her childhood experience about not speaking Khmer make her this insecure still?

"Well, my interest in Chinese is easy to explain," I say, to cover my curiosity about her past.

She seems glad to change the subject. "So explain."

"I married a Chinese man whose family did not speak English. I did not have much choice."

"What about him?"

"Oh, he spoke enough English for us to communicate. But his family and I relied entirely on their language. It was difficult, but I did all right."

"You met him where?"

She seems truly interested in my background but can't suppress a yawn.

I climb into bed and click off my light. "Sorry. But I'm exhausted. Can we talk about all this ancient history later?"

She had been sitting up in her bed, but her shoulders suddenly drop, and she slides underneath her covers. She yawns again and turns off her light. "Good night, Dara," she says. "Thanks for a wonderful day. I'm so glad we're making this trip together…"

"Good night, Barbara," I say, though she cannot hear me. She is already gently snoring.

❖

"This hotel pool can't compare to the beautiful ocean we just came from," Barbara tells me.

We have slept the clock halfway around, barely making it down for our international breakfast at the hotel—something from every conceivable culture and nation to choose from. Now she and I sprawl on lounge chairs on the shady side of the hotel pool.

"Uh-huh." I agree, though I never want to move again. Our long night's sleep has drugged me, and the pile of food I have just consumed has made me almost comatose. I could get used to this way of life.

"Death had her eye on me down there on Koh Rong, you know," Barbara says. "But Life seems to be trying to court me now."

When I manage to turn my head and my attention in her direction, she is staring into the long distance.

For a woman just turned seventy, she is easy on the eyes. I have not noticed her as an attractive, desirable woman before now. As her tour guide, I had to restrict my view. She was someone to deliver to a variety of interesting places, provide with pertinent information, and make sure she had an acceptable place to sleep and eat. And then, during our second encounter, I focused on keeping her clean, cool, and alive.

"I did not know Death was female," I murmur, too lazy and content to raise my voice to a normal range. "I suppose I was too busy wrestling you away from her to notice."

"Yes. You rode in on your black charger and whisked me away from her arms. She *was* wooing me, you know. Tempting me with invitations from my parents."

"Have you checked your temperature this morning?" I halfway mean it.

"Yes. It's normal." She laughs. "Don't worry. I don't plan to flake out on you again. We have an entire country to explore, and I wouldn't miss that chance for anything."

With more energy than I have, she jumps up from her lounger and strolls over to our rectangle of a swimming pool. It certainly cannot rival the ocean, but it provides a wonderful frame for my first picture of her as a companion. Her legs are long and sturdy, capable of gripping the sides of my Honda. Not many freckles or age spots on them. The skin is taut, not flabby. She has evidently spent time in the gym or on the track.

Her butt fills her red one-piece but does not ooze out and spoil the effect. I could probably run my hand from her bathing suit to her flesh and barely detect the change. Her suit is practically backless, so the long length of skin with its lovely texture is obvious. She has probably chosen a healthy diet and appropriate exercise. Her long neck leads up to a well-sculpted head, thick red hair feathering onto her shoulders and, as always, perfectly colored.

Suddenly, she turns around, and I consider cataloguing her from the top down now. But she strolls back to her chair and eases into it. I plan to save that snapshot of her on my inner hard drive.

Death is a woman. And Barbara is too. The reminder glues me to my chair. I suddenly desire this woman. But how should I deal with my attraction? I need to explore that question very carefully.

❖

I wake now. The aroma of coconut drifts toward me, makes me turn onto my side to watch Barbara smooth thick, white cream down her even-smoother legs. I want to help, but first I watch her through barely open lids.

"Like to do my back?"

Obviously, I have not fooled her. "Do you always ask your female pool companions that question?" I think I know the answer.

"Only if they're short and dark and drive a motorcycle."

She is flirting with me—out of boredom or genuine interest?

I jump in. "I suppose that qualifies me." I reach for the tan-and-brown tube she holds and read aloud, "Eco Tan, Natural Coconut Sunscreen."

"Yes." She turns her back toward me. "Smells great, has SPF 30 protection, and, most important, contains anti-aging properties."

"They certainly work."

She grows rigid as I rub the non-greasy cream onto her skin. Have my words or my touch caused her reaction? Or is it something else?

I stroke her skin, as I did her forehead and cheeks on the island of Koh Rong, my feelings nothing like the ones I had then. I felt almost motherly then, wanted to protect her, soothe her, nourish her.

But now? I want to get inside her, explore her. If I dared, I would investigate her shoulder muscle that stretches from her neck to her arm with my mouth. I would lick her warm skin. Then I would nip her, very gently. And—if she did not resist, but sighed instead—I would place a brief yet lingering kiss on the sensitive area I have created.

She turns around, gazes into my eyes for a beat longer than ever before, and says, "Want me to do yours?"

I do, I do, I say to myself. But then I, who speaks six languages fluently, simply nod and turn my back to her. I wish she would act on my fantasy. I am obviously unable to.

❖

I dream of fielding questions from a large audience, responding in French, Chinese, English to the varied crowd. The participants shoot questions at me faster and faster until—drip. I pause. Drip. Something is pulling me away from my intense interchange. Drip.

"Wake up, lazy bones," someone says. "Are you planning to sleep all day?" A soft hand is shaking me. Barbara. She is touching me where I wanted to touch her. But this is not quite what I had in mind.

I sputter awake, ready to tease her. "Can a woman not have any time to herself?" I mumble.

But she obviously does not understand my intent. Her hand drops. "I'm sorry."

Now I am wide-awake, sitting up and feeling terrible. She has regressed to the childlike figure I nursed on Koh Rong. I want the woman with the coconut lotion to return.

"What a nice nap." I stretch. "But I am glad you woke me up. Are you tired of being out here? Want to do something else?"

"I'm tired of being by myself." Her pout seems mostly pretense, because she laughs suddenly, and it vanishes. "Seriously, don't we need to discuss where we're traveling next? We do have dinner tonight with one of your friends, but do you want to spend tomorrow here too? Or should we plan our itinerary?"

I suppose she has obligations in Dallas and will have to return eventually. If this virus worsens, she might have trouble booking a flight home, and her visa—"Oh, my God. How long have you been here?"

"What do you mean, here? In Cambodia?"

I sit up straighter. "Yes. Have you forgotten about your visa? It is good for only a month."

"A month? Yes. I did forget. I'd planned to spend two weeks on our tour, then another one or so, tops, on Koh Rong. That would have given me enough time before my month ran out."

She stares at me, her dark eyes vast. "But Covid-19 changed all that. Will they throw me out of the country, or in jail?"

I shudder, then touch her arm, but not in the way I fantasized earlier. "No one is putting you in jail or tossing you out of the country. I can take care of this." My lethargy vanishes. "I have to get dressed, and I need your passport. Will you be all right if I leave you alone for a while?"

"I think I can manage."

She does not sound offended, merely amused that I am treating her like a child who requires constant supervision.

I jump up, already considering which of my associates to contact. "I will be back later this afternoon. This should not take long." *I hope.*

❖

My errand does *not* take long. I have a friend, Pich, who works at the police station in Kampong Cham. Luckily, she is on duty. She owes me a favor, so I have to wait only a few minutes.

"Hello, Dara. What is going on? Another tour group?" Pich looks behind her, obviously to make sure no one is listening, and keeps her voice low.

I shake my head. "No. It looks like most tourists are staying home right now. But I am escorting one American woman on a private tour."

Pich grins. "Is she rich and beautiful?"

"Of course. She is from Texas."

"Sounds like you have discovered a gold mine." Pich winks.

I have known Pich since I moved back to Cambodia with my husband twenty or so years ago. We were both proper wives and mothers and stayed in touch after we left our husbands and discovered how much we prefer the same sex instead of the opposite. She was wilder than I was, though, and still tends to like her women young and loose. She had a lot of affairs and got a position in the police force. Then she moved here from Phnom Penh. I do not run into her often, though I do try to get in touch with her when I stop here with a tour group. And when she has business in Phnom Penh, we sometimes hit one of the gay clubs there. Their drag shows are always worth seeing, and Pich likes to cruise the girls.

I do not mention Barbara's age or the way I am beginning to feel about her. Pich would tell me I am crazy, except that Barbara has money. Instead, I keep things light. "She is okay, Pich, but not your type."

"But she is yours?" Pich looks interested but glances around her office, as if she would like to talk to me but does not want to get into trouble. "How can I help you?" she asks in a louder tone.

"It is about the American woman. She has just recovered from Covid-19, but her visa has expired. Any chance you can help?"

"Give me her name and passport number, and I will call my friend at the GDI." Pich snaps her fingers. "They give out non-immigrant visa renewals all the time. All those old American hippies seem to love it over here, and we like to accommodate them and their life savings."

I hand over the necessary information, glad our General Department of Immigration is lax. It makes my job a lot easier. I do not consider Barbara an old American hippie, though I could be wrong.

In less than an hour, I am back at the hotel presenting Barbara with an officially stamped new visa, stapled in her passport.

She hugs me, a quick pull-me-to-her-chest move, which only makes me want to do it again. But this time, more slowly, so I can enjoy the burn. Maybe being around Pich has made me read more into a totally innocent gesture than I should. But when Barbara pushes me away too quickly, I wonder if she feels more for me than I think.

Or am I somehow hinting at my feelings for her, and she is trying to avoid a messy scene? She might have just realized I am gay. And if she has, she might decide not to share a room with me, or to cut our trip short. I need to be careful. I am so confused, but I am certain of one thing.

She is gradually making me want to act on my attraction. And I am not certain whether to encourage her. Either way, it will probably cause complications.

Chapter Eleven

We are sitting on the floor in the main room of my friend Leap's house. Our mats are thin, according to American standards, and I fear Barbara will be uncomfortable. At least her back is to the wall, so she can lean against it if she wants.

The floor in front of us is covered with a variety of dishes, placed one at a time on an ornate cloth. Fried chicken and shrimp, grilled beef and pork, rice, eggplant. She is sampling everything, talking about how good each dish is. She shifts her position often but does not seem to mind sitting here instead of in a chair.

We have eaten here before, with our tour group. And that time she did not complain, except about the noise. Another group sat on the other side of the room, so the volume was rather loud, but no worse than in a typical American restaurant.

She did not talk much the first time. But tonight, she appears relaxed and actively listens as Leap discusses his home. "I built this house from the ground up," he says. "Some friends helped me locate the trees and cut them. You cannot find many like them these days."

"Did building your house take long, Leap?" she asks.

"Oh, yes. We were all working at other jobs. But when we had a chance, we got together. And piece by piece, we created all this." He sweeps his hand around, indicating the large main room and beyond.

"Didn't you say last time that everyone in the family sleeps in this room?" She seems very engaged with him. I sit back and enjoy watching her.

"That is right." He beams at her—I suppose for taking an interest in what he had said on that occasion and remembering it. "We do not have to buy expensive bed frames and mattresses and, what do you call them, bedspreads, like people in some other countries do." He drinks from his glass, then continues. "Every night, after we eat, we pick up these floor coverings. And when we are ready, each of us spreads our sleeping mat on the floor, and we sleep. Then, in the morning, we roll them up again and store them out of the way."

"But that's just you and your wife and your sons and the young children. Isn't that what you said?" she asks.

"Yes. I partitioned off that little private room over there in the corner for our teenage daughters."

She nods. "I love the smart way you use space. And your front door is a work of art, Leap." She points behind him. "I looked at it more closely this time, as we came in. Surely you didn't make it yourself."

"Unfortunately, no. I am not that skilled at woodworking. The carvings you have surely seen in most of the older hotels on your tour require much more patience and ability than I have. And you will not find carvings like that in the new hotels. Cambodia is fast running out of the kind of wood you need to make them."

She sits up straight, no longer resting her back against the wall. "I've read about your deforestation problem. It makes me furious that foreigners and the wealthy here are cutting down your forests as if they'll always be here."

Leap nods. "Yes. But they are not the only ones. Our poorer workers can make a lot more money in one month from selling trees they illegally cut in the forest than they can make in a year from farming and other jobs. They do not see the big picture—just the hungry little mouths they have to feed every day."

At the end of our evening with Leap, he and Barbara shake hands with a warmth I have rarely seen her show. And his expression reveals a type of respect I have never seen him offer any of the many tourists I have introduced him to.

"I plan to do everything I can to help solve your problem here," she says. "I have friends in East Texas, which is still heavily wooded. It's one of the most beautiful areas in the state but has some of the same issues you describe."

During our ride home after dinner, in a tuk-tuk instead of on my cycle, Barbara says, "I had a wonderful time tonight, Dara. Thank you for the chance to talk to Leap again...and thank you for your company. I so enjoy being with you. The more I get to know this country and its people, the more I feel at home here."

She enjoys being with me? What does that mean? That I am a great tour guide, sensitive to her interests and meeting her needs? Or is she enjoying me the way she might enjoy a friend, and her hug earlier was just a hug? Does she even have close friends? If so, why is she here in Cambodia alone? For that matter, why is she not married? Maybe she was, and lost her husband. Or divorced him, like I did. Either one is possible. She is certainly a mystery I find myself wanting to solve.

"I enjoy being with you too." I squeeze her hand briefly and do not let go. We remain silent the rest of the ride back to the hotel, a full moon shining over the Mekong when we arrive.

"Want to sit out by the river and talk some more?"

Barbara's suggestion startles me. "Sure." I suppose our conversation with Leap has put her in the mood.

We find a bench across from our hotel, far enough away from the clubs and tourist cafés that their noise forms only a pleasant buzz. "Do you have anything particular on your mind?" I ask as we sit there, facing the lazy Mekong.

She surprises me. "Yes. Talking about Leap's house made me think about one I lived in a long time ago, in a run-down Dallas neighborhood."

She pauses, but I stay silent, let her memories unroll to match the pace of the river.

"The house was old, with high ceilings. I painted every room a vivid color—red, green, yellow, blue. Days of inhaling paint fumes and nights of smoking joints kept me in touch with those hues. As did the songs of the Beatles, Chicago, Simon and Garfunkel." She hums a bit of a song I used to love—"Bridge Over Troubled Water."

She falls silent, and I let the conversation drift. She will come around again, I am sure.

"My girlfriend and I were twenty-two," she says, "just out of college and enamored of the peace movement and free love. It was 1972."

Her girlfriend? A friend, she must mean.

She takes a deep breath, as if she is inhaling the color, the smell, the sound of those far-away years.

I was still living in Cambodia then, I recall, as I drift back too. Maybe I will reveal some of my own recollections later, but I want to hear hers now.

"I especially remember our dining room," she says. "The ceiling must have been twelve feet tall, and the room had an open entryway from the living room as wide as two doors, with fancy woodwork twelve inches high stretched across its top. I enameled it white, and it gleamed against the turquoise room."

I can visualize it, the blue and the white. "Those were colorful years," I murmur, and my comment does not distract her.

"My girlfriend and I had flown out to San Francisco five years earlier, for the Summer of Love, wearing bell-bottoms and flowers in our hair. During our two weeks there, we bought an erotic poster showing two nude women wrapped around each other, captioned COME TOGETHER. That was as risqué as we could conceive of."

Two nude women. Evidently her friend was her girlfriend.

I sigh loudly. "I wish I could have been at the love-in alongside you, with a girl on my arm too, and in my bed."

I hear myself say those words, and just like that, she and I are out to each other. The moon blushes above us.

She rests her hand on top of mine as she reminisces, my revelation not seeming to shock or concern her. "We bought a beaded curtain in San Francisco too—turquoise and green—just the width of a regular doorway, and four Japanese stools, made of wood and straw cord. They sat about five inches off the floor, each just wide enough for one person to sit on." She chuckles, mostly to herself, perhaps thinking how uncomfortable it would be to sit on those low stools now.

She lets go of me and stretches, as if recalling fond memories of the adventurous twenty-two-year-old she once was. "We bought a large square of plywood and four cinderblocks, plus a few yards of unbleached muslin for a tablecloth, complete with crayons for guests to use to sign or draw on it. That was our dining table, the four stools our chairs. The suggestive poster was tacked high on one wall, and the beads hung on the door that led to our bedroom." She laughs. "We thought we were so cool."

I take her hand, squeeze it the tiniest bit. "You were. And you still are." My throat aches a little as I ask, "What happened to those two girls and their hippie house in Dallas?"

Her smile is almost sad too. "They broke up, and they grew up. She had to work, and I played at work. My father cracked his whip, and I jumped to the tune of his money."

Barbara gazes at me and then at the river. "Where does all the time go? One day you're scandalizing your parents, and the next you wobble when you ride a bicycle."

I am caught in her moonlight mood and let it engulf me. "But we can still have our hippie houses and Japanese stools. The colors are just not quite as bright now and the stools not as low."

She laughs, as if breaking the spell she has woven. "Just look at me, sitting under the moon reminiscing, when I should be drinking in the wonders of Cambodia. And of you."

She jerks her head back, as if just hearing the words that have slipped from her mouth.

"And of you," I say, lifting her hand to my mouth and kissing the back of it. "Here is to new beginnings under new moons." I long to kiss her lips, explore her mouth with my tongue. But she is my employer, and I am her employee.

Her smile is radiant, and we slowly rise together, the river behind us. "Want to head north tomorrow? Toward the rain forests that are being pillaged," she asks as we cross the street, its traffic sparse now.

"Sure," I say.

"I'm certain we'll come across some adventures there." She gives a little skip, totally out of character for a woman her age. The remnants of her spell still shadow us.

"I cannot wait." I open the hotel's front door and then ring for the elevator. I mean what I have just said, and now I understand a bit better the part of Barbara that does not mind washing out her dirty clothes when she travels.

Like some Westerners say, she is getting under my skin.

CHAPTER TWELVE

At breakfast, I am enjoying my bowl of rice noodle soup when Barbara looks up from her omelet and bacon. "What rain forest should we head for? You're the expert on Cambodia's geography."

I swallow, then say, "I usually lead tours on good roads and focus on big cities. But I have sketched a plan in my head."

She breaks off a piece of a bacon strip and holds it up. "And? Tell me about it."

I take another spoonful of soup, which is still hot, and blow it before I raise it to my lips. Umm. I have added just the right blend of fresh onions and fried garlic to it this morning, and its sweet-zesty flavor makes my mouth feel alive. I relive the touch and taste of her hand when I kissed it last night—soft and fragrant.

She has already finished her bite of bacon when I hear her clear her throat. "Dara. Are you planning to tell me what you have in mind, or do you intend to sit here all morning?" She sounds impatient but may be teasing me.

I put down my spoon and try to focus on today instead of last night. Sitting and talking with her in the moonlight was so enchanting. I do not want to ever break the spell. I sip my hot tea, which I have stirred some coffee into. The combination should jolt me into the present.

"Do you think we'll have time to reach wherever we're heading today, or shall we wait till tomorrow?" She glances at her FitBit.

Americans can be so impatient and demanding…and charming. I like the way she has styled her hair. It is much longer than when I first saw her, which softens her face, makes her appear more youthful. Or maybe I am overlaying my image of her with the young hippie she let me glimpse last night.

The caffeine finally takes effect, and I sit up straighter. "We should head for Kratie. How long will it take you to get ready?" I am all tour guide now, have pushed our closeness by the river into the background.

She has cleaned her plate and almost finished her iced coffee. "Ten minutes, tops."

"All right. I am nearly packed so will check out and meet you at our room in eight."

"Don't be late," she quips, and I snap off a salute. We are up and out of the hotel restaurant in a flash.

Instead of sitting beside the mighty Mekong, we are now whizzing over it. I can feel Barbara turning her head to view one side of the bridge, then the other, evidently taking in every sight she can manage to spot on its 1.5 km span. Almost to the other side, she sucks in a breath as a salmon-red lighthouse juts up. I imagine her remarking that its French-inspired architecture makes its three tiers resemble those of a church more than a beacon for ships.

Today we follow the course of the Mekong, driving up toward Kratie by way of Chhlong. The road is not bad—tar in most places, with some gravel and dirt sections, ruts, and bumps. We have some beautiful views of the river, motor through flat land with some hills, ride several ferries, and encounter trucks, tuk-tuks, motorbikes, and a lot of school children in their uniforms pedaling bicycles near towns and villages.

We stop whenever Barbara taps my back—to take a picture, drink some water, relieve ourselves and buy gasoline at a station. The sun is blazing, but the breeze keeps us cool as we whiz along.

Every time we stop, her luminous eyes refuel me. She seems to take in everything with so much joy and excitement, plus a bit of mischief. Every new sight seems to engage her, as if she becomes part of it and it delights her. I want her to gaze at me that way, and when she does, I feel warmer inside than out. She seems unable to get enough of this country. The longer I am with her, the more I hope she feels that way about me.

After about 130 km on the road, we stand on the bank of the winding river. Only thirty more to go. She takes pictures. After she finishes, I ask, "What makes you want to look around at everything all the time? Most tourists get bored after a while, tired of the same thing." I touch her cheek.

She pulls away from my fingers slightly. Was last night a dream? But then she smiles slightly, reassuring me that it was no fantasy.

"I keep wondering where Meatea lived while she was here, what she wants me to see." She scans the river, a distant village, a solitary home shaded by giant trees. "Maybe she lived on a boat on the river, moving with the seasons, her family free to pull up anchor anytime."

I want to be involved in her search for her mother, her sense of adventure, her delight in the unknown, so I say, "Or maybe she lived in that village over there and walked to the river, imagining how she could get away from all this."

The glimmer in her eyes dims enough for me to wish I could take back my words.

But after a minute, she lets her suddenly rigid shoulders relax again. "Or perhaps she lived over there, in that little thatched-roof house on stilts, so poor and lonely she could hardly breathe. Then, one day, a tall, white-skinned stranger, who seems lost, asks her for directions to Kampong Cham, pointing at his crinkled map and gesturing. She takes pity on him."

I pick up the thread. "As best she can, she tells him how to get there, gesturing toward the village. But he seems helpless, so, as a good-will gesture, she offers him a banana from the stalk she is carrying to the village to sell."

She joins in. "He offers to carry the heavy stalk for her, she accepts, and after they reach the village, she takes her place selling fruit in the local market. He decides to rent a room nearby."

I am back on track. "He finds one, stays there, and begins to learn the language, resting from his travels in this part of the world. It is the first place he has wanted to stay, and—"

"She's definitely the reason. He sees her in the market every day, and they go for walks, up here on the banks of the Mekong—"

"And they fall in love. Her parents hate him, but she loves him, and you are the result." I sigh, basking in the romance we have imagined. "I like our story."

Her eyes shine. "I like it too. And I like you." She steps closer, puts her hand on my cheek this time, and I do not step back. Instead, I move nearer, stretch up on my toes—"Isn't it time to go?"

The magic of our story dissolves, and I back away. "We should do this again," she says as we retrieve our helmets and she mounts the cycle.

"Count on it." I climb on in front of her, and we are off toward Kratie. The heat inside me burns more fiercely than the sun on my face.

❖

Several kilometers before we reach Kratie, I turn left onto a gravel road and drive for a few minutes. We soon reach a village that reminds me of the one Barbara and I have just conjured up. I have called ahead and reserved a spot at one of the homestays we use on tours. Usually, we have to reserve weeks in advance. But now we are more than welcome on short notice like this.

Our hosts are scurrying around in the shade that the upper story of their cinder-block home provides. A long table with chairs fills part of the open-air lower area, which also contains a makeshift kitchen toward the back right. When this family hosts homestays, everyone except their teenage daughter sleeps in their enclosed kitchen and its adjoining room on the ground level.

Barbara and I climb the steep staircase to the second floor. Two thick mats already lie spread on the floor, mosquito netting hanging down to enclose each of them. The family's daughter will sleep in a walled-off area at the other edge of the large section where we are staying.

On tour, we usually have a similar situation, but normally the large upstairs room is covered with up to twelve mats and nets, travelers of both genders sharing the space. No one seems to care, except when some of them snore loudly and disturb the others.

We throw our backpacks at the foot of our mats, and she goes to inspect the bathroom. She is not that picky, though she did not shower at the homestay on our first tour. Those stark facilities must have seemed terribly primitive to her.

"I guess I'm getting used to Cambodian bathrooms," she says when she gets back. "It's not that much trouble to dip water out of a bucket and use it to flush the toilet. At least we won't have to squat on this one. My thigh muscles aren't what they used to be."

She is such a good sport. Who would have thought a rich, spoiled American would enjoy some of the things she does? But then I recall her youthful hippie phase, and the idea does not seem so preposterous. And her Cambodian side may play a role as well. Whatever it is, I am relieved she is not afraid to try new things.

❖

The virus has now spread, and people are afraid. Our hosts teach school for a living, so not only must they instruct students who cannot be close to each other, but they also have to deal with their own four school-age children. They are so busy they have no time to prepare a big, fancy dinner for us, as they usually do. We plan to eat a basic meal with them tonight and be on our own the rest of the time.

After we have washed up from our drive and gone downstairs to snack on a bowl of fruit I prepare from the bananas, mangos, and other produce our hosts have provided, Barbara yawns. "Do you mind if I go up and rest? That was a long drive, though I already love seeing a different part of Cambodia."

"That sounds good to me." Her yawn is infectious, so we both climb the outside stairs and stretch out on our mats.

She turns onto her side and props her head on her hand, facing me with gleaming eyes. "When are we going to visit some of those big, lush rain forests I've always associated with Cambodia? The scenery was pretty on the way up here, but I'm looking for jungles to explore. I didn't have a chance to do that on Koh Rong."

I have been lying on my back, staring up at the rafters high overhead, the ceiling fan that hangs there beating the air. I gaze at her, propping my head on my hand as well. I am frustrated that I cannot give her what she wants. "I wish we could turn back the clock and be here in the twentieth century instead of the twenty-first."

"Why?" She yawns and stretches out on her mat. She won't be awake much longer. "Because between 2000 and 2005, we lost about one third of our hardwood forests."

Her drooping eyelids rise. "I read about that problem but didn't realize it was so bad."

"Only Vietnam and Nigeria were devastated worse than Cambodia was." Just talking about this subject makes me queasy. It is larger than whatever is happening between Barbara and me.

"I don't understand. Everyone knows how important trees are to the planet."

"Money is the problem." I shake my head, feeling helpless. "People all over the world are demanding more luxury items. It is supply and demand."

"But surely things here slowed down after people realized what was happening." She blows out a deep breath, seeming concerned.

"I wish." I roll onto my back again, cynical. "People can break laws. And politicians can be corrupt."

She tucks her knees up against her stomach. "I know." I'm sure she's become aware of her government's failings. After all, LBJ and the Bushes were from Texas. Her eyelids are drooping again.

I try to lighten the subject. "At least some people did something positive."

She glances at me with what I imagine is the last remnant of her attention. "Which is?"

"Our government started assigning areas to local communities, who manage them."

"What do the communities do?"

"They are like watchdogs and have made some difference. But it is not easy to keep people from cutting down what they want in isolated areas." It is a complicated issue, and I am glad it interests her.

"Maybe we can visit some of the places where the jungles are being watched. What do you call them?" She sounds so tired but is still fighting sleep.

"Community forests. And yes. We should try to do that."

Her eyes close, and when she does not reopen them, I relax and let her soft snores and the thrum of the ceiling fan push me to sleep as well.

❖

The next morning, my eyes are still closed when I hear Barbara yawn. She rustles around, a board creaks, a door opens and closes, twice, and soon she is back beside me. But she is on her own separate mat.

I wish I felt free to reach across the space that divides us and pull her closer. Yet this connection between us is too fresh. And she is still my employer. Would she welcome my advance? Or would she stiffen, as she did when I touched her cheek on the way up here?

Warm and still drowsy, I decide not to risk it. Instead, I murmur, "Sleep well?"

"Mmm. Yes. Thanks. Did you?" Her morning voice is sexy.

"Yes. I did." I never sleep during the day on tour, like we did yesterday afternoon. Always something to do or someone's question or problem to deal with. I like this one-on-one, more relaxed approach to touring.

But my guide persona is hard to suppress completely. I resist my continuing urge to reach over and touch her. Instead, I say, "It is a little cooler outside now. Are you ready to leave this place, or would you like to stay here another night, perhaps walk around the village this morning?"

"A walk sounds nice."

She is ready before I am and leaves me to wash up and dress. When I get downstairs, she is sitting and reading her well-worn guidebook. "On second thought, I'm still a little tired," she says, the skin around her dark eyes appearing bruised. "Do you mind if we skip the village tour and just drive to Kratie today? Stay there a while? I'm not up for another long trip on the cycle just yet."

"Not at all." I am truly relieved. I have grown accustomed to having a driver on tour and am more weary than usual. "You are the boss."

She laughs. "And don't you forget it."

She is teasing me now, and a little wave hits my stomach, almost like a cramp but so much more pleasurable.

She is still holding her guidebook, a finger stuck into its pages. She seems to have regained some of her usual energy. "I have an idea for Kratie. In fact, several ideas."

I sit down beside her.

"You know I've enjoyed these homestays," she says, almost like she is apologizing for something. "It's really interesting to experience how the ordinary people of Cambodia live. But I found a place in Kratie where I'd like to spend a couple of nights."

"That is fine with me. Just tell me its name." I pull my cell phone from my pocket.

She opens her book and consults it. "It's not exactly in Kratie, but on Koh Trong island, nearby. It's called Rajabori Villas. The book describes it as 'drop-dead gorgeous' and says it looks like a traditional Cambodian village."

I am immediately intrigued. "I have heard of it but never been there. Does your book list a number for it?"

"Of course."

As she reads me the number, I tap it in and then talk to the owner.

"They do not have anything but a double, with one queen-size bed, available for the next few days. Is that all right with you? And it costs sixty-five dollars a night." Our tour company would never book a place this expensive.

She jerks back a fraction—because of the sleeping arrangement or the cost? But she immediately nods, and I am relieved.

"Okay," I tell her after I hang up. "The island is about twenty minutes from Kratie by boat. Then we have to drive to the north end of the island." She frowns, as if it might be too remote. "But it does sound like a good choice. Maybe I should hire you to be my assistant guide."

She flushes, and again I am unsure what she feels. Proud of her discovery, worried about its inconvenient setting, insulted to be considered a mere assistant, or something else? But she enlightens me this time.

"I'd love to be your assistant. What fun that would be. And let's don't forget my other ideas during our stay here. Maybe you'll give me a bonus for them."

"What are they?"

"Let's just say they involve dolphins and giant turtles." She smiles.

Hmm. She seems to like me and what I do. The little wave in my stomach becomes a tsunami.

CHAPTER THIRTEEN

The ferry from Kratie to the island of Koh Trong is crammed with locals and a few tourists like us. But it is nice to be on the Mekong, with its fresh breeze. The ferry pulls up to a huge beach, and I wheel my bike onto a makeshift walkway of old boards and plywood. It makes slogging across the deep sand much easier. Several bikes are waiting for the boat, and the drivers motion the other tourists to climb on behind them. Then they race up the hill we are trudging up, me pushing my cycle. I do not want to chance driving off the narrow path into the sand.

Always a good sport, Barbara follows me. And when we finally make it to the top, her eyes glisten. She has found her jungle. Trees and other vegetation of all description stretch as far as I can see. And the only motorized vehicles are cycles and tuk-tuks. Some of the tourists from our ferry climb into the tuk-tuks. Obviously, they do not want to ride the speeding cycles longer than necessary. I stop, board my bike, and Barbara gets on behind me. Then we are off, driving down the asphalt. The wind cools the sweat we have worked up on the beach.

The hotel is only a few kilometers away. And it seems worth the trouble to get here. We reach a compound of villas perched on stilts, each one made entirely of red teak and decorated with elaborate woodwork. I feel like I have stepped back into a typical village a hundred years ago.

I stop and hear her intake of breath. "How gorgeous all those birds of paradise and banana trees are. And the frangipani!" She is glancing around and identifying the flowers and trees that surround a huge swimming pool. It fronts what appears to be the main building of this breathtaking complex.

I go inside and chat with the manager, and when I return, she is on the other side of the pool studying the statuary and an organic garden. I wave her over and, pushing the cycle, lead her to our nearby villa and park outside it.

After we climb a short but steep flight of steps to the second floor, she gasps as we enter our deluxe room. "Now this is what I expected Cambodia to be like," she says.

The high-peaked ceiling and walls are all built of the same red teak we saw on the outside. And the floor is made of the same wood also. It is like standing in a very fancy carved box.

She walks around the room, inspecting the wall decorations, statuary, and other furnishings. "All these appear to be antiques," she says. "That armoire is outstanding." Then she checks out the bathroom, with its huge, white clawfoot tub, double-sink vanity, and modern toilet, approving of it as well.

Back in the bedroom, she tosses her backpack onto a nearby chair and climbs onto the bed—after I have removed all the fresh flowers and towels folded into the shape of swans arranged as a welcome. I have heard this is a common feature on a cruise ship but have never seen anything this extravagant in a hotel room.

Even when she lies down and looks up, she keeps gushing about how wonderful this place is. "Hmm." She turns from her back to her side. "The bed's just right, and I love that huge mosquito net."

I sit on the bed, which is as comfortable as she claims. Then I crane my head back too. "We should not have to use that netting. This far into the dry season, we may not have any insects at all, especially mosquitos."

I glance at the three-blade ceiling fan high above us but do not tell Barbara what I am thinking. When I checked in, the receptionist informed me that we have no air-conditioning and that the electricity cuts off about two a.m. The solar panels do not last all night, and it is too noisy to use generators while guests are trying to sleep. Barbara has been so excited about this place that I do not want to disappoint her. But after the fan shuts off, perhaps a cool breeze from the river will take its place. I hope.

We unpack our few belongings, and then she asks, "Want to walk around the remainder of the grounds? We didn't have to drive far today, so I don't need to rest."

"Of course," I say, happy to do whatever she wants. This is her trip, and I am delighted to be here in this hotel she has chosen. It is several steps above any I have ever stayed in, and I like its quiet solitude.

After we explore the grounds, she chooses two lounge chairs in a shady spot near the pool, and we stretch out. "How about a drink?" she asks, so I wave over a nearby waiter.

"What would you like?" I ask her. This is a new scenario for me. I never socialize with my tour members by the pool. I am always busy working behind the scenes.

"A Paradise Mule."

"What does it have in it?" I am not much of a drinker, especially of specialty cocktails like it must be.

"Hmm. Lime vodka, ginger beer, pineapple, and blue butterfly blossom. I had one in the Raffles lounge in Phnom Penh and asked the bartender to share the recipe with me."

I repeat the ingredients to the barefoot boy, who now stands beside me. Hopefully the bartender here is more sophisticated than the waiter appears to be.

"I will have one too," I say on impulse. I usually drink beer, but since this is a fancy place, I should try a fancy drink.

After they arrive, she takes a sip, the waiter nearby. She nods. "Perfect."

So I assure him that he has done well and try my own. "Ah. Just right for a lazy afternoon," I say. "Obviously, a Cambodian version of a Moscow Mule." I want her to know I can be cosmopolitan too.

We settle back in our loungers and watch the wind ruffle the leaves of the banana trees and the pool's blue surface. I soon doze off.

I wake up in a daze. "My mule must have kicked me in the head," I tell Barbara, and she laughs.

She seems in high spirits. "You know, Dara. I've been watching you sleep and thinking that I've told you a lot about my parents but don't know much about yours. You mentioned that they left Cambodia for the States right before the Khmer Rouge came to power. What made them decide to get out of the country?"

I stare at the pool, memories of the past hitting me, yet my surroundings and her presence softening them. I begin with my most comfortable recollections.

"My father was a history professor at Royal University in Phnom Penh, and my mother also taught history, at a French Catholic school there."

She shakes her head, as if startled. "I had no idea your parents were so well educated."

"Their families could afford for them to go to college. My father even studied at the Sorbonne in Paris, with the help of a partial scholarship."

"I'm impressed. When was that?"

"In the early 1950s, at the same time Pol Pot was there."

"Pol Pot? Did your father know him?"

"As a matter of fact, he did. But by his real name—Saloth Sar."

"What did he think? Were they friends?"

"Hardly. They were both in Paris on scholarship, but Pol Pot—I will call him that because the name is more familiar—had a background as a carpenter and received his scholarship to study radio technology in France."

Barbara nods. "I can imagine a history major would consider himself superior to a carpenter/radio technologist. Academics could be terrible snobs back then." She shakes her head again. "I remember my father talking about how his friends laughed at him when he decided to major in business."

"That is correct. Also, Pol Pot became enamored of the Maoist Communist movement popular at the time. He became so radical, he even lost his government scholarship."

"Ah. I think I know where you're going with this. When Pol Pot came to power, he had every academic and teacher and monk and even anyone who wore glasses declared an enemy of the state, tortured, and killed, didn't he?"

A chill runs through me in spite of the sun. "That is right, and he forced practically everyone else who lived in the city to move to the country and work on the land or join his military forces."

"As historians, your parents must have seen what was coming," Barbara says, "and acted immediately. You were lucky."

"I did not think so when it happened. At sixteen, I hated the thought of leaving my friends and my family and my home. I had never known anything else, so I put up quite a fight." I had rarely disobeyed them, so this memory was still vivid.

"Did your parents force you to go?"

"No. They sat me down and explained exactly why they thought it best for all of us to fly to America immediately, even though they certainly did not want to either." I miss their patient, rational attitude toward life.

"And you listened."

"I did. And I have never regretted it."

The memories of those last few days in Cambodia threaten to overtake me—those tearful farewells with my grandparents, my aunts and uncles, my cousins, and my school friends. When I finally returned after all those years, practically every one of those people I had known was gone, most of them bashed in the head or starved to death.

She takes my hand, and we sit, silent, surrounded by the beauty of nature. I recall the old woman with the banana leaves, how she cried as she spoke of her experiences during that terrible time.

This is the first time I have tried to describe how much leaving my home and almost everyone I loved affected me. I can still feel that ache, though sitting here next to Barbara and glimpsing the distant river and the leaves of the banana trees as they sway in the breeze helps.

Why am I almost willing to trust her with this damaged part of myself? She will be leaving soon.

❖

As we eat our main course in the hotel restaurant that evening, Barbara asks, "How about going to watch the dolphins tomorrow?" The fish we have chosen to dine on is fresh, fried to perfection.

"The famous Irrawaddy dolphins? You have obviously been reading your guidebook again."

I am beginning to enjoy teasing her. Sometimes she does not appear to know when I am kidding. But when she finally realizes it, her eyes light up with that glow from deep inside her that overwhelms me. At times like these I want to hug her, maybe kiss her, but something makes me hesitate.

The waiter arrives. "Do you want dessert?" I ask Barbara.

"No. Nothing on the menu strikes my fancy. Just a cup of decaf tea for me."

I order tea for her and a cup of Three Corner Coffee Roaster coffee for me. It is the best brand in the country, strong, and a real treat. Our waiter ambles away, wearing red flip-flops tonight. Evidently his formal attire.

As we wait, Barbara gazes outside at the sunset. Various birds are calling, and she is probably trying to identify them by sound. Suddenly, she pulls out her phone, hurries over to a window, and snaps a shot. Most likely she has heard one she wants to identify.

She is my employer, a wealthy American who can and will leave Cambodia when she finishes what she came here for. She could hurt me if she sees who I actually am and does not like the real me. Is that why I keep a certain distance?

She turns and smiles, apparently still caught up in the exotic bird calls outside. Yet she is now including me in her glance. She does seem fond of me.

Is she flirting, drawing me in so she can brag to her friends at home how she bedded her native guide? Will she take a picture of me similar to one of an unusual bird, display it as proof of her prowess?

Or am I being too skeptical? Maybe she also is afraid I will somehow harm her. She could have many reasons to remain detached.

"You tea, coffee ready, miss." The waiter places our cups in front of us. His English is basic, but at least he is trying. I am not. I am a coward when it comes to acting on my feelings for Barbara.

A voice in my head tells me I am in a safe place now, and so is she. We are both too old to let our emotions take charge and tug us around. We are seniors, and we should act our age.

But something inside my heart wants to hush that voice. She and I are both alive. We should wring out every drop of feeling left in us and enjoy each one to the fullest.

"You must have seen the dolphins a hundred times with your tour groups." Her eyes are shuttered. Did my teasing reference to her guidebook make her doubt her desire to visit them?

I miss that radiance in her glance again, that spark of anticipation, so I say, "I have never visited the dolphins but would love to. We used to spend one night at a homestay on the outskirts of Kratie but never took time for any excursions here. Everyone was too eager to reach Angkor Wat."

Her eyes switch to high beam immediately, and she pulls her creased *Rough Guide to Cambodia* from her pocket. Opening it to a bookmarked section, she says, "We should go either early or late in the day. And be sure to douse ourselves with insect repellant."

I nod and sip my coffee, which sends a jolt of excitement through me. Yet her enthusiasm may be the major cause. "That is a good idea, even this time of the year. With all that water and jungle, we will probably encounter something that wants to snack on us."

She grabs her phone, downs part of her tea, but leaves the rest. Then she scrapes her heavy chair back from our table. It pains me to leave my coffee, so I grab my cup. The management will not mind.

As we get up, I ask her, "What time would you like to leave? And how do you want to get there?" She straightens her back and seems even taller, more in charge

Evidently, she wants to plan this expedition, and I am more than happy to let her.

"Early," she says. "Let's go to bed soon so we can be there for sunrise, while the dolphins are still fresh and not many people are around." She heads toward our room, almost at a run. I follow at a slower pace, pausing in front of an interesting piece of furniture or sculpture or painting here and there, sipping the rest of my coffee and enjoying the moment.

I love seeing her this way. Not that long ago, she was so sick with the virus, and now she seems totally well.

"Slow down," I call to her, catching her hand. But she pulls me along, sharing everything she has read about the dolphins.

"Several years ago, they were on the endangered-species list, and now their population is growing," she says. "About twelve of them live north of here in the Mekong, near the town of Kampi."

She finally stops to examine a statue of a Buddhist goddess in the hall near our room. Her eyes sparkle as she walks around the sculpture, probably wanting to touch it but restraining herself. Then she is back at my side, and we are almost there.

I shiver. We will be sleeping in the same bed tonight, for the first time. What will that be like?

Chapter Fourteen

Ready to rest for the night, we are lying faceup in our queen bed, side by side. I am sweating, not sure what to do. Nothing has changed. I am uncertain what Barbara thinks of me. Does she view me as her tour guide, a person who probably saved her life? Or does she feel sorry for me? I am a refugee who deserted her country to save her own life and finally returned to discover a totally different place.

Her parents had an unhappy marriage. She rebelled briefly against her upbringing but then seems to have settled down and lived in Dallas. Yet what else? Is she satisfied with her life, or does she wish she had done things differently? I would like to know, so I simply ask.

"What happened after you and your hippie girlfriend broke up? You said you grew up. What did you mean?"

She stares at the ceiling fan, slowly circling above us. "Red bought me a house in the same posh neighborhood where he and Meatea lived. Not so close that they could spot any of my overnight guests, but near enough that I could keep tabs on how he was treating Meatea."

"Were you afraid he would mistreat her?"

"No. Not physically. That might damage his reputation. I simply didn't want her to be too lonely. Not that I made much difference."

"Tell me more about her situation."

Barbara jerks, seeming startled that someone would express interest in the subject, but then she evidently remembers who I am and why I might be interested in her mother.

She turns onto her side and begins to speak, at first seeming to search for words. "She lived in a small apartment attached to the mansion where Red reigned, so they basically lived separate lives. He was always involved with sports and loose women, and I hate to admit it, but I served as his hostess when he gave big parties for his various business associates."

I can envision Barbara playing that role. Did she feel like she was betraying her mother at those times or saving her from an uncomfortable experience?

"Meatea preferred to carve figurines and help landscape their huge yard. I spent time with her there occasionally, and as I grew older, she taught me to love flowers and birds." Barbara picks at a loose thread on our bedspread. "I truly don't know if she had a happy life. I would occasionally visit her and admire one of her intricate carvings, but we never had much to talk about until after Red died." She pulls the thread free and wraps it around her finger. "After he did, we stretched our wings like two doves freed from a cage, but by then it was almost too late to make up for all the time together we'd lost. I was so looking forward to traveling here with her. It might have drawn us together even more closely." She seems to have a hard time swallowing and pulls the thread tight.

Watching the moving fan, I let her draw me into a world I have never known, in a city in Texas—conservative, home to many wealthy people and even more poor ones. I try to picture the place and the people that molded her.

"When I was young"—she changes the subject—"I boarded at an exclusive, very expensive girls' school, from a very young age and graduated at the top of my class. From the late 50s until 1968, my world consisted of school, my friends, and occasional visits home. And, of course, my amazing two weeks in San Francisco."

"What did you look like?" I want to picture her during those years.

"Too tall, hair and nose too straight, too shy, too awkward. I probably resembled most of the other girls, but I believed I was the only one who thought she was so ugly." The thread breaks, and she twists her mouth into a smile as she flicks it away. "And Red chose the right school for someone like me. I was taught to appear as if I were lovely and charming and self-assured. The social graces, they called them at the time. I excelled in them, as I excelled in the classroom and on the playing field."

The ceiling fan draws me into its orbit, whirls me back to a time when young women were taught to polish themselves on the outside and ignore what they felt inside.

"I can relate," I say as those years before I left Cambodia unfurl. "But I was young and lived with my parents. They encouraged me to try to accept things, including myself, as they actually were. I tried not to gloss over my unpleasant thoughts and feelings."

Barbara bends her arm and rests her cheek on her palm. "You were lucky," she says, for the second time today. "At least I had one teacher who told the truth, and I adored her. The rest of my life seemed to be a lie, and that lie lasted a very long time."

I picture my own father and mother as they appeared when we left Cambodia—shoulders back, heads high, lips firm, eyes moist. They did their best, in spite of the horrible situation in Cambodia before the three of us left. I *was* fortunate to have well-educated, broad-minded parents—brave enough to leave everything they knew behind and give me a chance to live in a safe place. But I did not want to be there.

I turn onto my side too and face Barbara. Because of her age, she grew up in a world even more regimented than mine. Urban Cambodia was not that different from California when I arrived there in 1974.

"Back then," I say, "not many people admitted who they were, even if they knew. We all wanted to fit in. And we thought anyone who did not, especially homosexuals and people of color, were inferior. We lied to ourselves and each other, not recognizing what we were doing."

I glance over at the window in our bedroom, surprised at what I have just said. Is it true, or am I so caught up in what she is talking about that I include it in my view of the past?

She switches off the lamp on her side of the bed. Though I cannot see her or anything else, I can hear the soft thump of our fan. Lying on our backs now, we continue to talk, and the blackness encloses us in its intimacy. Our words seem to spring from a void, ramble between us, then wander away.

We discuss the women we have admired, fought with, loved, hated. We uncover similar jealousies and insecurities, as well as indiscretions and regrets.

In the darkness, we are weaving a web between us, a connection I can almost reach out and touch. I have never revealed my inner self like this before, not to anyone, in this slow waltz of words and memories and truth-telling.

I am calm yet exhilarated. As we finally drop our huge mosquito net around our bed and drift off to sleep, I am certain I will never forget tonight's conversation.

❖

"Are you awake?" Barbara whispers. "What time is it? I'm hot and sweaty." I hear the click of her bedside lamp, but nothing happens. "Shit. The electricity must have gone off." She turns on her phone light and heads for the bathroom.

I lie in bed, groggy. The coffee I drank last night was too strong, so I have not slept much. And now it is stifling in here and so very quiet. I should have told her about the solar panels, that they are not strong enough to provide power all night. What was I thinking? That everything would be fine? I have learned a lesson.

She must have stumbled as she emerges from the bathroom, and I hear a crash. "Shit. I stubbed my toe and dropped my phone," she mutters.

I grab my own and finally spot her scrambling around on the floor, holding hers up like she has won Olympic gold. "Good morning," she says, and I explain why we have lost power.

She takes the news better than I thought she would. "Well, since we're up, why don't we go visit the dolphins?"

I check my own phone and lie back down. "It is three a.m." The air is thick and heavy, and no breeze blows through the open windows. I hear the buzz of mosquitos and slap one on my arm. So much for it being the dry season.

"What do you think?" She is fumbling around, apparently looking for something to wear. "By the time we get there, the dolphins should be up." She walks over and pokes my arm. "Come on. It'll be fun."

"Okay." I drive my sleep-deprived self from bed and feel around for yesterday's clothes. Surely they are not too dirty to wear again. Water bottle? Check. Sun hat? Check. Money? Check. Ignition key? Check. "Do you know how to get there?" I ask her. After all, this is her expedition.

"Sure," she whispers. "It's all here in my guidebook. We have to drive to Kratie, then Kampi."

I hear her pick up her backpack and hope she has remembered everything she needs. "Ready to go?"

But she is already opening the door to our room. I grab my backpack too, and we are off.

It does not take long to reach my motorcycle, and I push it out to the front entrance to avoid waking everyone else at the Rajabori. I am really sweating now. But as soon as we begin to drive toward the ferry landing, we create a refreshing breeze.

It is about four a.m. by the time we catch sight of the landing. It is almost as dark as the inside of our room was.

"No one's here," she says, as if she expected a large ferry to be waiting just for us.

"Did you really think anyone would be?" I try not to sound irritable, but I would rather be asleep.

"Of course. We're on vacation, and I want to see the river dolphins." She is so cheerful and obviously teasing me now. Turnabout is fair play, I suppose.

By the time we locate the makeshift boardwalk and push the cycle down the embankment to the shore, I spot something shining out on the river. She holds her phone light up to make sure I do not veer off into the sand. And when we finally reach the shore, a flat-bottom boat is waiting for us.

"Can you take us to the mainland?" I call, and a boy splashes ashore and pulls a gangway toward the boat. I haggle with the owner, who grins when I pay him double his usual fare. But Barbara clearly thinks the dolphins are worth it.

We motor across the empty Mekong in the dark, and I think of our conversation last night. It shone a light inside me, like the stars that twinkle above us now. It made me hope my future may be brighter than I have ever expected it to be.

❖

We zip through the dark, deserted streets of Kratie, with its old French-colonial buildings, and I shout back at Barbara. "We should be watching the dolphins well before sunrise."

And we are, in spite of the choking red dust on the unpaved sections of road that slow us at times. Just outside Kampi, a woman on the shore agrees to watch my cycle while her young son takes us to enjoy breakfast with the dolphins.

He motors us out some distance in his noisy wooden longboat, toward a set of rapids in the wide, brown Mekong. Then he cuts his engine and rows the rest of the way, to where the water is the deepest. It is one of the animals' favorite playgrounds, he explains.

When the sky begins to turn pink, we are the only ones here on the water. We float in the gentle waves, the darkness lightening moment by moment as the blood-orange sun begins to rise. The boy suddenly says, "Yes, yes," and we turn in the direction he is pointing.

After we miss seeing the animals several times, Barbara nudges me. "There they are, I think." She is whispering as if they can hear us at this distance, and I whisper back.

"Yes. Over there. Rubbery gray, with a small dorsal fin?"

We are like proud parents watching our children play. And they do resemble children, very well-behaved ones. They do not leap and splash like most dolphins. They are more relaxed and shyer, rising when we least expect them, like porpoises do.

"Look. They're smiling at us," she says.

"That is probably because of the way their heads are rounded and their bulging foreheads stick out over their snub noses and straight mouths. And they have only a short beak, unlike the dolphins that live in the ocean. So that adds to the effect."

But she shrugs off my clinical explanation. Obviously, she prefers to think they are happy and grinning at us. I enjoy her enjoyment.

Then she says, "Listen. Hear that sound?"

"It is hard not to." Another of them breaks the surface of the water in a graceful upward arch, and it sounds like someone is suddenly taking a deep breath through a large tube.

"They're no longer a critically endangered species, thanks to people like this boy and his mother. They try to protect them from nets and noisy, dangerous boat motors." She consults her guidebook. "They mature around five years old and live in pods of about six. I wonder how many of them are in this area."

I ask the boy who is paddling the boat, and he immediately responds. "He says he has counted twenty of them and has a name for each one." Then the boy says something else, which I translate for her. "They are proud to have so many dolphins here. Only eighty live in Cambodia."

I nod to the boy and try to snap a picture of a dolphin that has just surfaced, but it disappears before I can get a good shot.

She is consulting her book again. "Did you know these dolphins can grow up to eight feet long and weigh 440 pounds?" She looks up and back out at them. "Wow. That's a big creature, but I can't imagine anyone hunting and eating one, like they used to. I'm glad the government finally woke up and started to protect them."

"Me too, though our driver just told me that China wants to build a series of dams on the Mekong." I gaze at the ancient river that stretches from China through part of Tibet and Southeast Asia, where it flows on through Vietnam into the South China Sea. "If they do, all these dolphins will die."

The boy gazes at them with noticeable reverence, as if communing with them. He tells me that many Cambodians believe these river dolphins are reincarnations of their ancestors. That is why he and the people who live near here do their best to tend to them. If I thought my grandparents were swimming out there, I would do the same. Also, they seem so self-contained, glad simply to be alive and move freely, that they inspire me to try to be my better self.

So what if I am sleepy and grumpy, that my mattress was rather hard, the room too hot, my cycle difficult to push across the sand? I am here right now with a woman I am beginning to feel attached to, watching these happy creatures play in the water, and suddenly my world is wonderful.

After an hour or so on the river, our boy asks, "Go back?" Barbara and I stare at each other, nod, and reluctantly leave the dolphins to their breakfast. The wide river's soft waves are rocking me to sleep, so I stretch out my legs on a wooden bench as the boy rows a safe distance away, then starts the clattering motor. Back to civilization.

"On our way to the hotel, would you like to stop in Kratie for our own breakfast and explore a bit?" Barbara asks.

My stomach growls, and I agree.

The boy returns us to shore, and he and his smiling mother search for someone else to share their ancestral dolphins with.

We take off on my cycle, and after we eat, we wander through the streets of the quiet town. It is best known for its rice whiskey, rice noodles, and bricks. But we do not need any of these items, so we drive back. There we have a long sleep and enjoy the rest of our stay at our idyllic villa.

This is by far the best tour I have ever led. Barbara and I are making many memories, which I hope are the beginning of many more. I am not sure about her, but I would love for this trip to never end.

PART III

BARBARA

Chapter Fifteen

Barbara woke up early and decided to watch the sun rise over the river near their villa on the island of Koh Trong. She dressed quickly, left Dara a note, and wandered down a shady path that led to a bench where she could enjoy the river and the sunrise. The breeze was fresh, rustling the large leaves, the birds cooing and clucking.

As she sat there, staring at the brown swells of water and the untamed jungle on the distant mainland, she heard something. They weren't words in either English or Khmer, but she could understand and respond to them.

"Do you enjoy being in my country, daughter?"

She looked around. "Is that you, Meatea? Have you come to me again?"

"Yes. I grew up in jungles and rivers. I can be here easier with you. In the city of Dallas I felt so foreign, with not many people like me except finally some refugees who fled from Pol Pot. But I found many companions among the people who worked for your father."

She couldn't view her mother, but the mental conversation she was having seemed to be connected with the tall banyan tree she sat under.

"I have been looking for traces of you, Meatea. Everywhere I go in Cambodia, I wonder if you visited there, or lived there."

The voice said, "It does not matter where I was, my Barbara. It matters where you go. Who you go with. You like this woman of Cambodia, this Dara Dith. Yes?"

Joy bubbled up in her, like a spring of cool water in the middle of the desert. "Oh, I do. She listens to me and seems to want to know me for who I really am, not who she wants me to be."

"I wish your father and I had been like that."

"What happened? Were you two ever in love?"

"We thought so. He once called me beautiful, kept saying I was 'exotic.' I did not understand. He was so handsome. But we were not wise enough. Should have listened to my parents. They said being apart would help us understand each other better. But I was young, silly. Was physical with him too soon and ruined our lives. Shamed our families."

She was the result of her mother's hasty decision. She was here, alive because two people had rushed into something neither of them was ready for. Barbara's throat constricted, ached, and her arms throbbed. "I wish I had never been born." She couldn't stand either her own tears or the truth of her mother's words.

Meatea beamed as she comforted her. "Hush. This is no one's fault. It is the way of the foolish world. Your father and I were impatient. Thought we knew more than our elders. But we were wrong."

Her words rang true. "Yet what does this have to do with me? With Dara? We're not young and impetuous. We're much older and hopefully wiser than you were all those years ago. How should we deal with these feelings growing between us?"

She could almost feel Meatea's soft arm around her. "You are older in years. It is easy for your body to age. Travel around my country, ask yourself how to become wise. Spend time to discuss every thought and feeling with Dara. Be truthful. Look inside yourself. Look inside others. Learn everything others teach you. Gain wisdom. Uncover your own hidden dreams."

She wanted to throw her arms around her mother, be close to her once again, but her mother was near her only like the soft breeze was—elusive yet present. Her throat tightened again, but now her tears contained more joy than sorrow.

The call of a bird startled her, and she looked around. The sun was riding high over the trees now, and Meatea had slipped away, leaving her alone yet filled with a warmth that soothed. Everything seemed so much closer now. She wanted to wrap her arms around the nearest tree, stoop and push her head into the heart of a frangipani blossom, inhale all its sweetness and that of the very air she breathed every second without appreciating the wonder of it.

"Gain wisdom," she murmured. "I will follow Meatea's advice."

❖

"Barbara. Where have you been? I woke up alone and read your note. But I have been wondering where you were."

Dara didn't seem worried or angry, merely curious. But perhaps the young dark-skinned woman Barbara had glimpsed talking to Dara right before she approached had distracted her. Yet who wouldn't want to spend time with someone as attractive and good-natured as Dara? Barbara dropped the little sting of jealousy she had felt when she first spotted Dara conversing with the attractive stranger.

She wanted to tell Dara about the appearance of Meatea, especially since she didn't have to defend herself or even explain where she'd been if she didn't want to and should extend the same courtesy to Dara. But she did want to confide in her right now. After their long conversation in the dark last night and then watching the dolphins play earlier this morning, she wanted to share with Dara everything unusual or exciting or even mundane that she experienced. She trusted that Dara wouldn't scold or censure her, wouldn't argue or disbelieve what she told her. Dara would accept what she said and help her gain the insight concealed in her experience. At least that's what she hoped, for that's the type of person she wanted as her lover.

They had met on the path back to their villa, so she took Dara's hand and led her toward the swimming pool. There they stretched out on lounge chairs once again, side by side.

"I've had another visit from Meatea," she said, watching closely for Dara's response. Would she lift a skeptical eyebrow, frown in disbelief, twist her mouth in impatience or scorn, shake her head in mock sympathy?

But she saw only a gentle smile that engaged Dara's mouth, cheeks, and eyes. "Tell me about it," Dara said as she squeezed her hand.

So she did, and Dara seemed to listen to every word, nodding at times, always with that same smile. After she finished, Dara stared into the blue depths of the swimming pool, as if drawing inspiration from its fluidity.

"I am glad your mother is so present to you, watching over you so closely. She sounds as if she gained a lot of insight from her unhappy experience with your father and wants to keep you from making the same mistakes and feeling the same pain she has suffered." Dara ran her hand through her long black hair, tousling it so that the white strands shone in the sunlight. "If you want to discuss anything she brought up, I would be glad to try to help us both understand what she means. This world, and the ones beyond it, holds many mysteries."

Barbara squeezed Dara's warm, soft hand and brought it to her lips, kissed it. "Thank you for understanding, Dara. I feel better now. That old cliché about today being the first day of the rest of my life makes more sense now."

Dara raised their joined hands to her own lips and kissed them where they intersected. "I am so glad we are here, now, together in this beautiful place. Would you not like to stay here forever?"

Barbara wasn't sure if it was her imagination, but she seemed to walk to breakfast beside Dara with a surer step, as if she belonged in whatever space she occupied instead of hesitating to be there. When she spoke, each of her words was distinct, as if it was important and worth listening to. As they moved down the line at the long buffet tables, she easily decided what she wanted for breakfast instead of hesitating to make each choice, as she normally did. And everything she selected was the right choice. She felt sure of herself, present in the moment, prepared to follow where life would lead her.

They didn't talk much during breakfast. She kept pondering her conversation with her mother. Had she changed enough for Dara to notice?

As they sat at their round table and gazed out at the light reflecting off the pool, Dara finally asked, "Do you want to remain here on this island longer, or would you like to move on?"

She drew a few deep breaths, filling herself with the enchantment the place had wrapped her in. "I'd love to never leave." She paused. Wouldn't that be wonderful? "But we do need to get going."

Dara raised an eyebrow, probably about to ask her why, but she quickly continued.

"I'm not sure why, but I'm still pulled toward the unexplored parts of Cambodia that take more effort to visit than the usual tourist areas do. On tour, we saw the big cities and well-known sights—Siem Reap and the whole Angkor Wat temple complex. Battambang, the gateway city to Thailand. And Kampot, with its access to the south of the country and to the islands."

"You know one major reason we visited those areas, do you not?"

She bit her lips. "No. Just that they're all famous."

Dara smiled and pointed at the bicycles and motorcycles parked outside their restaurant. "The roads."

"The roads?"

"Yes. In Texas, you probably take them for granted. You have multi-lane interstates. But did your father, Red, ever mention the motorways he remembered from his boyhood?"

"No. Though he did say that after the big East Texas oil boom in the late 1920s, the state paved the dirt roads quickly. Everyone wanted to access and truck out all that oil."

Dara nodded. "Cambodia is in a similar situation. Remember what I said about all the forests being cut down here during the early 2000s?"

"Yes. And it still infuriates me."

"I understand. The trees are so visible and so important, not only here but throughout the world. But drilling all that oil in East Texas evidently had the same impact on that part of the country back then that the commercial expansion we are experiencing in this country has now."

"What do you mean?"

"I mean the highway situation. Even now, only eight percent of the roads in Cambodia are paved."

"Do you consider gravel ones paved?"

"I do."

She shook her head. "That's unbelievable."

"Believe it. As a local tour guide, I am certain of that one statistic, though we are working hard to remedy the situation." Dara paused, probably thinking of all the construction south of Phnom Penh that she and the rest of their tour group had seen last month. "The more tourists we attract, the more infrastructure we need to build to show them our national treasures," Dara said.

She finally realized what Dara was trying to tell her. "So if I want to experience some out-of-the-way places, especially those that include a lot of jungle, I need to be prepared for some really rough roads?"

"That is correct."

❖

That afternoon, Barbara and Dara lazed around the pool during the heat of the afternoon, catnapping between brief conversations. Once, Dara had a brief business call and walked to the other side of the grounds so she wouldn't disturb her. Later, after the heat lessened, they strolled around the entire island of Koh Trong.

It was a five- or six-mile walk on a narrow road—mostly paved but made of dirt in some spots. Lined with banana, citrus, and coconut trees, it took them past private homes that resembled the wooden structures at their resort. They were all built high on stilts and had a wide overhang above a front porch. They also had shingles made of tile and roofs occasionally decorated with golden dragons along the very top.

Rural people lived in these houses, all extremely friendly, especially the children, everyone calling hello. One very old man, his teeth stained black, invited them to sit down and rest in the shade with him, then gave them some bananas. A young woman offered them a ride back to the resort on her motorbike, though that would have been a very tight squeeze.

They glimpsed rice paddies in the center of the island, though they were brown this late in the dry season. They also spotted several temples—one brilliant white with a red-tile roof and light-blue railing. On the beach sat longboats, shaded by palm fronds draped over long wooden frames. And cows roamed the cleared fields, as did chickens and hens.

At the southwest end of the island, they spotted a floating village of thirty or forty wooden houses built in a long line offshore. Each had a canoe, and Dara explained that the owners didn't have to pay for real estate to build on and didn't owe taxes.

They saw a group of men onshore near the village, working on a damaged boat, a woman enticing some hens and chickens into a boat with grain, and children splashing in the water. Most of the people waved and greeted them as they strolled past.

"This is the most restful, friendly place I've ever been," she told Dara as they caught sight of their resort in the distance.

"Yes. We should come back someday," she said.

"*We.*" Barbara liked the sound of that word. Had her parents taken such a walk after they first met, seen a similar beautiful, peaceful scene and been drawn together by it? And had they said the same thing about returning?

She glanced at the setting sun, the tree-lined Mekong gleaming with its golden light. A sense of loss combined with hope curled through her. "Yes. We should."

Chapter Sixteen

Barbara closed her backpack just as Dara finished brushing her teeth and started putting the rest of her stuff into hers. "How long will it take us to reach Stung Treng today?"

Dara worked quickly, then tossed her pack over one shoulder and glanced around. "It depends."

"Depends on what?"

She smiled, and Dara walked over and touched her left cheek. "You know, it's strange, but I've never noticed this dimple before. What else have I missed?"

"Well?" Barbara put her hands on her waist, pretending to be impatient, but she knew she wasn't fooling Dara. These last few days on Koh Trong had been good for them. Dara looked more relaxed and rested than she had ever seen her. They needed to keep on taking it easy like this, stop pretending they were still in their thirties instead of—"Are we going to stay here longer or—"

"Sorry. I'm just thinking how much I've enjoyed it here, with you. It's been wonderful, hasn't it? Like a dream…" Dara drew a deep breath. "But it *is* time to wake up. What did you ask me?"

Barbara chuckled. "How long?" She paused. "To get to Stung Treng?" Dara seemed to have finally begun to slip back into tour-guide mode, but she still didn't look very enthusiastic about leaving.

"It's about a hundred and thirty kilometers, eighty miles, but we have to catch a ferry back to the mainland, then drive through Kratie and a bit farther, and cut over to Highway 7. After that we have a new, *smooth* road all the way."

"How long?"

"Probably a couple of hours." Dara's tour-guide persona had obviously grown rusty during their downtime at this resort. "Do you mind if I go talk to the manager about having one of our more upscale groups stay here after tourism picks up again? I should be back soon."

Barbara wanted to leave right away but forced herself to sit down and try to relax. "Go ahead. I'll be ready when you are."

Glancing at her cell phone, she suddenly thought about her new friend Roland and, on impulse, located his number in her contacts and called him.

"Hello."

"Hey, Roland. I've been meaning to get in touch and say thanks for telling Dara I was so sick on Koh Rong. You probably saved my life, and I'm sorry for not getting in touch earlier. It's been crazy here. How are you?"

"Barbara. I can't believe my ears. I'm fine. We just started 'sheltering in place' here in the City because of the virus. How are *you*?"

She updated him on her situation.

"You go, girl. Sitting behind a hot woman on a cycle is a heck of a good way to get to know the country."

"Not too bad for a little old lady," she said, glad she'd called. She'd contact Roland after she went home and this virus mess calmed down. Maybe they could meet in New Mexico or Arizona or somewhere fun and get to know each better. Have a few laughs and a lot of drinks.

"'Little old lady'? I see you're still driving yourself crazy over how old you are. When are you gonna learn people think of you as the age you tell them you are, especially with your great dye job? You're still a sexy bitch."

"Oh, Roland. I've missed you." She loved the way he messed with her.

"Convince yourself you're young, girl. Tell everyone you're fifty-five, and they'll believe you. It'll make you feel a lot better."

"I can't lie."

She started pacing across their room. *Where is Dara?*

"Technically, dying your hair is lying. Think of it as enhancing an illusion."

She scratched her head. "Well, if you'd had a father who considered any woman over twenty-five not worth chasing, you might have a hard time too."

She heard someone talking and laughing in the background. "Do you have company?" *It should be about midnight in California now.*

"Yep. Lots. My apartment's crammed with beautiful men all craving my sexy bod."

"Yeah. I bet. You're trying to make the shelter-in-place order bearable, I suppose."

"Something like that. But listen to me, Barbara." He sounded serious for a change. "I realize I don't know you all that well, but we did have some good talks."

"We did, Roland." She'd had far too few good friends in her life and treasured each of them.

"Sounds like your old man was a jerk," he said. "Forget him. Women are as beautiful and as young as they think they are. Now that he's dead, stop letting him tell you how to think. Sounds like he did enough of that while he was alive. Let it go. What you have right now sounds like a dream come true, so enjoy your bike ride and your Cambodian woman."

She stopped pacing. Her wisecracking new friend was more astute than she'd expected. "Thank you, Roland. For everything. I mean it. Now I better let you get back to whatever or whoever you were enjoying before I butted in. Do keep in touch."

"You too, Barb. Congrats on beating the virus. Now tell your old man to get lost."

"I'll try. Stay safe. You're a pal."

"Remember what I said."

"Will do. Ciao."

"Bye. Be as bad as you want."

And with that, Roland clicked off.

Just as she was pocketing her phone, Dara walked in. "Ready to go?"

"Yes, but how was your meeting?"

"It went well."

"Great. And I *am* ready." After talking to Roland, she felt calmer. Yet she immediately asked Dara, "If we have just a two-hour drive today, can we make a stop or two?" She held up her guidebook, keeping her finger stuck inside it. "Remember when I mentioned dolphins the other day, after we first got here?"

"I think so, though maybe not. It seems like we've been here forever." Dara scratched her head. "At the same time, it doesn't seem long at all. Time can really play tricks on you."

"What did I say, along with the word dolphins?" She put her hands on her hips in mock impatience, still holding her book.

Dara seemed to be struggling to answer. "Turtles." She almost shouted the word. "You said turtles."

"And not just any kind of turtles." She prodded Dara, feeling like an elementary-school teacher with a slow student.

"Giant turtles. You said giant ones. I cannot believe I finally remembered."

She couldn't either. She stared at Dara and then burst out laughing. "Wow. I'm impressed."

"I am too." Dara laughed with her. "Anyway, what about giant turtles?"

She held up her book, opening it to the place she'd marked. "I just read about a conservation place near an old temple at somewhere called Sambor, not far from Kratie."

"Yes. We rode through there on our way to the dolphins."

"Oh. I didn't realize that."

"Well, it was dark and—"

"Anyway, these giants, the largest freshwater turtles on earth—Cantor's softshells, I think they're called—can grow up to six feet long. They lay twenty or more eggs deep in the sand, but not many of them survive."

"Yes." Dara didn't appear surprised.

"The mature turtles are critically endangered, as are many turtles in Asia, which are almost extinct. For centuries, people have been poaching them for food and traditional Chinese medicine. The turtle is the most revered of animals here, yet one of the most exploited."

"Yes. Now I recall that a monk discovered one on the temple grounds and realized what was happening—"

"And he helped found the Mekong Turtle Conservation Center." She looked up from her book. "Can we stop by there? Please?"

Dara put her hand on her arm and squeezed gently. "Of course. This is your trip. You are in charge and can do whatever you want, any time you want. I am just here to help make it happen."

She adjusted the money belt she wore around her waist under her somewhat wrinkled slacks, feeling more like the Dallas socialite she'd appeared to be when she first joined the tour group in early February. She hoped the glimpses of the little girl who still lived inside her didn't make Dara think any less of her.

"Shall we go then," Dara said, and they were downstairs and on Dara's motorcycle in a few minutes.

Barbara clung to Dara as they bumped toward the turtle conservation center. Maybe they should rent a car. Her head was whirling with so much information about giant turtles and her body vibrating so hard from hitting one pothole after another, she couldn't focus on how good it felt to have her arms around Dara's waist and her chest pressed into Dara's back.

Was Dara as afraid of being close emotionally as she was? She'd loved sharing a bed the past few nights and lying there in the dark confiding in each other about their failed attempts to find love. But she and Dara still seemed to have a wall between them that kept them from touching each other except in seemingly innocent ways. A cheek, a back, a hand—that's about all they could manage.

"We're almost there," Dara shouted as she slowed and turned into a driveway.

After they motored through an elaborate red-and-gold archway, she saw a pagoda, evidently the one near the turtle conservation center. Its walls and multiple columns shone white as they supported a glittering red-tile roof ornamented with gold frills and accents. It dominated the landscape, just as Buddhism dominated the lives of the people of Cambodia.

"I'm sure you've read the story about the princess eaten by a crocodile," Dara said as they climbed one of the temple's steep staircases.

"The one whose father had a hundred virgins killed and buried under the original temple, which he dedicated to his dead daughter?"

"Yes."

"But what are the facts about this place, Ms. Tour Guide?" she asked as they removed their shoes.

"Centuries ago, it was the site of a royal palace. Then it housed a Buddhist temple with a hundred columns that burned and was rebuilt, then destroyed by the Khmer Rouge and rebuilt again. After that, it was struck by lightning and repaired."

Inside the colorful temple, filled with vibrant murals, numerous statues of the Buddha, and people burning incense, she asked Dara, "So why the story about the princess? I like the idea of paying tribute to a woman, but killing all her friends? Have men always considered women disposable commodities?"

"I am really not sure," Dara said. "Shall we just say this is a sacred site?"

"I still prefer to say that this place shows how badly men have treated women for centuries and continue to do so, just as they keep recycling the temple here."

As they left the pagoda, Barbara spotted an unremarkable building with a corrugated roof and a small sign identifying it as the turtle conservation center. "Ah. I think I understand how they're connected."

Dara raised an eyebrow, and as they put their shoes on again, Barbara relayed some of what she'd read online. "After someone near here discovered a few giant turtles, members of an international agency tried to get the locals to protect them. They didn't have much luck, so they asked the monks here for help. The people listened to their religious leaders, and some of the natives even became volunteer rangers."

They were heading back down the stairs when Dara stopped. "I do remember, several years ago, talking to a woman who lived in Kampong Cham—where we spent our first night on the road—about turtle eggs. She said she used to love them, that they tasted a lot better than chicken or duck eggs. And they were easy to find and dig up because the mother turtle left such clear tracks."

"Really?" They started down the steps again.

"Yes. She said a monk explained how the turtles were in danger and asked her to help him protect them. And she agreed. She even caught one of her neighbors stealing the eggs on her property and convinced him to stop eating them."

At the bottom of the temple, Barbara touched Dara's arm, and they stopped, looking back up at it. "I've never been very pious, but a story like that makes me think better of religion."

Dara smiled. "Yes. It does have its good points. Ready to go visit the turtles?"

❖

The conservation center itself was shabby, but they joined a trickle of tourists, despite the growing scare the new Corona virus was causing. The informative posters that covered the walls of the center were written in English as well as Khmer. However, the woman who showed them around spoke very little English, so Barbara was glad Dara was with her.

They spotted some adult turtles of several varieties in a pen. But mostly they saw several rows of aquariums, some made of concrete and others of plastic. Blue plastic water pipes connected the tanks, each with its own orange spigot, to keep the sand wet. But that's about all they found—tanks full of wet sand.

She sighed.

Dara touched her arm. "Remember that these turtles take a couple of months to hatch, and the eggs are not laid until January. This is primarily a hatchery, to keep the eggs safe."

"That's right." She looked around again. "And even after they emerge, they like to burrow into the sand and don't have to come up for air but a few times a day." She searched up and down the rows of aquariums. "I'd love to see a little one with its cute face."

Just then Dara said, "Look. I think something is moving down there, in one of the aquariums near the end of the next row."

She rushed in the direction Dara had just pointed and let out a squeal. "Oh. It's so cute. Come look at its snout, like a tiny pig's. And its eyes are so black and intelligent-looking."

"I am sure you found pictures of adults online," Dara said. "After all, you spent hours on your phone researching them, did you not?"

She blushed. "Guilty as charged. But there's nothing like experiencing one in person, even if it is just a baby."

"Can you imagine an adult? A huge round blob with big flippers and supposedly quicker than a cobra."

"I'd keep my distance."

"Yeah. I would not want to be a fish that swam nearby."

They were walking along the rows of tanks once more to see if any other eggs had hatched when Barbara suddenly remembered a ceremony held each year that involved these turtles. "I'd love to be here in November, when they bless the babies and release them into the water. It would be like a mother sending her child off to school."

"You could stay."

She stopped, staring at Dara, who had also quit walking. Where had that come from? Which of them was more surprised by the three words that had somehow stumbled out of Dara's mouth, like a baby turtle hatching from the wet sand?

"Uh. Oh. Uh. I mean…" Dara obviously couldn't think of a way to explain why she'd made such a statement.

Barbara suddenly felt like she was back in Dallas, handing a saleswoman in Nieman Marcus her platinum credit card for a thousand-dollar purchase. "I'd love to stay, but I have to get back to my tennis and golfing acquaintances, and everything I've ever known." Still, she felt wistful as she looked at the empty tanks.

Dara flinched yet seemed to take a cue from her. "Of course. I just meant that I would like for you to be able to release one of those turtles with your own hands."

"And I'd love to. Truly, I would. But I can't be gone that long. You understand, don't you?"

Dara licked her lips and visibly swallowed, as if something were caught in her throat.

"I hope I haven't hurt your feelings, Dara, but the thought of living in a strange country makes me panic." Her chest ached. "I'm not sure how I could. Almost everyone I know lives in Dallas. My tennis partner, the women I golf with from time to time."

Dara seemed to have tuned her out, but she kept talking, unable to stop herself.

"I have women I shop with and go to charitable events with."

Dara stared at the empty tanks all around them, shifting from one leg to the other.

"I'm used to these...uh...I wouldn't exactly call them friends, but they are good acquaintances." She felt like she was in the muddy Mekong, flailing around, about to drown. "We understand each other, speak the same language."

Dara turned and faced her. "You and I do too."

"But I'll never learn Khmer. It's so difficult." She pointed to one of the posters thumbtacked to a nearby yellow wall. "And to read it? I can't make out a single familiar letter, much less a word or a sentence."

Dara nodded. "It does seem much more difficult to many people than French or German would. But once you really try—"

"Do you think I'll be able to find any trace of my mother? The French didn't keep records of the locals, and the Khmer Rouge burned everything historical they could find."

She left the baby turtle and walked down another row, searching for more. Dara followed, and Barbara stopped in a deserted aisle and faced her. "Dara. You lived in a foreign country for a very long time. Do you think I could ever feel as at home here as I do in Texas? If I wanted to take a long trip abroad, who would I find here to feed my goldfish?"

Dara chuckled, but her head had drooped, and she slumped, her cheek muscles relaxing, her eyes losing their spark. She reminded Barbara of a wilted morning glory.

"Would you really like for me to stay here? At my age?"

"I would, Barbara. But it would not be easy, no matter how young or old you are."

"You're right. It's silly to even think about it."

Dara didn't speak.

"You have your own life here, with a job you clearly love."

Dara nodded.

"You also have two sons, who will probably move back here after they get tired of living abroad. And they'll bring their wives and children." She adjusted her backpack.

"That could happen," Dara said, "but it would surprise me. When my sons decide to settle down, they will probably move to Shanghai, where their father lives. The standard of living there is much higher than in Cambodia, and they are fluent in Chinese."

"Still, you'll be a grandmother and will probably be involved in the lives of your grandchildren."

"Perhaps. But being a lesbian in this country and in China is not as easy as it is in America. My sons and their in-laws might not accept me."

"Do you think the Cambodians would accept me? Or would I always be an outsider? America has always supported your country, but we committed our share of atrocities here during the Vietnam War."

"That is correct."

"Besides, Cambodia is officially a communist country. China has supported it heavily for a long time and is a close neighbor and ally. Your government stands for everything I've been taught to oppose."

"That is also correct."

Everything they'd just discussed left her breathless, and she turned around and walked over to look once more at the baby turtle that had ignited this conversation. It was stumbling around in its aquarium, so new to the world, so helpless. Just like she would be if she stayed in Cambodia.

She had grown fond of Dara, would like to spend more time with her, but not forever, even if Dara might want her to. Which she doubted. She'd probably made that offhand comment about staying to release a turtle just to be nice.

"I suppose we better get back on the road to Stung Treng." The very name of the town sounded so foreign as she said it.

Dara had already turned toward the hatchery's exit, and as they walked outside and pulled on their helmets, the sun seemed to glare, its heat even more intense here now in March than it was in Dallas in August.

The road they drove over was still rough, but they soon reached National Road 7, which was as smooth as Dara had promised. Yet, as they sped along it, Barbara missed the wooden homes on stilts that had lined the narrow, older highway they'd taken during part of their journey north, with its lush vegetation and views of the Mekong.

On this road she saw only new Tela gas stations, road signs advertising Wing mobile phones and Anchor beer, buildings being constructed of cinder blocks, older houses with brightly colored aluminum awnings jutting out from tiled roofs, and dust-covered stalls where locals tried to peddle their wares in their traditional manner. This was the new Cambodia, expanding from its colonial, war-torn history into the twenty-first century. This far from Phnom Penh, the highway wasn't as populated and as busy as it had been farther south, but, like interstates in the US, they all looked the same.

She and Dara traveled north quickly on the new highway, which had been funded mostly by sources outside the country—entrepreneurs who sensed an opportunity here.

And before she knew it, Dara had driven past some breathtaking views of the Mekong, through a relatively small town, and, on its other side, wheeled into the parking lot of a four-story building, apparently a hotel.

They stopped and parked, then dismounted, removed their helmets, and threw their backpacks over one shoulder. "Welcome to Stung Treng," Dara said. "The gateway to the Wild East."

"The Wild East?" Barbara asked as she stood looking at the Golden River Hotel. They planned to spend a night or two here before they traveled east, toward the Vietnam border. "Is it anything like our Wild West back home?"

"In some ways, yes. But in others, no."

"You know, I just had a craving for barbeque and potato salad. Know any place around here that serves it?"

"No. But are you homesick? You have been away from Texas for well over a month."

"I must be. I've never lived anywhere but Dallas, except for my adventure in San Francisco eons ago."

"You don't still want to find your Cambodian roots?"

"It's probably impossible. And what's the point? Meatea left here seventy years ago. This country is totally different now. Even if I could find some of my family members, I can't change my past, my American heritage."

"And what is that heritage?" Dara seemed truly curious.

"We Americans are biased and flawed, but we also can be strong and decent."

"I do not think anyone would argue with that assertion."

"Why did you move back here? Didn't you have a good life in the US?"

"Yes. I would never complain about America. My parents and I would have not survived very long here if we had stayed here."

"And why are you here now?"

"I like my people and our history. America is young, but Cambodia is ancient, with a proud past. We have been powerless for quite a few centuries lately. I would like to help my country regain its strength and its pride after all these years." She squared her shoulders. "I want us to become a nation as tough as America, so we can govern ourselves in the ways that are best for us."

Barbara grasped Dara's arm as they stood in front of the hotel. "What a wonderful sentiment. You make me wish I were thirty years younger, so I could join your cause and help make a difference. But I'm too old to leave everything I've ever known."

That was what she said, but she wondered something else entirely. Did Dara have any deep feelings for her after such a brief time together? And how strong were her own feelings for Dara? She truly didn't know, so she decided to change the subject and dropped her hand to her side.

"Uh, Dara?"

"Huh?"

"The Wild East? What do you mean by that term?"

Dara appeared disoriented but then shook her head. She did the same. She would make the best of what they had during this trip instead of daydreaming about some "pie-in-the-sky" romance that would never have a chance of going anywhere.

"It *is* similar to the Wild West back in the States," Dara said, changing the mood entirely. "We are now about fifty kilometers— thirty miles—south of Laos, in an area bombed often during the Vietnam era. We are also near the old Ho Chi Min Trail, as the Americans referred to it back then. You can even take a tour of it if you like."

"No thanks." Barbara shifted her backpack to her other side, wiping sweat from her forehead, and Dara directed her toward the hotel entrance.

"War zones are notoriously lawless places," Dara explained, "as are borders." This area is also rather isolated, so people tend to do as they please more easily and readily here. From here, as we travel east, you will understand better."

She nodded as they reached the hotel, and they went through the check-in procedure they'd grown accustomed to. After they reached their room, which again contained only one queen-size bed, they both immediately used the facilities, washing away the dust from their trip, then unpacked, enjoying the air-conditioning.

"Did you find anything in your guidebook that appeals to you around here?" Dara asked.

She looked up from it, smiling. "What part of town are we in?"

"The east side."

"Great. Do you know of a place here called Mekong Blue?"

"Yes. Women make beautiful silk scarves there."

"Right. But it's more than that, isn't it?"

Dara nodded.

"Would you like to go there this afternoon?"

Dara nodded again. "I would enjoy that. How about—what do you call it—a catnap, first? I am becoming accustomed to them. Then we can pick up some street food on our way there?"

"Perfect," she said, and they flopped onto their bed to rest.

CHAPTER SEVENTEEN

D ara was right. The scarves at Mekong Blue were gorgeous. During their first tour, they had stopped at a local silk factory on their way to Siem Reap and Angkor Wat, where a young man led them through the entire process. On the first day, workers threw the cocoons of prized yellow silkworms into boiling water to kill the larvae.

"On day two, we dye silk with non-toxic German dyes," said their Mekong Blue guide, a young woman. "It must dry twenty-four hours."

Barbara remembered a discussion with an Australian woman on her first tour about how almost every guide they'd encountered on the local tours had been male, though Dara was certainly female. But Mekong Blue was different. She saw no one here but women, except one important man—one of its two founders—who appeared in a photo.

They entered a room where a group of women sat around chatting while they separated each clean, dyed cocoon into separate threads and rolled them onto plastic spools. "It takes one day to unravel enough thread for make a simple scarf," their guide explained. Just watching them made Barbara's fingertips hurt.

"Fourth day of the process is giving women plenty of exercise," said their guide. "Take more than five yards of thread to fill warp board. Woman must walk back and forth from one end to other, more than three miles for each scarf."

"I'll think of that when I hear someone complain how much one of these scarves must cost," she told Dara as they followed their guide through the immaculate workshop.

"On day five, warp board set up for weaving. Taking long time—four days for regular scarf. Many-color ones take much work. From eleven to fifteen days, depending on pattern."

Barbara mentally counted. "By this point, a woman will have devoted ten days of her life to making me a simple scarf to wear when I go out to a club meeting," she whispered to Dara. "My friends there better notice it."

Dara touched her arm. "I'm glad you appreciate what these women are doing. So many tourists have no idea how much effort it takes to supply them with a luxury item like this."

Dara's words and the feel of her warm hand made Barbara flame. If she were a color right now, she'd be a bright, pure yellow, like the silk threads stretched across the loom they'd just moved on to.

"After weaving begin, it takes woman one and half days to finish plain scarf. Six or seven days for one with many colors." They walked down a row of looms, the weavers chatting with one another, smiling and greeting them, their hands never stopping.

But Barbara was so busy counting again, she didn't completely understand what they were discussing. As they reached the end of the line of looms, she stopped and turned to Dara. "Eleven-and-a-half days, just to make one simple scarf. Can you believe that?"

"And three weeks for a multi-colored one," Dara said. "They create wall hangings here, too, and spend about three months just on the dying phase for them."

"Really?"

"Really. The hangings used to be restricted to royalty. But now, museums buy them. These silk products are the real thing—the finest quality, using techniques Cambodian women have passed from one generation to the next for centuries. Workshops like these are keeping this traditional art form alive."

To end their tour, they entered one final room. "What are they doing here?" she asked their guide.

"Women check, be sure no mistakes. Wash and iron perfect ones there." She pointed at a long row of tables, women bending over them and inspecting each piece slowly.

"Quality control?" she asked Dara.

"Yes. Nothing but the best in this establishment."

"Well, I want to check out the end product. I haven't bought many souvenirs so far, but that's about to end."

❖

"What do you think about this one?" Barbara held up a filmy yellow scarf adorned with fringe. "It's called Lemon. Isn't it gorgeous?"

"Here. Let me see." Dara arranged it around her neck and stood back. "Beautiful. It brings out the color of your hair and dark eyes."

"I love it. That's the most vibrant yellow I've ever seen. I have to have one."

They wandered from one display to the next. A local woman stood nearby and smiled, but she left them alone to shop.

"This is a nice change. In that factory where we stopped during our first tour, the saleswomen swarmed us, didn't give us a chance to find something we really liked. That's one reason none of us bought anything."

Dara pulled out her phone and tapped her screen. "I am making a note so we can do something about that situation. Thank you for the feedback."

Barbara found a rich-purple scarf for her neighbor back in Dallas who was feeding her goldfish. And she also found a deep-blue one, called Evening, labeled as an award winner, which she couldn't resist.

After she finished making her choices, she noticed Dara fingering a long scarf, half of it a lush Kelly green and the other a luxuriant turquoise. She walked over, picked it up, and draped it around Dara, tying it loosely between Dara's small breasts. "This is definitely you," she murmured, conscious of the earthy smell Dara exuded and the firm breast she'd grazed with her hand as she arranged the scarf. She gazed at Dara as if in a trance, until Dara started fidgeting and several women stopped and looked at them.

She tugged herself back to reality, and then, standing in front of Dara, almost close enough to kiss her pink lips, she slowly lifted the scarf from under Dara's black hair, again brushing her breasts.

Her breathing accelerated as she grew lost in Dara's endlessly dark eyes. If she weren't in a store full of tourists and saleswomen, she would have abandoned herself in those eyes, succumbed to her almost overwhelming urge to kiss this woman she'd grown close to so quickly.

"You have to have this one," she said as she added it to the other three in her stack.

"But—"

"No buts about it. Even the name says that it's meant for you."

Dara glanced at the placard near the remaining scarves like this one. "Seaside." She nodded, evidently thinking about visiting Koh Rong when she was so sick there.

"Every time you wear it, you can think about how you probably saved my life and how I'll never forget your kindness."

She choked up, her chest heaving. Dara had rescued her, but she would be leaving Cambodia soon. How could she forget those firm, small breasts and lips like pink plumeria petals?

She forced herself to motion to the nearest saleswoman and hand her the four scarves she'd chosen.

Dara stood to one side as she paid the cashier with her credit card and then dropped several bills into a nearby tip jar. "I'm impressed with these women and the quality of their work," she told Dara as she nestled the package of scarves in her nearly empty backpack that doubled as a purse during outings like this. "Can we visit the other buildings nearby? This shop is called Mekong Blue, and the cashier said they have a website where I can shop online. But evidently some other activities take place here as well, all centered on women. I'd like to see what else they have to offer."

She glanced at Dara and almost dropped her backpack before she pulled it over her shoulder again. She reached out to take Dara's arm to steady herself but stopped. Drawing a deep breath, she followed Dara through the shop door, careful not to touch her. Dara held herself erect, walked ahead quickly with a sure step. She tried to do the same. Dara turned and smiled as she caught up with her. If she stayed in Cambodia, would Dara always slow down for her and smile like this?

❖

"You know, Dara, the women working in that silk factory seemed a lot more content and engaged in what they were doing than the ones in the place we visited during our group tour. All that natural light that the floor-to-ceiling windows in the weaving room let in, combined with the large overhead light fixtures, helps create a better work environment than most factories I've seen in other underdeveloped countries. Including China during the eighties. Any other ideas why?"

"I know exactly why, which is one reason I am so glad you wanted to come here."

"Well, my guidebook didn't have much to say about Stung Treng. In addition to river sports and hiking, it recommended only visiting Mekong Blue and watching the sun set over the river. It's not like I had a lot of choices." She looked at the compound of buildings on the same wooded site where Mekong Blue was located. Is this where we'll find the other projects associated with Mekong Blue?"

"Yes. This is the Stung Treng Women's Development Center," Dara said. "One of the most worthwhile organizations in Cambodia, perhaps in the world."

"Really? Why do you think so? Is it similar to that place where you and I ate my first night back in Phnom Penh, with that cheeky teenage waitress, and the Australian-owned one in Battambang where most of us ate on tour?"

"Yes. They were all set up to help impoverished Cambodians and the entire country rebuild after the Khmer Rouge destroyed it."

"But that was in, what, 1975? That's forty-five years ago."

"True, but think of the area where you grew up. You cannot say that the American Civil War did not devastate the South. And it did not spring back very quickly. Am I correct?"

During holiday gatherings at her grandparents' home in Dallas, she'd heard some older relatives mention this or that ancestor who'd fought on the side of the Confederacy and been totally impoverished when their "glorious cause" was defeated. In fact, her father Red had mentioned how one of his grandmothers had never recovered from losing the war. The old woman had been vocal about how much she hated the "damn Yankees" until she died in the 1930s, which would have been more than sixty years after that war ended.

"You're right," she said. "And the Khmer Rouge era was much more brutal than our civil war in the States."

"Would you like to look around now?" Dara asked. "I want you to see these facilities for yourself, and tonight I have a surprise for you."

She had seen several young children in the room where the women were weaving, all so quiet and well-behaved she'd barely noticed them. But after Dara led her into a nearby room dotted with cribs and women tending babies there, she began to realize how unusual this place truly was.

"This is a community-based organization that offers a wide range of services to the poor women in this part of Cambodia. You probably read that in your guidebook, but you really do have to be here to realize what they are accomplishing." Dara pointed to the rest of the buildings that stretched out near the Mekong Blue retail shop, where she had just bought her scarves. "The organization also runs a clinic, where women in need can receive free health care, and provides daycare/kindergarten for both employees' and local villagers' children."

"That's impressive."

"Childcare and health care are just part of what this organization does. It also offers free English lessons and computer classes, as well as housing and lunch for the employees and their dependent children at no charge."

They walked through the grounds, looking at the various facilities Dara had just described. "Can we stay here for a while? This is a wonderful idea, and I'd like to do what I can to support it."

Dara beamed. "I hoped you would say that, but for now, I would like for you to simply get an overview of what is going on. As I mentioned before, I have a couple of other stops planned for the rest of the day, so we have a schedule to stick to."

"Oh, you and your schedules." She lightly thumped Dara with a loose fist. "You sound like a tour guide I once knew."

"Really? What was this guide like?" Dara adopted her light, teasing tone.

"Very competent, well organized, informative, easy on the eyes. In fact, I enjoyed being with her quite a bit."

"And what happened to this model guide?"

"She turned out to be a hero. Saved a woman's life and took her on some interesting adventures." Dara glanced at a variety of spaces as they passed them—a lunchroom with tables and chairs; a school containing a whiteboard, quite a few old computers, and bookcases crammed with books; and a clinic equipped with basic medical furnishings and supplies.

After they had strolled past the buildings that were part of the Stung Treng Women's Development Center, Dara stopped and pointed back toward her motorcycle, which they'd left in front of Mekong Blue. "You stay here, and a certain tour guide will pick you up and whisk you away to your next two interesting undertakings. At least I hope they satisfy you."

She almost purred. Dara was so much fun and full of surprises. "I feel like Cinderella, on her way to the ball." She gave a mock curtsey.

Dara returned a brief bow. "Be right back."

She watched Dara stride up the street, choking back tears. Had she finally found her Princess Charming?

Yet Barbara was tired. She leaned against a nearby wall and watched a child bounce a ball against a building several blocks away. She felt heavy, like someone was sitting on her head, almost rooted in place.

Having Covid must have taken more out of her than she'd realized. Granted, she was still in great shape and had never had many health problems, but she had lost some of her usual stamina.

"Is it okay if we stop back by the room before we go do what you have in mind?" she asked. Dara had pulled the cycle up beside her and was handing her the helmet that she took and put on almost automatically. "I must not have slept long enough."

"Fine with me. We don't have to be anywhere until about six thirty."

Back at the hotel, after an hour's rest, Barbara did feel better.

"I don't know what's wrong with me all of a sudden," she told Dara as she brushed her hair. It would be mashed again when she put her helmet back on in a few minutes, but she liked to be at her best for whatever surprises Dara had planned.

Dara gave her an appraising look. "You flew nine thousand miles across the Pacific to get here, didn't you? And before that, you probably spent several weeks packing and arranging for everything to be taken care of while you were gone. Right?"

"Yes. But I watched movies almost the entire way to Cambodia, except when I ate and slept. It was an easy flight."

"I am sure it was, but it is certainly not easy to fly that distance without feeling some effect."

"I suppose that's true."

"Then you spent two full weeks riding around a totally unfamiliar country with strangers."

"Plus, it was hot, and our tour guide made us walk till we almost dropped. And then she kept offering us even more interesting activities."

Dara grinned. "Guilty as charged."

"So, in order to rest before I traveled nine thousand miles back, I flew down to a gorgeous island, where I spent three idyllic days."

"But instead of lounging in the sun, as you should have, you had to go scuba diving, and snorkeling, and on a boat tour of the island—"

She laughed and put a hand on Dara's arm. "That's enough. You're right."

But Dara was on a roll. "Then you got sick with a mysterious new virus that could have killed you and turned around after you recovered and went back to Phnom Penh. And if that was not enough, the very next day you got on a Honda and headed out again."

"Yes. I realize now that a motorcycle's not the most relaxing way to travel, but it's certainly fun. I'll never regret visiting that little old woman or staying on Koh Rong, or seeing the dolphins and the turtles…Now I realize why I'm so tired. I'm not old. I have a right to be exhausted." She laughed at herself.

Dara frowned, lines showing in her forehead, and the skin at the outside area of both her eyes crinkling. "Would you rather not do anything tonight? I can cancel our plans. If you need to rest more—"

She put her hand over Dara's mouth to stop her rush of words. "No. I'm sure whatever you've arranged includes a sunset, which shouldn't require much energy to appreciate. But I'm looking forward to the surprise part too much to miss it. I can rest as much as I want after I get back home to Dallas."

There. She'd said it. She loved being with Dara, but Dallas was her home.

Dara's eyes lost some of their teasing luminosity, but she kept a smile in place as she picked up their helmets and turned toward the door. "Ready to go?"

❖

Barbara was right this time. Dara had driven through town and over to the Mekong. There she parked on a high, sandy bluff overlooking the river and led her to a fallen log. "We have the best view in the house," she said, like she'd just ushered her to a front-row seat in the Meyerson in downtown Dallas.

The sun slowly dropped behind a bank of steel-blue clouds over the distant forest, shining through cream-colored ones. White and gray wisps emphasized the fading light.

The river's metallic calmness on the far side, and the ripples near the bank where she and Dara sat, reflected the sun.

She grasped Dara's hand and breathed out a long trail of air. "I wish this moment would never end. Is it always this beautiful?"

Dara squeezed her hand and rubbed it slightly with her rough thumb. "Always. And each sunset is different. Tomorrow it could be as pink as it is blue today. And golden the next. That variety helps make it so spectacular."

"Life's like that, don't you think?" she said. "Experiences of so many different colors and shapes, but all with their own special beauty. I wish Meatea could be here. She would have loved to see this."

"As would my parents. We should enjoy it for them as well as for ourselves."

Still sitting on the log, Dara stretched up toward her as she lowered her head to meet Dara's, and heaven seemed to meet earth.

Dara's lips were as soft as she had imagined they would be—as smooth as the far side of the river, as warm as the sun on the water. Their kiss spread from Barbara's lips to her breasts, which prickled and tingled, then on to her rippling stomach. Farther down, she quivered inside, almost burning yet shivering.

The kiss kept flowing through her, like the meandering river.

But as they sat unmoving, tasting each other's freshness and desire, the light faded, the river breeze cooled, and they drew apart.

"I've been wanting to do that for a while," Barbara said, feeling as if she'd just awoken from a pleasant dream. Yet, too often, dreams like this one changed into nightmares. She normally couldn't keep such a kiss alive for more than a few months.

"So have I." Dara touched her cheek briefly, then let her hand fall to her side.

If only the sun would never set, would always keep both of them warm and wrapped in each other's arms. But Barbara had witnessed the end of too many sunsets. They were inescapable.

The wind from the Mekong grew even chillier, and she jumped up, wrapping her arms around herself. "I'm cold."

All the reasons she shouldn't have kissed Dara, shouldn't have enjoyed the experience so intensely, shouldn't have these feelings attacked her. She shivered. The river looked icy now, the cobalt sky like a metal shield designed to ward off the sun.

Chapter Eighteen

Dara drove back to the outskirts of Stung Treng, near the women's center they'd visited earlier. In fact, they passed the entryway to it, lit by small floodlights. A large sign announced, in blue and yellow script, STUNG TRENG WOMEN'S DEVELOPMENT CENTER, written in both Khmer and English.

Strands of barbed wire fastened to two timbers formed the beginning of a fence that seemed to stretch around the entire compound. Ferocious-looking iron spikes topped the two sections of the closed blue chain-link gate, an effective *keep-out* warning. These precautions probably provided the women and children there a sense of security. Barbara recalled Dara's comment about how this part of Cambodia was once a dangerous no-man's-land.

Just past the center, Dara stopped and hopped off the motorcycle, then helped her get off. After they secured their helmets to the back of the vehicle, Dara took her hand and guided her down a dimly lit winding path to the front of a spotlit red house, elevated on stilts, its roof multicolored. They climbed a metal stairway to the second floor, Dara's hand on her back.

"Why are you being so attentive? Afraid I'll fall?" she asked Dara.

"I just like touching you. I've never felt this connected and want to stay that way as long as I can."

Heat consumed her. "I know what you mean," she whispered, the door to the house in front of them. "Why are we here instead of alone?"

"I had already arranged for you to meet these people, and tonight is our only chance. After you talk to them, you should understand."

Curious, she watched Dara knock on the door, which opened almost immediately. A tall, thin man, about Dara's age, greeted them, dressed informally in a cotton shirt and long pants. "*Chom reap sor*," the man said, holding his hands together before his egg-shaped face and giving a slight nod, a greeting she had finally learned was called a *sampeah*. She returned it. Saying hello in Khmer was beginning to come more naturally. "Dara, welcome. And you must be Barbara. I am Kim. Please to come in."

After they entered the house, a petite woman, her short, black hair highlighted with red, rushed in and welcomed them, introducing herself as Chantha. Her dark eyes kind and wise, she seemed electric. Her dangling earrings moved as she greeted Barbara in the customary way, and then she said, in quite fluent English, "We are so glad to meet you. It is an honor to have you and Dara here."

As Barbara had come to expect, the room was bare, except for a low table, set for dinner. A wonderful fragrance had entered the room with Chantha, and Barbara suddenly felt hungry. In spite of her afternoon rest, it had been a long day. And while she was glad Dara had planned such a pleasant surprise, she wished she weren't still rather tired.

"Chantha has prepared some of her special dishes," Kim said, gesturing for them to sit at the low table. "She will be serving us but will have time to talk later at more of a leisure. Please to excuse her."

Kim asked her how she was enjoying her visit to Cambodia, then conversed primarily with Dara in Khmer. She didn't mind, gazing at the spectacular hardwood used in the room. But she kept returning to a wall hanging that looked to be six feet long or more. It shimmered in the dim light, its vibrant colors almost alive.

She was far from religious, but her grandparents had made sure she attended Sunday school and church every week as a child. Now, as she glanced at the wall hanging, she kept thinking about Joseph's coat of many colors from the Bible.

Dara and Kim must have noticed where she'd focused her attention, because Dara broke in. "Gorgeous, don't you think?"

"Oh, yes. I've never seen anything quite like it." She was drawn to its beauty, its simplicity, its originality, and its ability to stir memories of the past.

Just then Chantha bustled in again, holding a large, steaming bowl. "You like our wall hanging, I see," she said as she placed the container in the center of the table and sat down beside her. "Noodle and chicken soup."

"You are lucky. This dish is one of her best," Kim said. "Please to serve yourself."

She did as he suggested, suddenly realizing how hungry she was. "It looks delicious," she said, then took a spoonful and bit into one of the noodles. She almost moaned. "These noodles taste even better than they look. How do you make them?"

Barbara detected both pride and nostalgia in Chantha's smile. "Slowly, although not as slowly as my mother did. When I was a schoolgirl during the sixties, we ate them for breakfast every morning. She spent many hours each day preparing them. She mixed rice flour and hot water, which requires strong hands, and shaped each noodle individually." She smiled. "I take a shortcut and use scissors, which would appall my mother."

Barbara elbowed Dara. "Remember the noodles we helped make at our homestay on the way to Siem Reap during the tour?"

"How could I forget? Everyone got up early, long before our hostess had to be at her workplace, and watched her mix and roll out the dough," Dara said.

"Then we took turns cranking the handle of the cutter she ran the dough through. Those noodles were the best I'd ever had, at that point," she said, "especially served with those fried duck eggs. They're still the best eggs I've ever eaten, but your noodles win the prize, Chantha."

Chantha took another spoonful of her soup. "Using a noodle maker like that would have horrified my mother. She always said you need to do anything worthwhile slowly and mindfully. It is the Buddhist way, and I have always tried to follow her advice."

"Well, your mother must be appalled at how practically everyone who has anything to do with food is in such a hurry now, especially in America."

Chantha took another bite from her own helping of noodles and chicken, in a garlic-flavored broth, and didn't respond for a long beat, obviously savoring her handiwork. But her eyes looked dull when she finally did speak. "I lost my mother many years ago, in wartime Saigon, under the Communist regime there. My sister as well. I was only twenty-four."

"Oh. I'm so sorry." Barbara's heart clenched. "My mother died just this past year, in Dallas…"

"And you will never stop missing her, no matter how long ago you lost her." Chantha slowly chewed another bite. "I have so many fond memories of mine, most of them centering on her kitchen in our home in Battambang, before the Khmer Rouge took over. That is what made her and my sister and me to flee to Saigon."

"What a horrible time that must have been," she said. "It seems to have affected everyone I've met here. I suppose Dara and her parents were some of the lucky ones, to have been able to escape to the US."

Kim turned to Dara. "The academic background of your parents most likely helped them find a place there. Chantha and her family hoped for asylum in the US but failed to find any aid."

"You are correct, Kim," Dara said. "My father had attended several international educators' conferences, and his contacts with his American colleagues in California made it possible to get us out before Pol Pot forced everyone in Phnom Penh to evacuate the city."

"How about you, Kim?" Barbara asked. "How did you survive that awful time?"

Kim reddened. Apparently, he didn't like to be in the spotlight, but he responded readily. "I too left Cambodia, though I do not know how I survived. I went to Saigon as well and almost starved there. I also met Chantha." Kim looked over at her with a soft expression. "So something good did come from all that suffering."

"I would definitely have rather met you under different circumstances," Chantha said to him, "but we have done a lot together, have we not?" They exchanged another glance that made Barbara wonder if they were a couple, perhaps with grown children.

If they were, that meant they had met some forty-five years ago. She and Dara, even if they ended up together, would never have that kind of history. Was she foolish to think they could share many common experiences and memories except those of a brief interlude in Covid-19 Cambodia?

❖

Barbara gladly accepted another bowl of noodle soup, along with small helpings of other traditional dishes, and as she ate, she admired the wall hanging again. "Where did you find such a beautiful work of art?" she finally asked. Chantha, Kim, and Dara exchanged glances, as if deciding whether to let her in on some type of secret. Finally, Chantha put down her spoon and said, "I made it."

"You—" she almost choked on her soup. "You, but…did you work at Mekong Blue?"

"She and I founded Mekong Blue, almost twenty years ago, and she is executive director of the women's development center here," Kim said.

Barbara shook her head, amazed by what Chantha had accomplished. As she did, she spotted a wooden flute, intricately crafted, leaning against the other side of the room, and thought of Meatea's wood-carving skill. Beside it rested a *tro ou*, a two-stringed Cambodian musical instrument. Its sound box was made of a coconut shell covered with snakeskin, its stick-like wooden body heavily lacquered, with its long bow resting against it. Did Kim play it, or was it merely decorative? She had seen and heard one on the grounds near Angkor Wat on tour and thought how similar its whine sounded to that of an American fiddle. Dara had told their tour group that the *tro ou* often provided the music at weddings.

Kim said, "Making silk is a traditional art in our culture, which the Khmer Rouge almost destroyed. They believed everyone should wear clothes made of coarse, black material and that silk was part of Western decadence." He shook his head, as if such a simplistic generalization disgusted him. "When Chantha and I returned to Cambodia, in the nineties, with our son and daughter, this area was full of land mines, terrible roads, and armed bandits. Most of the women were illiterate and worked at menial jobs for one dollar a day."

"Or they had to become prostitutes in order to feed themselves and their children," Chantha said.

"Dara told me this was a dangerous place because it was so near the border, but I had no idea." Barbara thought of how easy life in Dallas had always been for her. As she did, she focused on a beautifully carved sculpture of a traditional *apsara* dancer sitting across the room. Depictions of these beautiful women covered the walls of many of the temples she had visited throughout Cambodia. Had Chantha encouraged their daughter to learn some of graceful moves and gestures these girls specialized in? Did their son play the *tro ou*? The traditional culture of Cambodia was obviously precious to them.

"All over this ruined country, we had to start building our roads, markets, hospitals, universities, and pagodas again. And the big cities recovered much faster than the small places like this," Kim said. "Chantha and I learned how to give basic medical care in the refugee camps in Thailand. And in 1993 we worked here in Stung Treng with Doctors Without Borders."

Kim paused to eat, and Chantha took up their story. "After that organization left, Kim and I established the Destination Center. It was a hospice for former sex workers, soldiers, and police infected with HIV, but we had no funding."

Barbara couldn't believe what she was hearing. If only she'd known, she could have raised money among her friends and contacts in Dallas to help such a worthy cause. She noticed a bowl full of yellow mangos perched on a small table on the other side of the room, shining against the polished hardwood of the dark wall. She had glimpsed both mango and cashew trees growing in their yard, several mangos lying on the ground near their front path. Kim was probably more at home outdoors—building, tending to the garden and their various plants, and other such activities—whereas Chantha seemed more suited for the social and political aspects of their various enterprises over the years.

"But we did not give up," Chantha was saying as Barbara focused on her again. "When Kim and I lived in wartime Saigon, the Communists kept preaching, 'You can turn your pain into strength.'" She put down her spoon, a stern expression lining her face. "At the time, I considered the phrase only propaganda, but when I saw the conditions of the people here in Stung Treng, especially the women, I finally made it work for me."

"So you founded the women's development center because you saw such a strong need here," Dara said.

"Exactly. I taught the women how to dye and weave silk, and instead of the technical terms for the two hundred and fifty colors we ended up using, I renamed them with words the women would understand," Chantha said.

Barbara thought of one of the scarves she'd bought this afternoon. "Lemon, for example?"

"Exactly. Instead of 'peach,' the name of a fruit these women have never seen, I used the term 'shrimp paste.' And I substituted 'ripe sugarcane' for the name gold. That way the women could visualize and remember these descriptions of the colors I was teaching them to dye."

"We made all our own equipment from old bicycle wheels and scrap lumber and anything else we could salvage, and gradually, the number of weavers increased," Kim said.

The strength these two must have to accomplish so much to help so many in need awed Barbara. She looked around the room, taking in two rows of colorful books lining low shelves. "So the women's center developed from there, and you added the kindergarten, clinic, classrooms, free meals, and so forth as you grew?"

"Yes. We were finally able to pay our best weavers at the center a hundred and fifty dollars a month, which is almost as much as a local medical doctor earns, thanks to the people both here and around the world who buy our scarves and other silk products," Chantha said. "I have been to trade fairs to display our products in several states in the US, including Texas and New Mexico. And I gave cooking lessons in Tennessee, where our daughter graduated from Sewanee: The University of the South."

Barbara stared at the wall hanging that had prompted this conversation. "You are amazing people," she finally said. "I am so very glad to have had this chance to talk to you, and to eat this delicious noodle soup." She placed her spoon in her empty bowl beside her plate and sighed with satisfaction.

Kim glanced at Chantha, then said, "Chantha is writing a memoir, collaborating with an American writer. But, during the course of this project, she is following her mother's advice about making good noodles. Her book is called *Slow Noodles: Recipe for Rebuilding a Lost Civilization*, and you can follow its progress at slownoodles .com."

Chantha laughed. "I keep telling my American writer friend that no one wants to know about what I have done. But she insists they do. So I try to dredge up my memories for her. That is not always easy."

"I wish I could have talked to my own mother about how to live life well," Barbara said, sadness engulfing her. "She also was victimized, in ways different yet similar to that of the women you've helped for so many years. Thanks to my father, I always thought my mother was weak. But you would have taught her to speak and read English, learn a useful skill, and make her own way in the world instead of remain a non-person in her own home most of the time."

She glanced at Dara, who put her hand over hers and squeezed. She thought of their sunset kiss and suddenly wanted Dara to be much closer to her, as close as her own skin.

CHAPTER NINETEEN

"Chantha is such an amazing woman," Barbara said as Dara helped her dismount their cycle back at their hotel. "I'd like to spend some time with her, get to know her better, and explore more of what she's doing at her women's center." But right now, all she could think about was Dara. She immediately missed having her arms around Dara's waist and resting her cheek on Dara's back.

"Yes. Despite how hard her life has been, she has done more to help women than anyone I know."

"She makes me proud of my Cambodian side, even though it's taken me seventy years to reach this point." Barbara gazed up at the moon, which had risen while they were at Chantha and Kim's home. "She reminds me of that moon, throwing light on the darkness."

After they pushed through the hotel entrance and took the elevator to their room on the top floor, they immediately powered up their A/C but clicked on only a small lamp. Then they walked over and stood at the rear window while their room cooled, enjoying the view of the Srepok River, which ran behind the hotel.

"Look how the moon brightens the river." Conscious of Dara's nearness, Barbara wanted to bridge the small distance between them. And then, as if reading her mind, Dara turned and put a hand on her wrist. That was all it took. The moon seemed to glow inside her, on her, all around her. She felt akin to the river, basking in the light of Dara's gaze, her touch, her aura.

"I cannot stop touching you," Dara murmured as she moved her hand from Barbara's wrist to her waistline and then around her waist.

Barbara settled into Dara, wanting to merge with her, empty into her as this tributary of the Mekong would soon mingle its waters with its source. "Did you slide down a moonbeam into our room?" she whispered just before Dara tugged her into a long kiss.

Their lips met, melded in a seamless connection. She tasted the faint remnants of the iced coffee they'd consumed earlier. She wanted to explore the kiss she and Dara had shared on the banks of the Mekong during sunset this evening.

Dara's tongue ran over her lips, and she opened them, slowly, welcoming Dara. She had waited so long for this moment. Dara's velvety, moist, warm tongue felt so right as it slid inside her. It searched, slowly touching the roof and walls of her mouth, her teeth, her tongue, seeming to familiarize itself. Dara finally withdrew and bit her lower lip gently, licked it, then nipped it again.

Barbara could have stood there all night, head bent, in the light of the moon. The river seemed to be streaming far below them, with no sound in the room except their deep breaths, thudding hearts, sighs.

She wanted to climb into Dara's mouth, curl up in it, spend her life meditating there, enjoying this closeness to Dara, to the source of the healing, the salve to her spirit Dara had provided these past weeks. If this leisurely kiss were the last one she and Dara ever exchanged, she would be content to languish in her memory of it.

But then Dara brushed her hand over her cheek, awakening another part of her. Dara touched her as if wondering whether they were actually here together in this time, this space. She saw fascination in Dara's eyes, sensed reverence in her fingers as they moved from her cheek to her nose—crested it, then slid down and over her other cheek. Dara inched over her mouth and traced the length of her long nose, up gradually to brush her eyebrows and, finally, her forehead, as if memorizing the features of a stranger.

In turn, Barbara cradled Dara's face between her hands, slid them up to Dara's closed eyes. Slowly, she ran her fingers over Dara's eyelids—so creamy, her lashes full and coarse, accenting the bright, dark eyes she knew so well. After she danced her fingertips over Dara's broad forehead, she let them drift back down over Dara's face, grazing each precious feature as she breathed in the light, musky aroma of this woman that reminded her of their busy day so far.

"I suppose we should share a shower, in case we don't have enough hot water for both of us. That would be a shame, wouldn't it?"

Dara looked up and then over at the window. "Should we close the drapes?"

"And shut out the moonbeam you slid into the room on? No. I refuse to let you slip away from me." She kissed Dara's lips lightly so she wouldn't be tempted to linger there. Then she reached down and grasped the bottom of Dara's ANGKOR WHAT?! T-shirt and tugged it up and over her head.

Dara's dainty breasts almost made her stop craving a shower. Dara kicked off her flip-flops, wiggled out of her denim shorts and underwear, and stood there looking as seductive as the statue of the apsara dancer Barbara had noticed in Chantha's home. Part spirit, part seductress, these women had long set the standard for elegance and beauty in this country, and Dara more than exceeded it.

"Come on, Ms. America," Dara said. "Show me what you have been hiding all this time."

"I didn't hide it when I was sick. You saw the entire package then. Nothing's changed that I know of."

"But *I* have changed. Then, I was looking at you with entirely different eyes. Now, I expect to see a desirable woman…"

Barbara stripped off her own clothes.

"And obviously I am getting what I expected," Dara said, as she pulled her close, skin to skin.

Barbara had to shut her eyes, steel herself to resist Dara's magnetic appeal. "Just a brief shower. I don't even care if the water's warm." She wrapped an arm around Dara's waist and towed her toward the bathroom. "I'm dreaming of a long night with you and want us both to enjoy every taste."

The shower's cool water practically sizzled on Barbara's heated skin. A question forced its way out. "Do you do this with many of your groupies on tour, Dara?"

"Can you keep a secret?"

"Always and forever."

Dara took one of Barbara's fingers and pressed it lightly to her own lips. "I never have, before now."

The words vibrated under Barbara's touch. She trailed a finger around Dara's lips, then kissed her, wet flesh against flesh, the water tepid now.

"In almost twenty years, you've never slept with anyone you've worked for?" She found that hard to believe. She drew Dara closer and gazed into deep, brown eyes. Not a ripple on the surface.

"Believe me," Dara said. "I would never jeopardize a job I love so much."

"So I'm your first?" Was Dara lying?

"My very first."

The water finally felt almost warm. "But you've had other women?" If she were lying, Barbara was glad. Being Dara's first indiscretion on the job thrilled her.

"Of course. How else could I learn the joys of loving my own sex?"

"Sweet young things?" At this moment, she trusted Dara with her insecurities.

"All ages. All colors. All sizes. A million women. Well, not a million."

"And what kind do you prefer?"

Dara filled her palm with body wash and ran it down Barbara's arm. "What do you think?"

"Older women, I hope." She flushed as Dara rubbed her hand back up her arm and grazed her breast.

"Women eight years my senior, to be exact."

"Because they're safer…"

"Wiser."

"Tamer?"

"Wilder."

She put her hand on Dara's shoulder, drew her closer. The water was hot now, a downpour. "Wilder?"

"Yes." Dara nipped her shoulder.

She bent, bit Dara's shoulder in return, then licked the red spot she'd left. "Surprised we're here tonight?"

Dara gazed up at her, spreading soap over her breasts. "I trimmed my nails this morning."

She laughed. "So did I." She filled her hand with the citrus-smelling soap and rubbed it over Dara's chest and down toward her navel. "The hot water won't last much longer."

"Neither will I."

"Where do you like to be touched?" she asked as she soaped near Dara's hips.

"My breasts. My feet. My head." Dara sighed as Barbara slid her palm up and down the butt she had admired so many times lately.

She caught her breath as Dara grasped her buttocks, pulled her nearer, eased a finger into her. Suddenly, water wasn't the only liquid dripping down her inner thighs.

Dara was kneeling before her now, soaping her legs and moving up toward no-man's-land again.

"I'm getting cold," she murmured. "At least my skin is."

Dara rose, grabbed the handheld shower from its holder, and sprayed her all over.

The shock distracted her from the bonfire blazing inside her. "Oww. The water's freezing now." She retrieved the sprayer from Dara and did the same to her.

More than ready for bed, she turned off the shower and bolted from the small enclosure, grabbing two towels and thrusting one at Dara. "I'm going to get you for that," she said as she swiped off the water.

Dara dried herself and was out the bathroom door almost before Barbara realized what she was doing. "You are going to have to catch me first," she heard from the bedroom.

"That's exactly what I intend to do, and a lot more," she said, dropping her own damp towel and rushing after Dara.

Dara already lay under the covers, her eyes closed and her back toward the center of the bed, obviously pretending to be asleep by the time Barbara could slip between the sheets. She lay on her right side, facing Dara, and slid her left arm over Dara's waist. "What have we here," she whispered. "A clean tour guide, waiting for me to molest her?"

Dara laughed and turned into her arms, fitting into the entire length of her as if they'd done this a million times.

Barbara murmured, "Have you read the *Kama Sutra*?"

"That is an Indian guide to lovemaking, not a Cambodian one."

"Aren't all Asians alike, especially the women? Meek and mild on the outside, but tigers in private?"

"Of course. Just like all Americans are alike." Dara chuckled. "And yes. I have read it. My mother gave me a copy as a wedding present."

"Did you pay careful attention?"

"Yes. But I did not care for it. Too much like working out at the gym. My husband wanted to perfect every position it described. But after a while I told him to go find someone else to exercise with."

She squeezed Dara closer. "And he did?"

"Multiple times. He often said it was a great suggestion."

"After you last slept with him, were you tested?"

Dara stiffened but then relaxed in her arms. "Yes. I am clean through and through." Dara reached up and pressed her hand along her cheek. "And you?"

"I had a close call several years ago, and since then I've been very careful. My last partner was myself, has been for quite a while. I've learned a lot about my own desires during the past fifty years." She took a deep breath.

"What have you learned?" Dara's hand strayed to her breast.

Now she stiffened, then tried to let herself relax. "That my breasts aren't very sensitive."

Dara stroked the one nearer her, almost tickling it. Then she leaned down and kissed it, finally circling the nipple with her tongue.

A slight tingle surprised her. "Maybe I've been missing something more special than I realized it could be."

Dara looked up and smiled. "What else have you learned during your years of study?"

"That I could indulge in oral sex forever—maybe because I can't have it by myself."

"That makes sense." Dara moved to her other breast.

She tensed again. "It takes me a long time to come." She hoped her admission didn't scare Dara away, so she continued. "When I do have a partner, I'm always willing to extend the courtesy to her indefinitely."

Dara kissed each of her nipples, then sifted her fingers lightly through her pubic hair. "That sounds delicious. I am glad you are so thoughtful. I will remember what you said."

Relieved, she said, "Anal sex is okay for me, but I need more experience with it."

"So noted." Dara let one hand drift over her derriere.

"I like to cuddle, and my thighs are very sensitive."

Immediately gliding her fingers down to her thighs, Dara said, "So you have come to know yourself well but need help with some areas you have been neglecting."

"And you're obviously a good helper."

Dara moved her arms up to her waist, and they lay facing each other, entwined yet still separate. "What turns you on about me?" Dara murmured.

"That's easy. Everything. But those silver threads in your black hair really attract me. They make you seem mature, sophisticated, experienced…You get the picture, don't you? And at the same time, they make you appear younger than you are. Want to know what turns me on about you the most?"

Dara cuddled against her. "I am listening."

"The way you do just that—listen, really listen, to me, and seem to understand what I'm trying to say even better than I do. That makes me want to let you inside every part of me."

"Which is exactly where I want to be," Dara whispered.

She allowed Dara's words to carry her away as if they were a return ticket to a vacation destination she couldn't resist. She stretched out her arms and touched Dara, who murmured, "I want you."

"I'm ravenous."

"Perfect word. I have been thinking about all the things I would like to do to you, with you, inside you."

"That's a tempting idea." Her mellow laugh sounded sexy even to herself. She rolled on top of Dara with a swiftness that surprised her. "I want you, in every way imaginable."

She ran her fingers through Dara's hair. "How can this be so coarse yet so supple," she asked. "Each of these silver hairs makes the remaining dark ones even more vivid. They remind me how long you've been alive and how long you still have to live. I just wish I'd met you sooner."

"I wish you had too. Think of all our missed opportunities." Dara raised her head, captured her nipple in her mouth, and sucked it.

Filled with regret, she massaged Dara's scalp and then kissed her forehead.

Dara released her nipple with a sigh. "Come to think of it, I would rather dwell on the opportunities ahead of us."

A rush of hope enclosed her. "Ahead of us" said everything she'd desired since she first saw Dara. Barbara wanted a future with her, however long it might last.

"I would too," she said as she kissed her way to Dara's lips and took full possession of them. Sliding her tongue into Dara's honey mouth, she savored its silken texture as she had earlier, by the river, and especially right after they'd returned to their room.

This time, as she ran her tongue over Dara's small teeth, the downy skin inside her mouth so very soft, she murmured to herself, "Only one other place would be more luxurious." Her breath hitched.

But first she wanted to worship somewhere else. "I believe you said you're a breast woman," she said as she kissed her way down Dara's throat.

"I am so glad you have a good memory."

After she had caressed Dara's breasts, she rose onto her knees and took them in her hands, one by one, sucking them until Dara whimpered with obvious pleasure. Then she scooted to the very end of their bed, lay across the foot of it, and cradled one of Dara's feet in her hands. "From one end to the other," she said, kneading the small foot..

"Oh. That feels so good." Dara moaned. "Please never stop."

She ran her thumb along the high arch of Dara's right foot, squeezed her slightly roughened heel as if it were a rubber ball, and pulled Dara's toes one by one, massaging each, then pulling it again. "Ah. I think I may come." Dara groaned. "That feels fabulous."

"Glad you're enjoying it." She bent her head and licked the bottom of one of Dara's feet.

"Ohh. That tickles."

She crawled to the middle of their bed, trailing kisses up Dara's legs as she moved from her thighs even higher and gently opened the moist folds surrounded by short, wiry, black hair. "You trimmed more than your nails this morning," she said.

Dara laughed. "Guilty as charged. What can I say? I am an optimist."

She touched her tongue to the reddish-pink protrusion between Dara's folds. Then she captured the ridge between her lips and sucked it, licked it, caressed it with her tongue until Dara whimpered. "That feels even better than my feet did. Sooo much better."

Lost in the smell and taste and sound and sight and feel of Dara writhing beneath her, she merged with her, lost in a sensation of riding the waves, then plummeting below the ocean's surface, becoming part of the water, part of Dara—engulfed and enwombed by this woman who lay squirming beneath her lips and tongue.

"Yes," Dara murmured. "Yes," she said. "YES," she screamed.

And then Barbara almost drowned, the salty gush covering her mouth, her cheeks, as she gently tasted Dara one more time and scooted up to enfold her in her arms.

Dara was shaking, breathing hard. "That was so good. I cannot wait to taste you, to be inside you. I have wanted you for so long now."

"What? A week?"

"It seems like a year, a lifetime. Desire does not know how to tell time. It is like a baby who wants to eat, *right now*."

Waves of desire rushed through Barbara, from her toes to her lips. Dara's words were as breathtaking as her kisses, pounding ashore, almost knocking her down with their force. "What's stopping you?"

"I hate for it to be over. If I do not begin, I will not have to finish."

"That's a pretty thought, but how about some action? Then after you finish, we can start all over again. And then again. For the rest of our lives." Barbara drew a shaky breath. "Did I just say that?"

Dara stretched up, unsealing their flesh that had seemed glued together, and blew in her ear. "You did. And I have an aural memory. That is like a photographic memory, but even more effective. I will never forget those six words. I will say them every night, mumble them forever."

"And I will listen to you say them, from whatever dimension I'm traveling in, and add two of my own: "For the rest of our lives, *and beyond*."

Dara blew in her ear again, and she breathed out, "How did you know to do that?"

"I am not sure. It just came to me. I have never done it before."

"That used to be the sexiest thing possible, the ultimate turn-on before I even experienced sex. Guaranteed to drive your partner into a frenzy of lovemaking." She chuckled. "Reminds me of backseats at drive-in movies, acne, fumbling hands under poodle skirts. You make me feel like a teenager again."

"You are. A teenager and the most desirable woman I have ever known. I crave to lick you until you scream for me to stop."

Dara slid down her, and then a lone finger circled her clitoris until she was afraid she would drown Dara with her juices.

"Slowly?"

"Yes. Yes. You're killing me, but I love it."

One finger became two, stroking and gliding.

Then a single finger inched inside her, feeling its way. "Yes." She couldn't stand much more. "You're a matchstick inside me. I'm burning, burning, on fire." She seemed to be flying, soaring through the clouds, looking down on herself lying there, heaving, coming all over Dara's wonderful searching finger, which gradually retreated, surely coated with her juices.

"Wow."

"Just wow?"

"That says it all."

Dara was suddenly beside her again, glued flesh to flesh once more. Entangled. She was still floating, slowly descending. Dara kissed her, then eased her salty finger into her mouth, the tang of her own cum making her stomach heave with desire again. "I have not finished with you," Dara said, moving to the bottom of their bed again.

This time Dara's tongue parted her neatly, like peeling a peach. Then it was licking, orbiting, sliding up one side and down the other.

"Does that feel good?" The question bubbled to the surface.

"Amazing. Just one thing."

"What?"

"Don't"—Dara froze—"stop…"

Dara began again.

"Ever."

Barbara was flying once more, the air rushing over her, nearing the moon now, past Venus and Mercury, into the sun. She was burning, burning, then exploding, caught in a solar flare, melting, dissolving, gone.

So this was what an orgasm felt like. Finally, she knew with total certainty. Before now, she had been wishing, hoping, trying. But this cataclysm had erupted without warning. She had done nothing except enjoy it.

"Barbara?"

"Yes?"

"Are you all right?"

Why did Dara appear so upset, kneeling there over her, stroking her cheek, her hair?

"I was afraid you had passed out."

"I thought I'd melted. Your tongue is unbelievable."

Barbara gasped. The experience seemed to have emptied all the old, stale oxygen from her and refilled her with a new, fresh supply. "Would you believe me if I told you that's the first orgasm I've ever had?"

"No. It seemed so natural for you."

"Well, it obviously is. You should be very proud of yourself."

"You are just flattering me."

"I'm being honest. But we don't need to talk about it. I'm more than satisfied to just lie here with you."

PART IV

DARA

Chapter Twenty

L et's stay in bed all day," Barbara says to me.

She gleams all over as she looks down at me. I see nothing but her, outlined by the early morning rays of the sun, bending over me, red hair falling into her eyes, cheeks flushed. A well-fucked woman. I throw my hands above my head, grab my own hair, stretch, and yawn loudly. "Ahhh."

She kisses the tip of my nose, and when I close my eyes, she touches each of my eyelids with another moist kiss. "You must be very proud of yourself," she murmurs as she settles down beside me.

"I most certainly am." I take a deep, satisfied breath. "I have never made love to anyone like you. You are the most responsive, combustible, lovely creature I have ever known."

"Creature?"

"Yes." I smooth my hand over her face. "As wild as a shark, as strong as a lioness, as graceful as a gazelle—"

"Hmm…you must bring out the animal in me." Barbara runs her hand from my neck to my hip. Then she draws me even closer and lets out a murmur that sounds like a snarl.

"Shall we stay in bed for the rest of our lives?" I ask.

"Let's do it. We can buy this hotel and move from room to room, try every bed, then start all over again." Her stomach growls. "Of course, we'll have to hire a chef—and someone to wash our sheets and towels."

"But not our clothes. We will never need any again."

"We could write a book. What shall we name it? *How to Have Multiple Orgasms While Touring Cambodia*?"

"What about *Eating Your Way Around the River Hotel*?" I ask.

"That sounds like fun," Barbara comments, "but my stomach is saying otherwise. Should we listen to it?"

I stick out my lower lip. "Noo. I would rather starve."

She nibbles my lip. "We should do this again." She bends down and circles my nipple with her tongue. "Like this." Then she does the same to the other one. "And this."

I pull her to me, squeeze her, want to never let her go. But I finally do. Yet I plan to make the interval as brief as possible. "Okay. I give up. I will run buy us something in the market to keep us from starving. But you stay here and prepare to be molested sooner rather than later."

"Is that a promise?" she asks.

"Cross my heart."

What have I done? Barbara lies here beside me sleeping, her red hair tousled, smelling of sex. She is finally sated, I suppose.

How long before she decides she has had enough and wants to go home? Back to Texas, where she speaks the language, knows the routine. Maybe she even has a lover waiting for her there, wondering why she has been gone so long. Surely not, but most of all I hope she does not have a husband she has "forgotten" to mention.

I have broken a promise to myself that I have kept for almost twenty years. *Never sleep with the boss.*

I should have known better, put the pieces together sooner. She recently lost her mother, then almost died herself. So I let her talk me into driving her around on my motorcycle like we are teenagers. And I end up in bed with her having the best sex of my life.

What will I do when she grows tired of me?

I try not to disturb her as I move her hand from around my waist and slip out of bed without a sound. She looks so peaceful lying there, chest rising and falling, a sheet draped over the lower half of her. So innocent, like she appeared to be when she was so sick.

Can I believe a single word she has said after we fell into each other's arms last night? Especially the word promise. At least the L word did not come up. Not that I would have expected it to. Last night, and this morning, and most of the afternoon were all about sex. Yet, I have to admit, the L word did hover on my lips once or twice. Thank goodness I was cautious enough not to be sentimental and let it slip.

A cold shower. That is what I need. Try to wash the layers of sweat and dust and regret from myself. My back is sore, one knee rug-burned, my hair filthy.

The water is barely warm now. I am soaping my hair when the bathroom door creaks open. She pulls back the shower curtain and steps in like she owns me, wraps her arms around me, and I am lost again—falling into her kisses, abandoning myself to the bonfire she ignites in me. Let its purifying flame burn.

"What now?" I say as we stand there toweling off, the hot water long ago turned chilly.

Barbara hangs her towel on a hook, rakes her still-damp hair out of her blazing eyes, arouses me with a stare. My stomach lurches, from which kind of hunger I am not sure. We could so easily fall into bed again.

"Shouldn't we try to find something to eat? We've had a lot of exercise." She keeps us from starving to death.

Am I the lust-crazed one in all this, craving her more than she does me?

"We definitely should," I say. "Have something in mind?"

She looks me up and down. "Yes. I do." She kisses me, pressing her nude self against the full length of me. "But we really should eat something else now."

I chuckle, squeeze her, then force myself to hang up my towel beside hers. I go rummage through my backpack and find a decent T-shirt. Trying to anchor myself in a safe place, I ask her, "Do you have many clean clothes left?"

She is halfway dressed in an outfit I recognize from two days ago. "No. Should we leave our laundry at the front desk? I've let things get away from me and am not in the mood to rinse out this many dirty clothes."

"That is fine with me." I make a pile of practically everything I brought to wear, and she does the same.

"Let's just put all our clothes together," she suggests. "It's easier that way."

I nod. It is a weak symbol of our apparently new status as equals. But I will take it, fool that I am. Something tells me I will regret it when she finally does leave. But I am weak when it comes to her. We have maybe one more week together, at the most, before she flies away. Why not make the most of it? She will most certainly abandon me, break my heart. But after I recover, our lovemaking will be a pleasant memory.

I scoop all our dirty T-shirts, jeans, shorts, underwear, socks, and nightshirts into my arms. "We probably will not need any of these for the next twenty-four hours, will we?" I ask.

"Definitely not." She grins.

"Then shall we go find something to eat?"

After we locate some decent food in a nearby restaurant, we wander through the open-air market in the center of town. Tin roofs cover part of it. Umbrellas, tarps, and other portable shade protect the rest of the stalls.

"Look at all those fish," Barbara says. "I've never seen so many different types and sizes."

"Most of them come from the Mekong. Next time we eat, we should try one."

"Sure. We don't have such a wide variety in Texas, and most of these seem fresh."

Many of the vegetables for sale are spread out on tarps on the ground. And their sellers are almost all women, squatting near them, always ready to bargain.

"Such a variety of greens, and a million vegetables I've never dreamed of, much less eaten." She prefers the fruit and buys several bananas and mangos, conversing with the vendors in her very broken but nevertheless improving Khmer.

"I am proud of you," I tell her. She has made a deal with an older woman who appears happy with their bargain. "You are beginning to enjoy the spirit of the marketplace."

"Interacting with these people is so much easier than I thought it would be. And the women are all so nice. No one's overcharged me too outrageously, that I know of."

"It is an honor for the ones you buy something from. It shows that their produce is worth more than the other women's. So you are helping them build their pride as well as their income." I have no idea if that is an accurate statement, but it sounds logical to me. I do know that Barbara seems to be building some confidence in herself, which is what matters to me at this point.

The heat and the dust are beginning to bother me, so I say, "Ready for a nap? You have gotten me in the habit, you know."

Her eyes flame with that expression of pure joy I cannot resist. "Glad I've been a good influence on you. And yes, I'm ready."

The spark of desire in her glance tells me she is ready for more than that, again. And so am I. We are insatiable.

"I need to make a quick stop," I tell her. "Meet you back at the hotel in half an hour."

She glances around and spots our hotel in the distance. "Oh. Okay. I know where I am now. Make it an hour. I want to run by the women's center and visit with Chantha for five or ten minutes. But I'll see you soon." She walks off through the noisy crowd.

I head for the best massage parlor in town. The street is lined with such businesses, but I refuse to patronize most of them. A friend, Harini, owns the Pure Gold, though, and I can trust her.

Once I enter the parlor, she heads over to me. "Hi, Dara. What are you doing here? I thought your company had canceled all its tours because of the virus."

"It has." Harini leads me toward the back so we can talk in private, catch up a little. She is a gorgeous woman, and we have had our good times together, particularly when I was first coming out and she owned a parlor in Phnom Penh. She taught me things about myself I had no idea of, but then she found someone much more experienced.

I was devastated for a while, and then we started hooking up again—when we were in the mood. But after she moved up here to open a business with a new girlfriend, we lost touch. Several years ago, we bumped into each other and have finally realized we make better friends than lovers.

"Anything particular on your mind?" she asks after we talk for a while.

"In fact, there is." I explain what I need, and she grins and supplies it, though her tone tells me she is curious, maybe even concerned. She could want to be sure she can have me again, if and when she wants me.

"Have fun, Dara," she says as I leave. *But not too much.*

I hope I have grown beyond her, and the fact that I am back at the hotel with ten minutes to spare tells me I may have, finally.

"Where have you been?" Barbara asks as I burst through the door. "I've missed you."

"I have missed you too." I grab her and kiss her until she gasps for air. Then I hold out the package wrapped in white paper, which I had clutched in my sweating hand as I hurried back here.

"Oh. Did you buy something special?"

"A surprise you might like."

"Really? I love surprises. What is it?"

"Let me get it ready first, while you make yourself comfortable. Preferably in the bed."

Her brown eyes glisten. "This sounds exciting."

"I hope it will be." I kiss her again and walk into the bathroom, closing the door behind me. Then I turn on the faucet and unwrap my package.

When the water is hot, I pour some special soap into my palm and wash my surprise for her. After that, I dry it with a piece of paper towel.

Cradling it in my hand, I open the door and walk over to the bed. She is where I expected her to be, where I want her—stretched out on her side, the sheet pulled up to her bare waist.

After I place my gift, wrapped in the paper towel, on the bedside table, I shuck off my clothes.

"What are you being so secretive about?" she asks as I slide in next to her, kissing her as if I have never tasted her lips before. I run my hands up and down her side, reacquainting myself with every curve and crevice of her, enjoying how she undulates under me, surging and swelling like the sea. She moans. "Oh, what you do to me. I'll never get enough of you."

Now I bend, kiss my way up her legs, and massage her until she grows pliable, unresisting. Then I reach over and unveil my secret. "Surprise."

She gasps. "Where did you get that dildo?" she asks as I hold it up.

"I was unsure what size you would prefer. If you want another one, we can shop together later. But I thought you might enjoy trying this one and seeing what you think."

"It looks perfect. But I do need to give it a trial run. That's only sensible, don't you think?" Her smile has a Cheshire-cat quality, though I keep the cliché to myself.

I nod and reach for the lube I have also bought, squirt a generous amount into my hand, and coat the toy thoroughly. Then I bend over her stomach and run my tongue through her wiry hair to her wet lips and insert our new toy into her as deep as I dare. After that I pull it out and kiss her down there. When my face grows wet from the liquid she is secreting, I pick up the toy again, rub its head around her entrance, and whisper, "Feel good?"

"Wonderful. Divine," she whispers back. "You're an angel."

I press it hard, and she seems to draw it into her. In and out, I inch my way inside her, checking constantly to make sure she feels no pain. "Deeper, harder," she says, again and again, so I take her at her word. But now I am thrusting in, then pulling out, and she keeps repeating those two demands—"Deeper, harder"—until she finally screams. It is a long, primal howl, like that of a panther. She was correct earlier. Obviously, I do bring out the animal in her, and I am so proud to do so. She is the most perfect woman I have ever met. Perfect for me, and I cannot get enough of her, will never let her go, ever. Harini is history.

She finally stops moving, and I carefully draw the dildo from her, glistening with her juices. I watch as it leaves her, want to go where it has been. All at once she pulls me to her, squeezes me, runs her hands up and down me, kisses me like this is the first time we have ever had sex.

"I don't know what to say," she tells me. "I've never experienced anything like that before. You've released something in me that I've always been afraid of. You're ruining me. I'll never want anyone but you." Her arms grow slack, and I turn us so we face one another.

"I feel the same. And if I have my way, you will never want anyone else."

"You better not either then." She glares but softens into a smile.

We kiss again, a long, relaxing embrace, and fall asleep in each other's arms. This is the happiest, the most content I have ever been. Harini is definitely history.

I wake up, but Barbara sleeps on—her hair mussed, one hand tucked under her cheek—and I let her. She still needs to rest. I get up and dress, dash downstairs to check on our laundry, then visit the market again. After bargaining for some tamarinds, green oranges, and a jackfruit, I pick up some sticky rice, and we are set for a while.

Then I wander around, chatting with the children who have spent the day here with their parents. The market is like a giant home. In many of the booths, various family members are involved in daily activities like shaving and cooking, while one of them sells their wares to townspeople and tourists.

After I return to the hotel, Barbara says, yawning and stretching, "Hmm. I missed you. What do you have there?"

"A few things to tide us over until we feel like going out to eat again." I pull my purchases from the string bag I never leave home without and display them on the bed.

"Aren't those oranges still too green to eat?" she asks.

"No. A lot of oranges in Cambodia never turn orange. That color is to fool the Irish into buying them."

She laughs at my corny joke and then points at the tamarinds. "Those brown things that look like huge dried peas still in the shell. What do they taste like?"

"They are sweet, when they are ripe like this, and they can make a mess when you eat them." I crack the brown shell of one and scrape out the sticky pulp, then hold it up for her to taste. "And really sour when they are green."

She runs her tongue over her lips, cleaning off the resin left on them, and I am instantly wet.

"That's a jackfruit," she says of the large green, knobby-skinned piece of fruit about the size of the cantaloupes I grew familiar with in the States. "I've seen them and wondered if I'd like them."

"They taste like a blend of an apple and a banana, except you should try not to eat them in public. If you belch them, people nearby may be offended."

"Offended how?"

"They will probably think you have just eaten a piece of goat meat gone bad."

Barbara laughs. "Okay. I'll indulge in them strictly in private. And only if you will too."

"All right. We can belch at the same time to cancel each other out." We chuckle together. "Hungry?"

She yawns. "I'll say. I've certainly had my exercise today, and more. Want me to cook since you did the shopping?"

"Not this time. Stay right where you are, and these will be ready in a few minutes."

I peel and cut up several oranges and one of the mangos she bought earlier, slice off a piece of jackfruit, and arrange everything, along with some unshelled tamarinds and a banana, on a large plate I borrowed from the desk clerk downstairs. I have also bought a large container of water, which I pour into the water bottles we carry everywhere with us.

"Dinner is served, madam," I announce as I set the plate in the middle of our bed. I strip off my clothes and sit as close to her as possible without tipping over our food.

"Now this is my kind of meal," she says, reaching for a segment of a green orange. "Hmm. You're right. It tastes perfectly ripe."

Juice coats our hands from it, plus the drippings from the mangos and jackfruit. I even let some drop onto one breast, anticipating the aftermath. She peels the banana seductively, and I savor the bites she gives me as the piece of fruit disappears inch by inch.

By the time we finish, we have made such a mess, we have to take another shower, which leads to washing each other to ensure both of us are clean.

Then, while she completes her toilette, I sneak into our bedroom and exchange our wet, sticky sheets for some fresh ones I retrieved from the maid earlier, leaving her a generous tip, of course.

Barbara emerges from the bath with her hair unmussed, so we cap off our meal with our sticky rice. After that, we proceed to spend the rest of the night and next morning staining our sheets again.

Chapter Twenty-one

Barbara just went crazy, and I am not sure why. But let me explain what happened.

We have been having the most wonderful time fucking our brains out, as she calls it, and this morning she decided she would like to try some other sex toys. Stupid me told her where I bought the dildo. I also said she could go with me to pick out some other playthings.

So off we go, detouring through the market to check how ripe the mangos are today and shop for the colorful variety of fruit she seems to love. She tries them all and has even threatened to buy a durian. I warned her that the hotel management would probably make us leave, because durians smell like a combination of rotting onions and cat shit. But she is determined to taste one. I suppose we could go down by the river and cut it there, someplace with no one nearby to complain. Some people say they taste all right once you get past their odor, which almost knocks you down. She is one determined woman, so I will probably give in, like I usually do.

Anyway, we have made it past the fruit area and shopped our way through the section where women are selling clothes. She has fingered I don't know how many cotton outfits, the traditional ones she fantasized everyone would be wearing here in Cambodia. But she has yet to buy one.

She keeps picking up T-shirts, though, colorful ones with funny sayings on them. Her latest is black, with a picture of Angkor Wat, in white, in the center. Above the picture it says, "I Don't Need THERAPY," the word therapy colored red. And under the drawing is written, "I Just Need to Go to CAMBODIA," the word Cambodia in red too. She says she loves how soft the shirts are. Between those and all the silk scarves she keeps buying at Mekong Blue, I am not sure how we will ever get back to Phnom Penh.

Not that I am in a hurry. I could spend the rest of my life living this dream. She is still unquenchable, like she has never had sex before now. She wants to try everything, as many times as she can, before she almost passes out from exhaustion. She has taught me a lot, and I certainly do not mind indulging whatever whim she suggests. I just hope she does not overdo it.

We have been here in Stung Treng about a week now. And when we are not in bed, which is not all that often, Barbara is at Mekong Blue or some other part of the women's center. She is obviously becoming great friends with Chantha, because she is always saying Chantha this or Chantha that. And her Khmer is improving. Of course, I encourage her every chance I get. Learning to speak the language is high on her list.

While she is at Mekong Blue, I either hang around the market looking for little things I think she might enjoy eating or wearing or whatever. Or I stop by the Pure Gold to reminisce with Harini. With the lull in the tourist trade, she has more time on her hands than usual. We talk about the old days, after I first moved back here, how the gay club scene in Phnom Penh has evolved but still has a long way to go, mutual acquaintances, and so on. She is hard to resist, but I have every reason to do just that.

You know how it is with old girlfriends. Unless you break up on a really bad note and cannot stand to be around each other, you still have a connection—special memories exclusive to the two of you, gossip about the old crowd. You also spend a lot of time just dwelling on how things in general have changed and how they used to be so much better or cheaper or well-made or whatever.

The one thing Harini and I have *not* discussed is Barbara. I refuse to. Harini has always been possessive—seeming glad to see me with someone she can feel superior to and turning on the charm when she wants me to pay attention to her.

But Barbara is the most special person I have ever met, and I want to keep her all to myself. No one, especially a self-centered ex like Harini, would want to hear about how crazy I am about Barbara.

She amazes me on so many levels. If I began to talk about her, I would have a difficult time stopping. Plus, I am sure Harini would not want to listen to me describe how fabulous my sex life is right now. She and I were okay together, but that is exactly the right word—okay. I have already said she is gorgeous—willowy and graceful—but she is also self-centered and prejudiced, especially against Americans.

I have no idea where my brain was this morning, when I gave in to Barbara about the sex toys. I refuse to take her to some cheap, sleazy place that will try to overcharge her and give her a bad impression of Cambodia. In many ways, she still has a tourist's view of this country, and I want to let her discover for herself how difficult life here is for a lot of people. She is really caught up with Chantha and her mission to save the women of Cambodia from having to work for almost nothing or prostitute themselves. So she would have a difficult time understanding how a lot of people here live by the law of supply and demand. If foreigners come here demanding sex in any form, these people do their best to supply it.

I am not saying that the Pure Gold offers more than massages. It does not. But it took Harini a long time to build up a business that can survive by offering only legitimate pleasures. She has sex toys in the back room to supplement her income. Yet along the way, she has developed a bad attitude toward foreigners, especially wealthy American males. You know the type. The obnoxious ones who think they can buy anything here in Cambodia—or anywhere else—even Harini on occasion.

As we leave the market, Barbara says, "Chantha told me the best place to buy sex toys is the Pure Gold."

I stop and stare at her. "You discuss our private life with Chantha? I did not realize you two are that close."

"I don't go into any detail at all, baby." She looks at me with those glowing eyes that always melt me. Then she lowers her voice. "Anyone with eyes can see how well-fucked I am."

How can I stay upset when she says something like that? Harini always made me feel like I was merely adequate in bed.

"I simply asked her where I could find some adult toys, and she drew her own conclusions. Like I said, she thinks the Pure Gold is number one in that area. Besides, that's where you told me you bought the first one, and it's held up well."

I panic. Why did I have to mention where I bought it? Harini will be furious if she finds out I have been sleeping with an American and that American is wealthy and more alluring than she is, though I would never use that word. But Barbara wants to choose her own toys. And I truly do not want to buy anything like that anywhere else in this town.

I have not spent enough time with Harini to know her schedule, so I try to distract Barbara, stall until I can make sure the two of them do not run into each other. I know both of them well enough to realize they will instantly despise each other.

"We've put this off long enough," Barbara says. "Besides, we're already out of the hotel and don't have anything else to do. What's the problem? It's simple. Go to the Pure Gold, buy a few toys, then go back to our room and try them."

My stomach ripples, flares with heat. I cannot resist. Maybe Harini is off today, or gone on a break, or has broken her leg. Anything so she and Barbara do not meet. I hate to think of what might happen.

"It is not that simple," I tell Barbara. "Do you not know sex toys are illegal in Cambodia?"

She stops right there in the street. "Illegal?!" She turns pale.

"Keep your voice down." I am whispering because you never know who speaks English. "It is not a major crime. But the law is on the books, and I have heard that the police actually enforce it on occasion."

"Enforce it how?"

"Confiscate the illegal items. Sentence you to twenty days in jail, or a fine of forty dollars, or both."

She laughs. "High crimes and misdemeanors? We had an anti-sodomy law on the books in Texas until not that long ago. And a lot of fundamentalist people there still consider oral sex, not to mention anal, to be deviant acts."

"Hmm," I say. "Not that different from here."

"We also still have an odd law regarding sex, passed less than fifty years ago, that our lawmakers haven't bothered to excise yet."

"What is it?"

"It's illegal to own more than six dildos at a time in Texas."

I have to laugh. "Why six? To discourage people from inviting all their friends over for an orgy?"

"I have no idea. Too much of a good thing?" She chuckles. "It's just some trivia a lawyer friend once mentioned."

"So you are not afraid of doing something illegal here in Cambodia?"

"Does what we do feel illegal to you?"

She has a point. "Not at all. Being with you is one of the most freeing things I have ever done."

"Exactly. When I was young, I was afraid to even masturbate, mainly because my church and my culture in general didn't exactly encourage any activity related to sex." She frowns. "Not letting a young person get to know her own body should be illegal."

I nod. Embracing my preference for women has been one of the most liberating events I have ever experienced.

"But back to the subject," she says, and I am afraid I know what is on her mind. "How were you able to buy a dildo here in this small town? You must have more pull than I knew."

The blood rushes to my face, and I grow hot all over. This is exactly the question I have been trying to avoid.

"Uh, yeah, well, I guess I do. Come to think of it, maybe it would be best if you just describe what you want and let me buy it for you. That would be a lot simpler."

She is quiet for a minute. "Maybe you're right. But why are you acting so strange about all this?"

"*Strange*. Why do you say that?"

She gives me a hard look. "You've been acting weird all morning, though I can't put my finger on it. Nervous. Like you've done something wrong and are afraid to admit it."

"What are you talking about? Maybe I am a little uneasy about this silly law. You never know how seriously some people take such things." I resort to a little joke. "I would hate for us to get thrown in jail for something so personal. I can just picture the headlines."

She laughs. "*Respectable tour guide and her foreign client sentenced to three years of hard labor in the banana plantations for breaking the anti-sex-toys law in Cambodia.*"

I have to chuckle. But some people might not consider what she is joking about so funny. Specifically, my old flame Harini, who could lose her business and be thrown in jail as well, though I doubt it.

Just the thought of having her meet Harini makes me want to end this conversation, go back to the hotel, and make love to her again and again. We are safe there, just the two of us in our perfect little world. I do not want anything to ever disturb it. But how long can I avoid what might happen?

"The Pure Gold is right up there." I point to the attractive shop, advertised by a professional sign: BEST MASSAGES IN TOWN. TEN DOLLARS.

I have lost the argument, so I pray Harini is not here. Of course, that thought is silly, because she is the only one in the shop that I know. No other person in charge there would even admit they have a back room where you can buy illegal goods. At least Harini does not speak much English. Maybe I can serve as an interpreter and keep this encounter all business. I hope.

"Why do they call it the Pure Gold? That's an odd name for a massage parlor."

"Sorry to say, it is meant to appeal primarily to men. We have an old saying here in Cambodia: *men are gold, and women are cloth.*"

She stops, a question in her eyes. "What does that mean?"

"It has different interpretations, but I have heard people explain that if pure gold gets dirty, it can be cleaned. Yet if cloth is soiled, it is stained forever."

"In other words, the double standard, wrapped up in a cryptic statement."

"I agree." I wonder what Harini thinks about the name of the place where she works. Or has she even thought about it? She is a what-you-see-is-what-you-get person. She does not enjoy dealing with life's subtleties. She probably likes her type of business because it gives her an excuse to dress up and look gorgeous, it provides her a decent living, and she does not have to kill herself with hard, repetitive work or do anything disgusting. I imagine she does not care about its name.

And there she is, as beautiful as ever. She is in her forties, slender, her black hair streaming down her back, her molten eyes revealing a trace of ancestors from China and India. She is dressed perfectly, as always, her blue silk blouse of the highest quality, her tight black skirt cupping her butt in all the right places without being too obvious.

This parlor even has private rooms with real massage tables in them, so different from the flop joints she worked in when she started out in Phnom Penh.

She told me that most of those places charged just a few dollars for a massage on a mattress thrown on the floor in a room full of them. For a little extra, some of the girls would slip in a hand job on the guys, which made up most of their customers. For a short while, she had been one of those girls.

But she was smart and worked her way up, speaking enough English to fool people into thinking she was fluent. In fact, as I mentioned earlier, she truly hates Americans, mainly because she has had to interact with so many rude, demanding ones.

As I stand here, it flashes through my mind that I should have told Barbara all this beforehand, just as I should have warned her the electricity would go out in our villa on Koh Trong. I also should have explained that Harini prefers women, and I was one of the ones she preferred—for a while—long ago. Barbara seems to have a jealous streak that I would prefer she keep in check, and I am afraid Harini will trigger it.

What can I say, though? I am a coward.

When I bought that first toy, I thought that would be the end of it. That Barbara would be satisfied, and I would be her hero.

But now, when I witness the way the two of them lock eyes in instant hatred, I realize my mistake. It is too late to grab her arm, turn around, and walk out the door. If only I could do exactly that.

"Welcome to the Pure Gold. How may I help you?"

Harini is speaking in Khmer, though she has memorized these opening lines in English and always uses that language when a tourist walks in.

This is her way of making Barbara invisible. Harini obviously does not like her and has decided to ignore her. That is the wrong move.

Barbara refuses to duck her head like Harini apparently expects. Instead, she glares. A sign beside the front door clearly states, ENGLISH SPOKEN HERE. Her Cambodian half can apparently sense an insult. What is more important, she clearly can sniff out a potential rival, even if the danger was buried a long time ago. She does not know that, and I admit that Harini may still be able to sway me, if she tries.

In comparison to Barbara, Harini has thirty years and a face and figure like a Bollywood actress on her side. Barbara would have to be the Buddha's mother not to feel somewhat threatened. And as shaky as she seems to feel about her age, she most probably does.

Why did I get out of bed this morning? More important, will I have a bed to sleep in tonight?

I try to intervene, saying, in Khmer, "My friend would like to view your best room before she decides whether to have a massage." That is the code for requesting to view the store's sex-toy display, hidden from any authorities who might be bored enough to search for illegal goods.

Harini's small nose flares like a water buffalo's. "Our best room is occupied. Maybe you could come back later." She speaks in Khmer, obviously intending this message for me and still ignoring Barbara altogether. The way Harini finally glares at her says, in an international nonverbal language, "You can go to hell."

Barbara understands that language as if she has a PhD in linguistics. And I suppose she does, in a way, given the way her father's family treated her mother like she was a leper, and he denied Barbara the right to learn her "mother tongue." Also, Barbara possibly thinks Harini considers me her property, whether she still wants me or not. And she might be right..

I feel like a piece of raw beef two strays are baring their teeth and snarling over. A few toys are not worth it, so I take Barbara's arm, say our good-byes, and guide her out the front door, leaving Harini in her kennel.

"Who the hell was that?" Barbara spits out her question.

"Someone I used to know a long time ago. Her name is Harini."

Why am I so embarrassed, and why do I feel so guilty? I have not done anything except try to please Barbara. Yet I am practically apologizing for having a girlfriend years before I even dreamed Barbara existed.

"Have you seen her since we got to town?"

I know what she is asking, but I choose to play stupid. I obviously know how to do that well. "I bought you a present from her, one you have clearly enjoyed more than a little, on several occasions."

I cannot keep from using a smart-ass tone, even though her frown should warn me not to.

"Did you try it out first? On her?"

I grab her elbow and propel her over to a side street, where no one can overhear us. "Are you out of your mind? For starters, that would be unsanitary and a gross insult to both of you." My tone is still sharp, but my mind is noodle limp. Do I still have some type of attachment to Harini?

Barbara is not backing down, her gaze like a knife slicing through all the trust we have built together.

"She and I did have an affair, ages ago. She was my first, and not exactly a good choice for a virgin lesbian wanting to learn how to live the life." I take a deep breath, the memory of those years still painful. "As soon as she realized how unskilled I was in practically everything that matters to her, she tossed me aside for someone more experienced."

I start to touch Barbara's arm, but she is a stone statue.

"Have you seen her since you two broke up?"

I spot a hint of daylight after the stormy, dark night she has resembled up until now.

I refuse to lie. "We were both into the Phnom Penh club scene back then. It was impossible not to run into her from time to time."

"And did you sleep with her then?"

"Once in a while. After I broke up with someone, I might be at a bar having a drink, and there she would be, all sympathetic and listening to my sad story."

"So it was more comfortable to tell it to her in the place you were both familiar with—her bed."

I bite my lip, try to remain rational. "At first, it was. But we gradually drifted apart, especially after she moved up here and bought a respectable shop. I have no idea what her home life is like right now. And I do not really care. She is simply an old friend, someone familiar. We live our own lives, and I am happy with mine. Deliriously happy." Maybe I am exaggerating, but it is the truth. Yet is she only a friend? Do connections like ours ever lose all their edge?

Barbara seems to calm down. She lets me ease my hand over hers for a few seconds, bump shoulders with her. The storm seems to have passed.

"I'm sorry," she finally says. "But that woman is just so beautiful, and obviously experienced, and so…young. I could never compete with her. If you're still hung up on her, tell me. I'll back off, catch a plane home to Texas right away. Just say the word."

I know she means what she says. She is right. Harini is definitely younger than she is and, to a lot of people, more beautiful. But not to me.

I wish I had the words to tell Barbara why she is so special. At times she seems like a child, with her quest for her mother and her memories of how shamefully her father treated his foreign wife. At others she is the wealthy Dallas socialite I do not care for—pretentious, superficial, haughty. And she will admit it, even laugh at that bossy version of herself that she presents to the world. That is obviously the version her father helped her shape.

But I do have a faint idea why I care for her so much. She will admit who she is, or pretends to be. And from there she keeps trying to grow into the person she would like to become—instead of the one she was abandoned to be or groomed to be.

She nudges me in the ribs. "I'm sorry." And her tone, her expression tell me that she really, truly is. "I'll try not to be so jealous from now on. I don't know what happened. I just snapped when I saw that woman—the way she looked at you, and the way I was afraid you wanted to look at her."

I move closer, stroke down her arm, and rest my hand on hers again. "Do you think you can do without some new toys until we get back to Phnom Penh? I have some sources there too."

"Are they as young and beautiful as this Harini person?"

"Not in the least. They are all big, ugly guys."

"Thank goodness." She draws a deep breath. "I'm exhausted. Want to go back to our room?"

She is not as exhausted as she claimed to be. Make-up sex truly is the best.

PART V

BARBARA AND DARA

Chapter Twenty-two

BARBARA

Barbara gazed at her hair in the bathroom mirror. Her roots were shining like a narrow gray ribbon in contrast to her red hair. She grabbed a handy plastic bottle from her makeup kit to take care of that situation, noting that it was almost empty. Where would she buy a replacement?

Dara called out. "How long have we been here in Stung Treng?"

"A little more than a week?" She'd lost track of time. She glanced at her fingers as she tucked away her nearly empty bottle. Her cuticles had grown, and several nails looked ragged. Even worse, her clear polish had worn off them, leaving them dull and lifeless. She needed a manicure, soon.

She'd been so busy lately. Her relationship with Dara had exploded, and she'd also become increasingly involved in helping Chantha at the women's center. It seemed like she'd been here ten years instead of probably ten days.

"Getting ready to head east yet?" Dara sounded like the tour guide she was. Obviously, Dara didn't realize how invested she'd become in the women's center, and she hadn't mentioned her indecision about that project to Dara. She wanted to wait before she committed herself long-term to this cause.

Right now, she was surer about her feelings for Dara than she was about working with Chantha at the center. She ached all over with what might be love for Dara, who took such good care of her in every way. She checked every box on Barbara's perfect-woman-for-me list.

But again, wasn't it premature to declare her never-ending love before she was certain it would last? What if it was just sex? What if Dara didn't feel as deeply for her as she did for Dara? How many old flames like Harini would turn up? Young, beautiful women seemed to be drawn to Dara.

"How about staying here a while longer?" she said. "I really like this town and want to learn more about what Chantha is doing at the settlement. How about you?"

"It is your trip. I am happy to be wherever you want to be, as long as we are together."

She hurried into the bedroom and glanced at the digital clock on the nightstand. "I'm sorry to rush off, but Chantha texted me early this morning in a dither. One of her teachers is sick, and she asked if I could fill in until she's better. I'll be teaching basic English, which I figured I could do. Besides, it might help me learn Khmer faster. I have no idea how long I'll need to be there."

"Oh. Okay. Have a good time." Dara's kiss was long and hungry, and Barbara almost regretted her promise to Chantha. But she pulled herself away. It wouldn't hurt Dara to relax and get some extra sleep. Only heaven knew how active they'd both been recently.

Teaching the class hadn't taken as long as Barbara expected, and she hadn't even stopped to chat with Chantha. She'd missed her usual early morning activities with Dara more than she'd imagined she would and was looking forward to enjoying some catch-up sex.

While rushing down the street, she bumped into a well-dressed, gray-haired man whose crewcut, erect posture, and aroma of nicotine reminded her of her father, Red. "Sorry, ma'am," he said. His drawl could have come only from someone born and reared in Texas. He had just emerged from a massage parlor that even she knew was a front for an illegal, very active back room. Scowling at her when she simply nodded, he spit on the sidewalk and strolled away like he knew he could buy just about anything in this town.

His appearance shook her. Was he real, or a vision, like her mother at the fancy resort where they had stayed on Koh Trong? It wasn't difficult to imagine what he would have said to her if he were actually here.

"Dara's conning you, Barbara. Don't you realize that? Like your mother did me. All she wanted was a free ticket to America and for me to support her in style for the rest of her life. I gave her everything money could buy, and she never had to strike a lick. All she had to do was not make you into a foreigner like she was. I saw to that and did it for your own good."

The sun overhead seemed to be burning a hole in Barbara's brain, so she stopped in the shade of a nearby awning.

The words of her father rattling in her brain had taken hold of her, as though she'd accidentally watered a seed and a giant beanstalk had burst from it, mushrooming toward the heavens. They pounded in her head.

"Don't you see what's going on? Open your eyes, girl. Most likely she and that Harini bitch are partners and take advantage of innocent foreigners like you whenever they get a chance. Remember how she contacted that official back in that first big town y'all stayed in and got your visa extended? Gave herself more time to milk you dry."

Barbara's head began to ache. She shouldn't listen to Red, but he wouldn't shut up.

"That gal's only after your money, little lady. Why would she want to be involved with some old woman like you when she can have a looker like that Harini you met the other day? Better get out of here while you can. Fly straight home. That's where you belong. You speak Texan, and deep down you feel the same way about foreigners they do."

Barbara put her palms on both sides of her head, trying to stop Red's nasal twang, but he was gaining control over her.

"That woman you're involved with here is a notch above most people here, with her fancy degrees and living abroad, but she's still different from you. You'd never make it if you decided to stay. She'd get her hands on all your money or make you give it all away, then leave you high and dry. You'd end up looking as bad as that old woman squatting and cutting banana leaves." Red wiped a piece of tobacco from his lip and flicked it to the sidewalk. *"You got off easy with her, daughter—a little cash and some ice cream—but Dara has her hooks in you. I'm giving you one last warning. She's gonna drain you dry."*

Barbara shook her head and took a series of deep breaths until the image of her father vanished. But his words kept echoing inside her.

She started walking, needing to see Dara, to strip out the hateful things she'd just heard. But then she glanced through the window of a familiar restaurant. Something had caught her eye, and she didn't even realize it until someone came into focus. Long black hair, piercing eyes. The person looked familiar. Harini.

The despicable woman glared at her, her red lips twisting into a smirk that seemed to say—if Harini could speak English—"You better pay attention to me, loser. I have your woman, and I'm not letting her go."

Barbara froze and burned at the same time. "RUN," she thought. But only after she confronted the bitch.

DARA

I was sitting here in a restaurant near our hotel eating, when who do you think showed up? If you said Harini, you guessed right. Yes. Like she was playing a bit part in a bad Hollywood movie, there she stood, complete with tight skirt, red nail polish, and lipstick. I could not ignore her when she smiled and waved like nothing had happened the other day between her and Barbara. Then she insisted on sitting at my table as if we met for breakfast every morning. I could not say no, although I wanted to. But what could it hurt? We are old friends.

She keeps talking while we eat. I do not say much. Have never had to around Harini. She can converse with anyone about anything without a problem. I usually just sit and listen, let her do as she likes. I plan to finish my noodles, make an excuse, and head back to my hotel as soon as possible.

Instead, the bad script plays out exactly as you would expect, and Barbara appears. She must have spotted my back through the window and walked in without realizing who was sitting here with me. Or maybe she did spot Harini, because when Harini half turns in her chair and looks at Barbara, Barbara glares at her as if she would like to put a knife through her heart and throws one phrase at me as if it is a live grenade. "I hate you." Then she whirls around and is out the door in an instant.

She is halfway to the hotel by the time I catch her. "I had no idea how long you would be gone," I tell her, panting and now side-stepping next to her.

She keeps walking. "So, as soon as you can get rid of me, you hook up with *her*?"

Her face is as red as her hair, and sweat covers her face and arms. I want to hug her and tell her what really happened and how much I would rather have been sitting there with her and everything I really feel. But my mouth works faster than my brain.

"I did not do that. But what if I had?" I blurt out the question.

Barbara is clearly irrational and insecure. But I do not want to have to apologize for something I did not do. If I give in now, will I spend the rest of my life doing the same thing? Will I be forced to avoid every young, attractive woman I know forever?

Yet it is too late. She explodes. Obviously, she did not hear me deny her accusation.

"That's just what I thought. She's beautiful and *young*. You're just like everyone else. You can't resist that combination."

Her tone could freeze the Mekong. I almost shiver, though the late-morning sun is already blazing down on us. "You do not know what you are talking about," I say and immediately regret my words, again. I would not be surprised to see snowflakes falling on this town, which has never witnessed such a sight before.

I try to be calm, reasonable. "Let me explain."

That approach does not work either. She begins to head toward the hotel again. But I refuse to give up, so I walk beside her. "I was just sitting there—"

"And Harini shows up out of the blue, with no idea you're there. And since you're old friends, you—"

"That is exactly what happened." My tone is beginning to chill too. "Though I do not suppose you believe me."

She walks faster. "Do you think I'm stupid?" The temperature shoots up a hundred degrees.

I trot beside her and answer her question. "Of course I do not. You are one of the smartest—"

"Save it."

We stop and square off.

"You do not trust me, do you?" I ask.

"Would you trust me if you saw what I just did?"

"Maybe. Maybe not."

"Well, right now, I don't. I trust my own two eyes. You had to know that seeing you with her would upset me."

"You are so right. I deliberately invited her to meet me in a place where I was certain you would notice us on your way back here and get upset. Is that what you think?"

"You must be tired of me."

She is almost talking to herself now, spinning her own truths to convince herself her first impression was correct. How can I break through her delusion?

She stalks off again, and I run around in front of her and put my hands on her shoulders, try to stop her. "Barbara. I care for you. A lot. Do you not get it? I am crazy about you."

"About me or my money? You're like all the rest of them. I'm an easy mark, always have been. Well, your sugar mama just turned to salt. I'll give you everything I owe you, plus a more-than-generous tip for all the 'extras' you've provided, but I'm out of here."

She looks around as if deciding how to make good on her threat. And she does. "I'm taking a tuk-tuk to the rinky-dink airport here, flying straight to Phnom Penh, having the hotel deliver my bag to me at the airport, and heading home to Dallas. Thanks for showing me the *real* Cambodia, especially the night life."

I step to one side and drop my hands. I am almost staggering, like she just hit me in the head with an ancient statue. I do not say a word as she rushes past me and down the street toward the hotel. Maybe she will change her mind, or maybe she will actually do what she threatened.

Anyway, I stumble over to a wooden box someone has left there beside the street for some odd reason and sit down. And I stay there until my head begins to clear. Everything has happened so fast, I am not sure this situation is real. Maybe I will wake up in a minute, reach out, and there Barbara will be, all warm and cozy.

But that does not happen.

I do not trust myself to walk, much less run after her, so I let her go. If she distrusts me this early in the game, we need to call it off.

At least she did not lay claim to my Honda, not that she could handle it. When I feel like driving back to Phnom Penh, by myself, I will.

Or maybe I should stay here another day or two. She may come to her senses, and we can try to repair the damage. It is a crap shoot, and I am not much of a gambler, but I will take a chance this time.

Surely this is not what Barbara's mother wanted her to discover during this trip. Or perhaps it is.

BARBARA

Barbara filled her backpack in five minutes. That was the beauty of traveling light. She left a huge amount of money for Dara on their bedside table, wrapped in her favorite ANGKOR WHAT? T-shirt. She wanted to give Dara what she owed her for this amazing trip.

Dara! She'd probably be here soon, and Barbara didn't want to be near her again. At least not right now. She didn't want to totally lose control like she just had, blurt out things she didn't mean and would regret later. She needed to get away, find somewhere she could think so she could sort through everything they'd said. Somewhere safe, with someone wiser than she was.

Chantha. She'd go over and say good-bye. She and Chantha had really bonded. What an amazing woman. Her compassion, her organizational skills, her work ethic. Barbara had never met anyone like her, had wanted to spend much more time with her. She could trust Chantha, even if she couldn't trust Dara.

DARA

I finally snap out of my daze and am still sitting on that wooden box on the side of the street. What did I do to upset Barbara so completely?

I did not kiss Harini or even hold her hand. I did not ask her to meet me at the café or join me at my table. I was decent, sat there and listened to her ramble.

I had wanted Barbara there with me, silently eating her fruit and cereal, drinking her juice. Gazing at me with those eyes that told me she desired me as much as I desired her.

I never had anything worthwhile with Harini. If I had, I would probably still be with her. She is more about show and blow, a phrase I have heard Americans use. That is fine, if that is what you like. But it is not for me. I truly believed Barbara had everything I wanted.

What could I have done? Stayed in the room until she came back? Bought something to eat on the street, nearer the hotel? Or should I have stood up when Harini walked in, told her I was just leaving, though I had eaten only a bite?

Yet is Harini really the problem? Barbara may be tired of me and simply wanted a way out. She could be dishonest. Maybe she had to find some other reason to leave me so she could blame it instead of telling me the truth.

My brain feels like the noodles I halfway ate this morning—cold, soggy, ready to be thrown out with the rest of the garbage.

I push myself up off my box and then stretch. I feel old and tired.

But I unkink myself, trudge back to our hotel, and insert my key into the lock. Maybe Barbara has not left. Maybe she is lying on our bed, waiting for me, ready to apologize and forget this unfortunate incident.

I open the door, but she is not here. Only one toothbrush and one comb. Only one backpack. Only one pair of shoes. She has left the helmet and mask I loaned her. But what will I do with it? I want to throw it away. I will not be able to look at it strapped on the rear of my cycle. It should be protecting her head all the way back to Phnom Penh.

I should leave too, drive to the city before it gets dark. I can make the ride in one afternoon, though I will have to stay sharp, eyes on the road. That should keep me from thinking about Barbara and what has just happened. If only I had been stronger, made some excuse to Harini and left the restaurant alone.

I grab my backpack from the closet and shove my toiletries into it. Then I pull out my clothes, put the dirty ones in one section and the clean ones in another. I have worn my ANGKOR WHAT? T-shirt only briefly and pick it up from my bedside table. Something is wrapped inside it.

Money. Piles of it. More than I have ever had, than Barbara agreed to pay me for our entire trip. Is she saying she is sorry and still cares for me? Or is she telling me she has bought and paid for me and my services, both in public and in private?

I sink to the side of what has been *our* bed.

I jump up and rummage through every drawer, examine every shelf, every cabinet, even dump out my pack, searching for any trace that she has been here. Nothing except her money.

God. Everything is so messed up, and I am so tired. I will sleep for a while. Then I will leave.

Chapter Twenty-three

BARBARA

Chantha already stood at the door of Mekong Blue when Barbara arrived. "You texted that you are leaving Stung Treng, and Cambodia?" Chantha probed her with her gaze.

"Something just happened between Dara and me." Her voice was still shaking, her throat tight, and she began to sob. God. How humiliating, embarrassing. Her father, Red, had always insisted that she be in control, stressed that people would take advantage of her if she let them view her real feelings. So she rarely did. Even with Dara she held back, focused on her physical response to their lovemaking instead of how vulnerable she felt when she tried to open herself emotionally.

Chantha took her in her arms, and a rush of comfort enveloped her. She'd never experienced this feeling around Red, remembered him touching her only once during their long life together. It had been after his own mother died. Barbara had been out of town, and she'd flown in for the funeral. He'd met her at the airport, and she'd never forgotten how he hesitantly reached out and touched her arm with his large, freckled hand and then removed it immediately. The unexpected contact had stunned her so completely, she'd pretended to ignore it, and it had never happened again, though she would have welcomed such a sympathetic gesture at other times of crisis.

She lingered in Chantha's maternal embrace, drinking it in like she had gulped down the glasses of cool water Dara had first given her when she was so ill. She inhaled the warmth of Chantha, the fresh smell, her feelings of contentment, safety, acceptance as long as she dared. Then she finally forced herself to pull away, though she wanted to stay in that soothing space forever. She could almost hear her father say, "Don't get too dependent on anyone, Barbara. You never know when they'll turn on you. This is a hard, cruel world."

Chantha's mouth and eyelids drooped. "I am so sorry you are leaving. I was hoping you and I could be great friends. You have become very special to me during the past few days. I cannot recall ever feeling such an immediate kinship with someone."

Her throat tightened. "I don't want to. There's so much more of Cambodia I want to explore, and I feel the same about you and what you're doing here at the women's center. It's like I've finally found the purpose I was sent here for, a way of making amends for not bringing my mother back here as soon as I became an adult. But I never had any money of my own. I mean, I had money, but my father controlled it. Yet that's no excuse. I should have gotten a job, declared my abhorrence of his power, not only over Meatea all her life, but over me. I'm just now realizing how its poison invaded me. Yet now…" She couldn't say any more and tried to swallow the boulder in her throat, but it kept expanding. Chantha probably had no idea what she was trying to express.

Chantha rubbed her back. "Sit with me. No need to rush off. You have been very busy for the past month and more. Toured, survived a near-fatal virus, motorcycled here and worked for me…and maybe even fallen in love?" She patted her shoulder and pulled away with an expression indicating that she seemed to know her most secret thoughts and actions, like a mother would, like her own mother probably had. But Barbara had been too sucked in to Red's world to notice, too busy trying to prove she was the smartest student, the best athlete in every area she attempted.

For that's when Red noticed her, heaped praise on her for winning yet another trophy or ribbon or medal to add to her collection. He was an athlete and expected her to follow his example. So she'd spent her life outdoors on the tennis courts and the golf courses, and indoors playing bridge and chess and mah jong and whatever competitive game her set of friends had indulged in at the time. Her father had insisted that she be the best, and she spared no effort to prove to him that she was. And all that time Meatea worked in her flowerbeds and gave all her affection to whatever stray dog or cat might end up in their yard and she could slip food to, as well as the various workers and whoever else she associated with.

"You stay here," Chantha said, "and I will go tell your tuk-tuk driver you do not need him right now. I will even get his cell number so you can call him later if you need to. The poor man is probably excited about a fare to the local airport."

Barbara reached into her pocket and pulled out a wad of bills. "Here's enough to make up for his trouble, and more. Thank you."

She couldn't stand without Chantha's arms around her, didn't want to, so she stumbled over to a garden table sheltered in the shade of bamboo and sank onto a bench there. Chantha returned and sat beside her again immediately, hip to hip, hand on her arm.

During the last six months of Meatea's life, after Red died, Barbara had begun to realize that she and her mother should have been as intimate as she and Chantha were now—two halves of a whole, two sides of a peach growing together around a single seed. If only they had been that close when she was a child, her life might have been different. *She* might have been different—more at ease with others, with herself. Instead, she had been half of a bad apple, Red the other half, hanging from the same tree.

Chantha sat beside Barbara silently as these regrets washed through her. "You do not have to tell me what has happened to change everything so drastically. But if you want to, I will be glad to listen."

The words helped reduce the size of the boulder threatening to choke her, and she blurted out, "That woman. It's all her fault. I hate her. Dara and I were so happy, but she couldn't stand it. Had to take back what she'd thrown away. Couldn't stand for Dara to be happy when *she* isn't."

Chantha's arm was around her again, inviting her to rest her head on her shoulder, so she did. "Tell me who you are talking about, what she has done to you." Chantha's voice was like a croon, a chant.

"Harini. She works at the Pure Gold. She and Dara were involved ages ago, but she dropped Dara, then toyed with her, and now she's evidently staking her claim again. Dara acts like she can't resist her.

She and I have been so happy. I've never felt this way about anyone before. I have to get away. I can't stand for Dara to be with anyone else, especially someone like Harini." She ran out of breath, her lungs on fire, almost like the virus had resurfaced inside her.

"Hmm. You became jealous? If you feel comfortable confiding in me, would you tell me what happened?"

The words flooded out—how she was rushing to be with Dara, the strange appearance of the man who reminded her of Red, her irrational reaction to seeing Dara sitting at the restaurant with Harini, her own outburst and accusations.

She had jerked away from Chantha while reliving her experience, but now her shoulders dropped on their own, and she leaned against Chantha again, as if resting after setting down a heavy backpack.

Chantha stroked her hand, held it between both of hers. "Your encounter with the strange man evidently watered your seeds of anger, bitterness, and jealousy."

Barbara stiffened, tugged weakly against Chantha's grasp.

"Shh. It's merely the Buddhist way to help explain the strength of our negative emotions and how to try to keep them in check."

Curious, Barbara remained silent.

"Many of my people believe that everyone carries seeds within them, inherited not only from our parents but from their parents and before them. If we water the positive seeds of love, generosity, hope, and so on, they will grow and blossom. But if we neglect them and cultivate the negative ones—"

"Such as anger, bitterness, and jealousy—"

Chantha nodded. "Exactly. They will flourish. Apparently, your encounter with the man who reminded you of your father, imaginary or not, shaded your good seeds and made your bad ones shoot up."

Barbara inhaled deeply. "So I'm not a bad person. I just let part of myself that I'd rather suppress take over at an unfortunate time."

"Exactly. We have to be mindful in order to live a life of peace and tranquility." Chantha gave a small smile. "And you're certainly not a bad person. Emotions come and go. You need to learn to identify what you are feeling, acknowledge each one with a smile when it appears, and then step back and let it go. You can control how you respond. Sometimes, simply taking a deep breath can help. Evidently, you let your jealousy take over and control you at an unfortunate time."

"I sure did." Again, Barbara inhaled slowly and then exhaled gradually between pursed lips.

"Yes. That's the way to manage your breath. But tell me why you came here, to Cambodia. We can talk about Dara later, but right now I am more interested in you." Chantha's voice—deep and low, soft and strong—helped cool the heat in her chest, enabled her to pour out her story about Red and Meatea, how he'd treated her with such disdain, how he'd forced Barbara to fit into the mold he wanted her to fill.

"You never really knew your mother until after your father died, did you? Yet you wanted to all those years. You felt like half of yourself was missing, and then after she died, you traveled here to find that part of you that is her. Is that correct?" Chantha wasn't simply a mind reader. She was a heart reader.

"I had six months alone with Meatea, and we began to discover what we could have been to each other. We had planned a trip here, together, so she could rediscover her country, witness how much it has changed yet remained the same."

"What happened?" Chantha's voice was a breath on her face.

"Her heart gave out two weeks before we were supposed to leave. It happened so suddenly. I was numb with shock, grief."

"So you decided to make this trip in her memory."

"That's right. And I've succeeded more than I ever thought possible, though I do wish she had been able to be here too. I did bring a small part of her with me." She fingered the little red heart-shaped vial that hung around her neck alongside her treasured glossy shell. "I had her cremated, and although she'd asked me to use most of her cremains to fertilize the roses she loved and cared for, I brought a bit of her with me, to leave in a special place. The container is in my makeup bag. I haven't even told Dara about it because I couldn't bring myself to—"

"I will help you find just the right place to sprinkle her ashes, if you want."

Her deep sigh seemed to clear some of the rubble from Barbara's chest, her throat. "I do. Thank you."

"You are most welcome. Your mother links you to this country as closely as the memory of mine ties me here. And it just may be the place where you belong. You should stay, at least until you are satisfied that you have found what you came here searching for."

"Even if Dara has already packed up and is on her way back to Phnom Penh?" She wanted to believe Chantha, but would it be possible to stay here without Dara? Or would it be too unbearably sad to be so near her yet never be close to each other again? To know that Harini had seduced Dara once more and would drop her again on a whim.

"You are welcome to stay with me as long as you like. I have a little guesthouse on my property, where you could have your privacy yet continue to learn Khmer, along with the ways of our country and its women."

Barbara's head seemed a little less fuzzy now. She could have a home base here near Chantha. She could slow down, settle down, absorb this experience gradually until she could decide the best course to take.

Chantha took her hand and tugged her to her feet. "Let me show you my guest quarters. Maybe that will help you reach a decision, though you can simply stay overnight, or a few days, if you want. Long enough to be sure what you want to do."

They strolled through the grounds, covered with fruit trees, some flowering and others offering mature cashews, bananas, mangos. The faint noise from the women's center faded in the distance, the hum of insects and chirp of birds now filling the warm air.

"Here it is. Just within sight of mine. Go on in. I will go fix us something cool to drink. It is beginning to heat up."

The little house was neat, clean, simple, with a small kitchen and bath, a larger room with a small statue of the Buddha in one corner and a clear area for sleeping at night and eating or sitting during the day. A thick, rolled-up mat with a mosquito net draped over it would unfurl and serve as her bed. Could she adjust to these conditions, so different from her plush surroundings in Dallas? The word yes kept sounding in her head, so she laid her backpack next to the sleeping pad and walked back outside.

Chantha had set up a small Western-style folding table and chairs under a nearby mango tree and motioned her over. "Have you had anything to eat?"

"I forgot all about it. I rushed to the classroom after you called, hoping to have a meal with Dara after I returned to the hotel. But Harini beat me to it."

Chantha patted the back of one of the chairs. "Let me get something for us to eat along with our drinks, and then we will talk some more. Or you can rest if you want."

She started to object, but Chantha had already turned to leave, and Barbara was suddenly hungry. Chantha was right. She would be able to think more clearly on a full stomach.

Chantha returned with two bowls of what looked like the same type of noodle soup she'd served when she and Dara had eaten with her and Kim. How long ago had that been? And did he and Chantha live together? Or were they simply old friends, linked by the existence of their children. It hurt to think about being there with Dara, just after their first kiss. She'd lived a lifetime during that short span of time, of new experiences, new feelings and sensations, filled with the dream of Dara and all things wonderful. But she refused to go there.

"Do you plan to eat?" Chantha interrupted her musing. "I have brought some green tea as well. Over ice, it is refreshing this time of day. The monks drink it, cold or hot, to help them meditate and try to achieve spiritual enlightenment."

She sipped her glass of tea and attempted to be sociable. It tasted bitter yet sweet, like her life at the moment. But after several more sips, her mind began to clear, and she focused on her bowl of noodles, still warm.

"Hmm. These are so good. I don't think I'd ever get tired of eating them."

Chantha smiled. "When I was a child, I reached the point of never wanting one again. But then, in exile in Saigon, when I was starving, I could think of nothing else."

Guilt stabbed her. She was having a meltdown over a failed love affair, and this amazing woman had lost both her mother and sister under unbearable conditions, also suffered other unimaginable deprivation. How ironic to think that two women who had valued food so highly and centered their lives around feeding others should starve to death. What an entitled, ignorant fool I am, she told herself.

"I'm sorry for being such a baby. I've led a privileged life and have no right to complain about..." She didn't know how to continue.

Chantha put her hand over hers and gently squeezed. "We are all babies, deep inside, all wanting our mothers. Do you miss yours very much? I grieved for years after I lost mine."

Tears sprang from her eyes. She did miss Meatea, terribly. Her throat ached again now from trying to hold back the tears dripping from the corners of her eyes and rolling down her cheeks. Her breath came in gasps as she mourned the loss of the mother she'd never had during all those many years while Red was alive and dominating both their lives. The tears suddenly poured from deep inside her stomach, pushing their way up and making her struggle for breath, then sniffle as the first wave of grief subsided.

Chantha sat there silently, a witness to what she had lost, eyes wet also. No doubt she was honoring her own mother and sister, ripped away from her so long before they should have been.

Barbara couldn't stop the tears now that they'd finally begun to surface. She surrendered to them, exhaling a shaky breath after they finally seemed to have stopped. Wiping her face with her palms, she gazed at Chantha, who still sat beside her quietly, as she had throughout this emotional outburst.

"It is important to grieve...and then to forgive ourselves," Chantha said. Then she grew silent, seeming comfortable to just be there as long as Barbara needed her. Chantha's presence filled her with reassurance.

They sat quietly for a long time. Gradually, the very air she breathed became different—fresher, cleaner, clearer. She inhaled deeply, visualizing her lungs losing their congestion, their staleness, growing stronger, more resilient. The sensation spread throughout her, curling like a mist, changing her cell by cell. She lost track of time, let the transformation overwhelm her, breathing quietly and steadily, her heartbeat slowing, steadying her as she simply sat there, content—Chantha by her side.

Slowly, she returned, as if from a long journey. "Could I have some more tea, Chantha?"

Chantha eased up and soon returned, carrying her tea and what appeared to be a small photo album. "I do not share this with many people, but I would like to show it to you."

She took it and looked at what appeared to be a happy, prosperous family, dressed in the Western fashions popular during the mid-1960s. An older man and woman stood with a girl on each side of them.

"That is me, at about twelve, with my sister and parents." Chantha flipped through several pages and pointed. "My sister, and mother, and I, in 1974. This is our last picture together, ever." Her eyes glistened. "My father had died several years earlier. I was twenty-two when we had to leave Cambodia because of the Khmer Rouge regime."

"How horrible. I can't even begin to imagine—"

"And here is one of my parents on their wedding day, in 1950. I enjoy looking at it."

Barbara studied the black-and-white photo. A happy couple in formal dress—their smiles huge, love beaming from their faces. Chantha's early life had been most likely a pleasant one—cooking with her mother and sister, an affectionate father coming home from a long day at work, delighted to be with his girls. She inhaled slowly and pulled her wallet from under her shirt, where it rested on a long cord near her heart.

"I haven't even shown this to Dara. But I want you to see it, if you'd like."

"Of course. I would be honored."

She'd had the old photo laminated to preserve it from growing even dimmer. "It's the only picture I have of my parents together. It was evidently taken here in Cambodia, on their wedding day as well."

Chantha held it reverently, gazing at the tall, thin man and his short bride beside him. "How wonderful that you have this memento. I can understand why you would carry it close to your heart. But something about it is strange. The background is the same as the old one of my parents, and..." She turned it over. "Look. Evidently they are from the same photographer. I can tell by this stamp, written in Khmer." Chantha removed the one of her parents from her album and held it out for her to see. "I never paid attention to who he was, but apparently they were both taken in Battambang, where I grew up." Chantha examined her photo more closely. "And something else. Look how much our mothers resemble each other."

She took the picture and scrutinized it, then reexamined the one from Chantha's album. "It could almost be the same woman—their eyes, the way they hold their heads, the slope of their shoulders."

Chantha paled. "Wait a minute. When did you say your mother married and left Cambodia?"

"About 1948."

"I cannot believe I did not think of this before. It has been so long, and so much has happened in the meantime, but—"

"What?"

Chantha took a long drink of her own tea. "I recall my mother and aunt talking, in hushed tones, about a cousin who left home in disgrace and ran away to America with a soldier she had become involved with. Even after all those years, they were whispering, refusing to say out loud that she had to get married because she was pregnant. Evidently, no one in the family ever heard from her again."

Chantha sat back and stared at her. "But here you are, and that helps explain why I have felt so close to you ever since we met, as if we were—"

"Cousins. Part of the same family. That's what we'd be if all this were actually true. And I'd have an even bigger reason to stay here in Cambodia. Wouldn't that be unreal, and wonderful, and amazing?"

"I am certain it is true, Barbara. I have a gift for knowing when something is true and right, and this definitely is."

She could barely assimilate Chantha's revelation. She'd found what she'd come here to search for. Now what should she do? *Dara.*

"Chantha, do you think I deserve to be with someone as wonderful as Dara? Or will I treat her like my father did my mother? All my life, people have told me I look and act just like him."

Chantha gazed at her without blinking, obviously considering the importance of her question and her revelation. "Of course we cannot alter our physical resemblance to someone, Barbara. But we can change our thoughts and actions, even at our age. It is not easy, and it takes time and hard work and determination."

"Maybe it would be better for Dara if I left her alone. She deserves someone much less flawed than I am."

"That is possible, but the fact that you said that makes me wonder if you are as flawed as you fear."

"So I might be able to have a healthy relationship with her?"

"That is entirely up to you and Dara. Perhaps you would be better off alone. Maybe she would be. Each of you has to decide if you want to walk the road of life alone or together. But at this point, you should definitely discuss your options."

She was in a turmoil. None of her relationships with women had ever lasted very long after the initial stages of attraction, pursuit, and conquest. She had worn them out, chasing the ever-elusive orgasm that everyone claimed to have enjoyed but she had never truly experienced, though she'd tried over and over. Maybe she'd tried too hard. Sex apparently wasn't a competition. At least it shouldn't be. But that's how she'd always viewed it, until Dara showed her a new, more relaxed approach.

Maybe Dara would truly be different from all the others. But probably she would just wear Dara down and wear her out. Wouldn't it be kinder to let her go at this point, before she hurt her any more deeply than she already had? Besides, that way she could return home a winner—she'd solved the riddle of Meatea's identity, survived the deadly Covid-19, and experienced exciting adventures riding a motorcycle with a desirable woman. What fun she'd have bragging about her conquest, what stories she'd have to tell her friends in Texas.

She caught herself. Wasn't that how Red would react to this situation? He'd always done everything he could to be a winner. And where had it gotten him? Did she want to be like him for the rest of her life? At her age, could she change even if she wanted to?

As if reading her mind, Chantha said, "You need to decide who you want to be, Barbara, and visualize yourself being that person. You could live thirty more years, or an hour. You cannot let time decide who you want to be. A minute can seem like a lifetime, or a lifetime like a minute. Search inside yourself, listen and observe. We all are sleeping Buddhas. We can reach past the influence of others, such as our parents, and awaken to the Buddha inside us—to who we are and what we can be. We simply need to have the courage to face reality, the truth, things just as they are."

Barbara pondered the words of this woman who had suffered and endured so much. If only she could learn to be more like her. Or, if she followed Chantha's advice, she needed to become acquainted with her own best self, try to become it. Did she have that type of courage? What was her reality, her truth?

"I've been giving a lot of thought to doing something to honor my mother, Chantha, and have decided that I'd like to endow a charity in her name, Ree Ngoun. It will be dedicated to helping Cambodian women who need a hand up in being able to live a decent life here. Can you help me arrange something like that?"

Chantha nodded. "I would be more than happy to. But you don't have to give only money to others. You can gift them with other things, beginning with how stable you can be. The people we love need us to be solid and stable. Try visualizing yourself as a mountain as you breathe in and, as you breathe out, think, 'I am solid.'"

Barbara followed her directions and, after a few exchanges, said, "I already feel stronger. That really works."

"What about freshness? Would you like to feel newer, more alive, and share that quality with others?"

Barbara grinned. "Who wouldn't? Especially the newer part. How do I do that?"

"Simply take a slow, deep breath and say to yourself, 'I see myself as a flower.' Then push your breath out gradually while you think, 'I feel fresh.'"

After she followed the simple instructions, Barbara said, "Amazing. I feel so different, somehow renewed. Thank you, Chantha. Any other tips?"

"Let's try one more. And remember that you're not doing this for yourself alone. Think of your solidity and your freshness as gifts you share with others, especially those you love."

"Right. That makes sense, and they're so much more personal than money. That attitude could be better for everyone involved."

"Yes. Being able to relate to others securely and happily is a wonderful gift. Last, how about peace?"

"Of course. I could use a lot more of that for myself right now, but I'd be glad to share whatever I can find. What should I do?"

"As you breathe in, say, 'I see myself as still water.'"

After a moment, Barbara, following Chantha's lead, repeated, "I reflect things as they are" as she slowly released her breath. A serenity filled her that she hadn't experienced since she was a child standing in Meatea's rose garden, inhaling the honeyed fragrance of the blossoming plants. Their aroma filled her now and seemed to bathe her with its sweetness. "Ah, I never realized what peace smells like until now. Thank you, Chantha. I will practice what you have taught me and share these wonderful treasures as well as some of my money."

Chantha beamed. "Welcome to our country, cousin. Now let us go track down Dara before she does something foolish, like leave town. I do not want to have to drive all the way to Phnom Penh to persuade her to come back up here. You two need to have a long talk."

Chapter Twenty-four

BARBARA

Barbara and Dara sat on the same log on the riverbank where they had shared their first kiss. But this time the sun was rising at their backs, turning the darkness into light.

"You didn't answer my texts yesterday."

Dara took her hand. "I was asleep. Watching you throw a jealous tantrum took a lot out of me. Especially since you had nothing to be jealous about."

Her face heated as the sun's first rays hit the Mekong. "I realize that now. But I've never been that jealous before. Or if I ever was, I denied it to myself and to everyone else."

"Why would you do that?"

"Because jealousy is bad. Like hatred and greed. At least that's what I was always taught. Chantha has given me some new thoughts about that subject."

"Oh, sweetheart. They are all just feelings." Dara traced the blue veins on Barbara's hand. "They do everything from alert us to danger to help us form meaningful connections with others. They are just tools, neither good nor bad. Did you never take a psychology course?"

"No. I didn't get around to it. Red always said psychiatry was a waste of time and money and that therapists were frauds."

Dara gazed at the river, frowning. "Why were you jealous of Harini?"

"I was afraid she would take you away from me."

"Did she?"

"No. I didn't give her a chance. I took myself away from you."

"So, your jealousy was a warning and made you act. What would have happened if you had simply said to Harini, 'Dara and I have something special, and I refuse to let you destroy it'?"

"She probably would have laughed at me, and you would have had to make a choice right then and there."

"And who do you think I would have chosen?"

She shook her head and stared at Dara. "Me?"

Dara nodded. "Right. Your jealousy would have helped us both deal with a difficult situation. But when you refused to honor it, everything became confused and out of control."

"You make it seem so easy. I feel like a fool."

"You are no fool. Life is never easy when you are caught in the middle of a feeling. It is a frightening and confusing and difficult place to be." Dara smiled. "But after things calm down, it is not that hard to think about what has happened and what you could and should have done differently."

She gazed out at the river, flowing peacefully, as it had in Kampong Cham when she first confided in Dara about her fear of speaking Khmer.

"This river seems to inspire us to tell the truth about ourselves." She studied Dara. "What's the truth about you?"

Dara took a deep breath. "That I am crazy about you. But…"

"But what?"

"I am not sure what we are doing."

"What do you mean?"

"I cannot continue to be your employee. If we have a future together, I must feel that I am your equal." Dara looked across the river, where a large, white bird had settled on the distant bank. "We both evidently need to be free. But if we ever decide to build a nest together…"

She kept her eyes focused on the other side of the river too. "That's a big 'if,' isn't it?"

"Just a small word we can both pronounce, *if* we decide to."

"I've done a lot of thinking since yesterday," Barbara said.

"Yes."

"And I've decided to stay in Cambodia."

"I am surprised, and your mother would be pleased."

"Would you?"

Dara gazed at her, eyes dark and serious. "Yes."

"But…"

"But what?"

"I've decided to rent Chantha's little guesthouse and help her at the development center. As I texted you earlier, she and I are related. Isn't that amazing? Of all the people who have lived and died in Cambodia during all these years, it's a miracle that you should introduce me to one of my cousins, especially one who remembers what happened to my mother."

"Yes. It is like a fairy tale. A dream come true. I am so very happy for you. You deserve this wonderful gift of knowing."

But Dara's eyes had hardened. "You are staying here in Stung Treng? Is this the end? Is everything over between us?"

"I don't want to let you go. Not unless you want me to. It's taken too long to find you. But I need to learn to do something except merely dole out my father's money as if I'm the Lady of the Manor. I did nothing to earn my wealth except sell my soul to him." Her laugh tasted like an unripe lemon. "I want to be able to give something of my real self to others."

"What do you have in mind?"

"Chantha's helping me learn that I can offer intangibles such as stability, freshness, and peace to others. Maybe even love. I never thought I had anything like that to share with anyone, but she's made me think I might." Barbara flushed. She felt naked, as if she were exposing herself on the town square, and rushed to discuss goals that were more down to earth.

"Studying Khmer is high on my list. I have to be able to communicate with my own people in their language. And perhaps I'll learn to weave beautiful scarves and wall hangings alongside these women. The world can always use more beauty. Besides, neither language nor weaving is a competitive sport, as far as I know. The change will be good for me."

"Those are some interesting goals."

"And surely during my lifetime I've picked up a few useful skills to share with the women who come to the center to try to better themselves."

"All that sounds like a good plan for everyone involved."

"I agree. Also, I want you to know that I have finally realized what those several 'business' calls you had on the way up here were all about. At my lowest, I thought you had been talking to Harini or some other woman. But then, yesterday, Chantha mentioned that she had recently put you in touch with an international agency, and they have offered you a rather prominent position as a liaison with the Chinese government. Your language skills seem to have paid off."

"Yes. I have been considering their proposal." A ray of new sunlight hit Dara's face.

"Oh, Dara. I'm so happy for you. You should accept their offer. And if you do, it looks like we'll both be busy for a while."

Dara's smile faded. "Too busy for each other?"

"Of course not. I can't wait to visit you in Phnom Penh. After all, it's not that far, and Chantha travels down there all the time. But I need to spend time alone too. This trip and my conversations with you and her have made me realize how much I need to get to know myself and change some very old patterns."

"I will give you all the time alone that you need. But you do want to continue to see each other?" Dara asked. "I do not know what the coming years may bring, but I do know that I hope to spend part of them with you."

"Yes. I've never felt this way about anyone before now. I love you, you know, as best I can. And I'd like for us to have a future together. But all this has happened so quickly…"

"I love you too, Barbara. The flirtation and sex have been outstanding. But the possibility of having a long-term relationship with you is satisfying in an entirely different way. I am looking forward to the next part of our adventure together."

"Me too." She sighed and shifted to a more comfortable position. The air had already begun to heat, and Dara had a long drive back to Phnom Penh today. She hugged Dara's words to herself. "I hope you have a good trip. Please call me when you get there. And I'm looking forward to visiting you."

"Riding there alone will be different, and sad. Yet I will definitely be thinking about our future."

"As will I, Dara Dith." She rose. "Thank you for everything. You've helped me reach this new point in my life, our life."

"I have enjoyed every minute of it." Dara grinned. "And I hope I have many more chances to do the same."

"As do I. With all my heart."

They got up together, and, arms encircling each other's waist, they walked back toward the motorcycle that had brought them here, gleaming in the rising sun.

About the Author

Shelley Thrasher, a BSB editor since 2004 who lives in East Texas between Dallas and Shreveport, has a PhD in English and taught college composition and literature. During the 1960s, Shelley hitchhiked from Glasgow to Baghdad, and after retiring early, she led student tours in Europe and the Middle East. She has published nonfiction as well as fiction. Her novels include *The Storm* (2012), a Goldie finalist; *First Tango in Paris* (2014), set in 1972 Paris; and *Autumn Spring* (2016), set in East Texas and a Lambda finalist. Her book of poetry, *In and Out of Love* (2016), won a Goldie.

Books Available from Bold Strokes Books

A Woman to Treasure by Ali Vali. An ancient scroll isn't the only treasure Levi Montbard finds as she starts her hunt for the truth—all she has to do is prove to Yasmine Hassani that there's more to her than an adventurous soul. (978-1-63555-890-6)

Before. After. Always. by Morgan Lee Miller. Still reeling from her tragic past, Eliza Walsh has sworn off taking risks, until Blake Navarro turns her world right-side up, making her question if falling in love again is worth it. (978-1-63555-845-6)

Bet the Farm by Fiona Riley. Lauren Calloway's luxury real estate sale of the century comes to a screeching halt when dairy farm heiress, and one-night stand, Thea Boudreaux calls her bluff. (978-1-63555-731-2)

Cowgirl by Nance Sparks. The last thing Aren expects is to fall for Carol. Sharing her home is one thing, but sharing her heart means sharing the demons in her past and risking everything to keep Carol safe. (978-1-63555-877-7)

Give In to Me by Elle Spencer. Gabriela Talbot never expected to sleep with her favorite author—certainly not after the scathing review she'd given Whitney Ainsworth's latest book. (978-1-63555-910-1)

Hidden Dreams by Shelley Thrasher. A lethal virus and its resulting vision send Texan Barbara Allan and her lovely guide, Dara, on a journey up Cambodia's Mekong River in search of Barbara's mother's mystifying past. (978-1-63555-856-2)

In the Spotlight by Lesley Davis. For actresses Cole Calder and Eris Whyte, their chance at love runs out fast when a fan's adoration turns to obsession. (978-1-63555-926-2)

Origins by Jen Jensen. Jamis Bachman is pulled into a dangerous mystery that becomes personal when she learns the truth of her origins as a ghost hunter. (978-1-63555-837-1)

Pursuit: A Victorian Entertainment by Felice Picano. An intelligent, handsome, ruthlessly ambitious young man who rose from the slums to become the right-hand man of the Lord Exchequer of England will stop at nothing as he pursues his Lord's vanished wife across Continental Europe. (978-1-63555-870-8)

Unrivaled by Radclyffe. Zoey Cohen will never accept second place in matters of the heart, even when her rival is a career, and Declan Black has nothing left to give of herself or her heart. (978-1-63679-013-8)

A Fae Tale by Genevieve McCluer. Dovana comes to terms with her changing feelings for her lifelong best friend and fae, Roze. (978-1-63555-918-7)

Accidental Desperados by Lee Lynch. Life is clobbering Berry, Jaudon, and their long romance. The arrival of directionless baby dyke MJ doesn't help. Can they find their passion again—and keep it? (978-1-63555-482-3)

Always Believe by Aimée. Greyson Walsden is pursuing ordination as an Anglican priest. Angela Arlingham doesn't believe in God. Do they follow their vocation or their hearts? (978-1-63555-912-5)

Best of the Wrong Reasons by Sander Santiago. For Fin Ness and Orion Starr, it takes a funeral to remind them that love is worth living for. (978-1-63555-867-8)

Courage by Jesse J. Thoma. No matter how often Natasha Parsons and Tommy Finch clash on the job, an undeniable attraction simmers just beneath the surface. Can they find the courage to change so love has room to grow? (978-1-63555-802-9)

I Am Chris by R Kent. There's one saving grace to losing everything and moving away. Nobody knows her as Chrissy Taylor. Now Chris can live who he truly is. (978-1-63555-904-0)

The Princess and the Odium by Sam Ledel. Jastyn and Princess Aurelia return to Venostes and join their families in a battle against the dark force to take back their homeland for a chance at a better tomorrow. (978-1-63555-894-4)

The Queen Has a Cold by Jane Kolven. What happens when the heir to the throne isn't a prince or a princess? (978-1-63555-878-4)

The Secret Poet by Georgia Beers. Agreeing to help her brother woo Zoe Blake seemed like a good idea to Morgan Thompson at first…until she realizes she's actually wooing Zoe for herself… (978-1-63555-858-6)

You Again by Aurora Rey. For high school sweethearts Kate Cormier and Sutton Guidry, the second chance might be the only one that matters. (978-1-63555-791-6)

Coming to Life on South High by Lee Patton. Twenty-one-year-old gay virgin Gabe Rafferty's first adult decade unfolds as an unpredictable journey into sex, love, and livelihood. (978-1-63555-906-4)

Love's Falling Star by B.D. Grayson. For country music megastar Lochlan Paige, can love conquer her fear of losing the one thing she's worked so hard to protect? (978-1-63555-873-9)

Love's Truth by C.A. Popovich. Can Lynette and Barb make love work when unhealed wounds of betrayed trust and a secret could change everything? (978-1-63555-755-8)

Next Exit Home by Dena Blake. Home may be where the heart is, but for Harper Sims and Addison Foster, is the journey back worth the pain? (978-1-63555-727-5)

Not Broken by Lyn Hemphill. Falling in love is hard enough—even more so for Rose who's carrying her ex's baby. (978-1-63555-869-2)

The Noble and the Nightingale by Barbara Ann Wright. Two women on opposite sides of empires at war risk all for a chance at love. (978-1-63555-812-8)

What a Tangled Web by Melissa Brayden. Clementine Monroe has the chance to buy the café she's managed for years, but Madison LeGrange swoops in and buys it first. Now Clementine is forced to work for the enemy and ignore her former crush. (978-1-63555-749-7)

A Far Better Thing by JD Wilburn. When needs of her family and wants of her heart clash, Cass Halliburton is faced with the ultimate sacrifice. (978-1-63555-834-0)

Body Language by Renee Roman. When Mika offers to provide Jen erotic tutoring, will sex drive them into a deeper relationship or tear them apart? (978-1-63555-800-5)

Carrie and Hope by Joy Argento. For Carrie and Hope loss brings them together but secrets and fear may tear them apart. (978-1-63555-827-2)

Death's Prelude by David S. Pederson. In this prequel to the Detective Heath Barrington Mystery series, Heath discovers that first love changes you forever and drives you to become the person you're destined to be. (978-1-63555-786-2)

Ice Queen by Gun Brooke. School counselor Aislin Kennedy wants to help standoffish CEO Susanna Durr and her troubled teenage daughter become closer—even if it means risking her own heart in the process. (978-1-63555-721-3)

Masquerade by Anne Shade. In 1925 Harlem, New York, a notorious gangster sets her sights on seducing Celine, and new lovers Dinah and Celine are forced to risk their hearts, and lives, for love. (978-1-63555-831-9)

Royal Family by Jenny Frame. Loss has defined both Clay's and Katya's lives, but guarding their hearts may prove to be the biggest heartbreak of all. (978-1-63555-745-9)

Share the Moon by Toni Logan. Three best friends, an inherited vineyard and a resident ghost come together for fun, romance and a touch of magic. (978-1-63555-844-9)

Spirit of the Law by Carsen Taite. Attorney Owen Lassiter will do almost anything to put a murderer behind bars, but can she get past her reluctance to rely on unconventional help from the alluring Summer Byrne and keep from falling in love in the process? (978-1-63555-766-4)

The Devil Incarnate by Ali Vali. Cain Casey has so much to live for, but enemies who lurk in the shadows threaten to unravel it all. (978-1-63555-534-9)

His Brother's Viscount by Stephanie Lake. Hector Somerville wants to rekindle his illicit love affair with Viscount Wentworth, but he must overcome one problem: Wentworth still loves Hector's brother. (978-1-63555-805-0)

Journey to Cash by Ashley Bartlett. Cash Braddock thought everything was great, but it looks like her history is about to become her right now. Which is a real bummer. (978-1-63555-464-9)

Liberty Bay by Karis Walsh. Wren Lindley's life is mired in tradition and untouched by trends until social media star Gina Strickland introduces an irresistible electricity into her off-the-grid world. (978-1-63555-816-6)

Scent by Kris Bryant. Nico Marshall has been burned by women in the past wanting her for her money. This time, she's determined to win Sophia Sweet over with her charm. (978-1-63555-780-0)

Shadows of Steel by Suzie Clarke. As their worlds collide and their choices come back to haunt them, Rachel and Claire must figure out how to stay together and most of all, stay alive. (978-1-63555-810-4)

The Clinch by Nicole Disney. Eden Bauer overcame a difficult past to become a world champion mixed martial artist, but now rising star and dreamy bad girl Brooklyn Shaw is a threat both to Eden's title and her heart. (978-1-63555-820-3)

The Last First Kiss by Julie Cannon. Kelly Newsome is so ready for a tropical island vacation, but she never expects to meet the woman who could give her her last first kiss. (978-1-63555-768-8)

The Mandolin Lunch by Missouri Vaun. Despite their immediate attraction, everything about Garet Allen says short-term, and Tess Hill refuses to consider anything less than forever. (978-1-63555-566-0)

Thor: Daughter of Asgard by Genevieve McCluer. When Hannah Olsen finds out she's the reincarnation of Thor, she's thrown into a world of magic and intrigue, unexpected attraction, and a mystery she's got to unravel. (978-1-63555-814-2)

Veterinary Technician by Nancy Wheelton. When a stable of horses is threatened Val and Ronnie must work together against the odds to save them, and maybe even themselves along the way. (978-1-63555-839-5)